Thank you, be
and I will you
thinking o this
while reading
them bright -Abraham

ACKNOWLEDGMENTS

This book is dedicated to my husband, Brig.Gen. (Ret) James M. Abraham. P.E.; and my children, Michael, Deborah, Pamela and Scott, who have always brought joy into my life. And also, to my step-sons David and Thomas.

Many people assisted in this endeavor, and they deserve recognition. My gratitude to Alice Hornbaker, Mary Lord, Sharon Courtney, Patricia Hadley, Mary Jane Palmer, Richard Nunlist, and others for their encouragement and support. They know who they are.

A special commendation to Jack Howard for agreeing to design and create the dust jacket.

First Edition
Library of Congress Catalog Card Number (Pending)

<u>This Story of Garland and its People</u>

.........is a book of fiction. *The names of people, places, companies or other entities do not correlated to any that are living or dead, existing or non-existing. Events and dates also are not factual, and are included to facilitate the story of a non-specific people in a non-specific place. The purpose is to enlighten and entertain, by sharing a perceived message from the past that life goes on into the future.*

THE TEMPERING SEASONS

by

Irene H. Wright-Abraham

People, like communities, can be tempered into
Pure steel if they have the strength to emerge
After being thrust into their inevitable crises.

CHAPTER ONE

August, 1934

Rain could have relieved the suffocating August heat that lingered into the steel mill's second shift, but that blessing had only been a muttered prayer or curse by steelworkers for over two weeks.

Kentucky transplant Martin Bradford leaned over the metal railing to glance at the night sky during a break near the end of his three-to-eleven shift. He was drenched in sweat, and not just from the night's heat or the nearness of the open hearth furnace behind him. He also had the shakes. It was not just beers from the night before. His dread and fear of the plant worsened each work day.

It's a death mill, he thought, despite the fact that technology had steadily improved over the 34 years since the metal buildings began marring the Midwest landscape in 1900. Improved working conditions didn't stop the terrifying fright for Marty, his dread of the steaming vats of molten steel and the craziness of workers who liked nothing better than stupid, life-threatening jokes.

Marty shielded his eyes from the furnace's strawberry glow behind him to gaze away from the plant into the night. Drops of sweat dripped from the 22-year-old's beard-stubbled chin and sizzled on the hot railing.

The vividness of the many stars dashed any hope of clouds gathering for a drenching coolness. No clouds were in the sky tonight.

At the open hearth, pit men lacked any faith in any kind of relief. It was just hotter than hell all the time. Through their shifts, they moved as grime-coated, glow-reflecting images. Their numb purpose was to tap the "heat", or pour the batch of lava-like steel out of the open hearth, guide the flow into molds and get the next track of molds ready to start over again.

They tried to think cool - like visualizing an iceman splitting a frozen fifty-pound chunk with a jabbing ice pick or feeling the crispness of a spring morning in a fishing boat out at Stone Point. The reality, as long as they were on the job bundled in layers of clothes that ranged from itching long-johns to woolen pit jackets, was that heat was as much a part of their existence as sweat-matted eyebrows and lashes.

Marty loosened the red bandanna around his neck, shaking out the silvery-flaked "kish" from the cotton handkerchief that he wore over his nose to keep from breathing the glittering particles that surrounded him. He would need the cover again when he returned to the open hearth, where the kish sparkled in the hot air like Tinkerbell's fairy dust.

Marty squeezed moisture out of the bandanna with hands so grimy he could barely detect his fingernails.

"It's not a pie factory", they had told him when he waited in line for one of the mill's scarce jobs. The Miami Valley Steel Co., (MVS plant) was the City of Garland's primary job attraction for Briars from Kentucky, Hunkies and Pollocks relocated from Europe, and colored folks from the southern United States.

"If you can stand the heat, you can work here," Marty was told along with the others job hopefuls."If you can't, other people are in line behind you."

The mill was the only place in town that paid a living wage or even had jobs to offer. Everybody had hoped 1934 would be better, that the depression would be left behind, but lot of men he knew were still laid off. Jobs had not recovered since the financial market's crash. But the mill job for Marty meant being a dripping human sponge, spending a maximum of a half hour at a time in volcanic temperatures while a heat of steel was poured.

Marty hated it. A half hour of pure purgatory. Get me out! Get me out of here, he pleaded, although lacking faith that aid would come from any higher power.

He turned his stern profile toward the night sky and sought cooling, deep breaths through a nose slightly bent from lost fist fights in the past. There was no relief. What was making it so damn intolerable for him and other mill hands tonight was the Dog Day's heat both inside and outside the quarter-mile-long metal building.

The ninety-five-degree autumn temperature, combined with the nearly three-thousand-degree heat waves rolling out of the furnace, could cook the skin and steam the eyeballs.

Marty could not control his frustration at the over-powering heat, or his increasing habit of continually glancing over his shoulders defensively, in anticipation of threats. That nervous gesture overcame him now and his attention was jerked to the silhouette of a bundled figure shuffling toward him.

"Shit. This is one of the worst," shouted Marty's work partner, Elgin, with an exaggerated wipe of his brow as he neared Marty. He was more appropriately known as "Pig", short for "Pig Iron", but co-workers knew the shortened animal description better described the crusty veteran.

He had tackled various mill jobs over the years from working railroad coal cars to shoveling at the open hearth. He did not last long in any one job, but he was strong and showed up on time.

"Gonna take a piss," Pig shouted, pointing his arm toward the toilets and waddling off like a penguin in his heavy clothes.

Marty, relieved to be alone, suddenly craved a cigarette badly. He needed to feel the sucking of smoke into his lungs, and pursing of lips to blow it out. Hell, it would taste a lot better than the grit he sampled each time he licked his lips.

He reached into the back pocket of his clammy coveralls, and fished out a crushed red package. He caught a cigarette in his slightly over-lapping front teeth, then tapped it against his palm to tighten the loose tobacco before slipping it back in his mouth. The glow of the match faded into the color of the open hearth behind him.

Time was pressuring Marty. The next heat was coming up. All he could hope for was this moment's break and hugging the platform to catch any kind of breeze. Not much hope, but just the gentlest breeze was welcomed by mill hands. Marty needed it. He felt the air stirring suddenly.

Leaning as far as he dared over the railing, facing a twelve-foot fall to the ground if he lost his balance, he felt the first cooling wave of the evening sweeping from the hills west of the city.

The wafting breeze was so slight towns people probably missed it if they were pumping back and forth in their porch swings to find a little relief in the late evening hours. To pit men, weighted down with drenched protective clothes, the slightest breeze could feel like a twenty-degree temperature drop.

Martin felt a shiver in the slight drying effect of the air movement. Strange to think of shivering in heat that smothered down like a down-feather pillow, but he welcomed it, knowing what he had to face in returning to the pit.

He took a deep drag on the cigarette. His dark, tangled eyebrows pulled closer together as his face tightened into a frown.

In a moment or two he would be pulling his heavy coat back over his bib overalls and plaid shirt, but he needed this brief delay. It was a momentary escape. His thoughts rarely strayed far, however, from the maiming threats of the mill.

There was too much exposure to the potential of lost limbs and disfiguring burns. Mill workers' stories always lead off with their worst memory, that was when a steelworker fell head first into a red hot vat of molten steel. There was nothing left of his body to recover.

When the entire mass cooled, it was buried as his memorial.

The cigarette in Marty's hand was getting so short he felt the heat on his fingers. He sucked the last drag from the matted paper and tobacco before dropping it to be crushed under his work boot. Marty shuffled in his heavy clothes back across the platform.

"I was about ready to come and git ya, Buddy," bellowed Pig, yanking on his stiff, blackened gloves. "What the shit were ya dreamin' about out there? I saw you starin' at the stars. You wantin' to be somewhere other than a fuckin' steel mill?"

"I was watching the time. We're doin' all right," Marty yelled, striving to be heard over the metal-scraping, steam-hissing sounds of the mill.

* * *

5

CHAPTER TWO

People's faces were ugly.

That was the first thing Rachel noticed. She was already seventeen and had been in large crowds before, she reassured herself, but that had not prepared her for this day.

Mostly back home she had been in crowds at rural church picnics or county fairs. Those were happy times. People laughed, shared stories and slapped each other on the back. The only concerns were when a child seemed to be lost or someone tipped the bottle too often.

But this mob of job seekers, predominantly men, wore faces that were harsh in the reflection of the mid-morning sun. Not many jobs were available as the depression lingered. Puckers around eyebrows deepened as the men and women continued to wait in front of the tobacco company's loading platform where jobs regularly were assigned if any were available

The steel company had not hired anyone for months, so the unemployed masses huddled each morning outside the tobacco plant so they could continue to live in their Ohio hometown of Garland and not have to migrate to a strange location.

They had no jobs, did not really expect jobs, but they also had nothing else to do.

Rachel saw mouths pulled to one side or lips sucked in and mauled between grinding teeth. Any one face seemed to expressed the emotions felt by all - hunger, anger and suspicion.

Hostility was all around her in tense, hunched bodies which Rachel feared could spill over with emotions and trigger shoving or trampling.

She was wedged into the herd. Her left hip was pressed uncomfortably against the fender of a Model T Ford parked along the curb. She preferred to be there, rather than surrounded by bodies on all sides. She pressed harder against the car, away from the rancid-smelling men oozing stale body sweat.

Several other cars were parked along the street in the shadow of the block-long, red-brick tobacco factory. The searing autumn sun, still moving over the four-story building, would be directly overhead in another hour to intensify the heat. The crowd had endured the wait for nearly two hours.

Across the street, leaning against the plate-glass window of a delicatessen, Douglas Hodge scribbled brief notes on a pad. He watched the crowd, gleaming bits of conversation and appearances of the people so he could include them in a story he would write when he returned to the newspaper office. He had kept his distance so he could get an overview, yet he mentally absorbed what the crowd was experiencing.

People generally thought the still-unseasoned reporter was older than his twenty-three years. That reflected his generally serious attitude. Also his intensely dark, almost black, eyes commanded the attention of viewers and his quiet demeanor seemed to help him relate to individuals of any age. They could talk to him and sense he was sharing their agonies, pain and yearnings.

Just now, he was weighted down with sympathy as he watched the restless swarm of humanity overflowing the sidewalk into the street. He was separated, but wrapped in the anguish of all of them.

"When do they start?" a middle age man, wearing a red-plaid shirt, complained as he stood next to Rachel and about fifty feet from the observing reporter. Rivulets of sweat seeped down the man's temples into his shaggy sideburns and down his open shirt front to mingle with damp, matted hairs on his chest.

"No set time," snorted another man, shorter by a head than the older one. "I stood here more'n three hour sometimes. They don't care nothing."

Rachel studied the man's thin face and long neck which he stretched upward to compensate for his size, making him resemble a turtle straining out of its shell. All of it repelled her, the stench of unwashed bodies, closeness of the crowd, the fall heat and above all the agonizing need for a job.

She *had* to find work, *had* to move out of her sister Alice's place, and *had* to find her own direction in life. Her impatience in all this flowed through her fingers as they clasped her cloth bag, unclasped the handle, twisted and gripped the handle repeatedly.

The pressure of the car fender continued against her side, but now she sensed a new discomfort of a sharp object gouging into her back. She glanced around and down at a small pale woman whose frowning face was framed with blond hair.

Rachel's first thought was that the woman was totally out of place in the dark, swamp-like mass of people. She was softly rounded, her complexion glowing, peach-blossom like. A little paper doll, Rachel thought, suddenly aware of the comparison of her own tall, slender body.

"Sure am sorry. They're jist shoving into me." The woman's voice was timid, with a heavy Kentucky accent that carried the last word of each sentence to a higher pitch. "I wish they'd stop pushin'. This is the worst I seen it," the young woman said, although smiling in acceptance of her lot.

"You been here before?" Rachel asked, shifting her body slightly to ease what she realized was the woman's handbag jammed against her.

"I'll try to move it up a little," the woman said, looking down at her handbag, "but I don't want to call any attention to it. I got two dollars....." She stopped, fearing her words were being heard by the men around her. She adjusted the square straw handbag nearer to her breasts. The clutching fingernails, bitten into the quick, contrasted with the prettiness of her face.

"Why are so many men here?" Rachel asked. "I thought they hired mostly women for the factory."

"They do," the woman responded in a soft voice that Rachel strained to hear over the gruff male conversations around them. She almost whispered now. "But men think they need work most. They ain't much around, so they jist show up wanting anythin'. And there's

8

never any coloreds. They never hire any coloreds here at the tobacco plant. You been here before?"

"Three days. Only hired two in that time." Rachel couldn't take her eyes off the woman's hair. The paleness of the blond curls turned almost gold in the sun light that was now creeping over the factory.

A few freckles were spilled irregularly across the young woman's cheeks and nose. Blue eyes, almost the color of a Robin's egg, looked up at Rachel.

She's too fragile to work in this factory, Rachel thought, eyeing the young woman when she caught her looking the other direction. The delicate features and body of the woman made Rachel self-conscious of her own mass of dark hair that was hard to keep confined, of the hollows under her high cheek bones, and her chest which she wished would start maturing like her sisters.

Although Rachel's eyes also were blue, and people told her they were startling with her dark hair, she knew her eyes failed to match the sharp brilliance of the doll-like woman beside her. She's about my age, seventeen or eighteen, Rachel thought.

The woman's dress - a pink floral design - was vivid in comparison to the dark gray and brown clothing or faded coveralls worn by most of the crowd. Rachel's own Navy blue skirt and white blouse seemed drab in comparison.

It didn't take much study of the fabric of the woman's high-necked, puff-sleeved dress for Rachel to recognize that it was one of the cotton feed sacks known so well to Midwest farmers. The colorful print sacks were used to package chicken feed, but were stitched by farm wives into aprons and bonnets. The woman's dress was of a particularly pretty pattern but, still, Rachel knew for a fact that it was the loosely-woven, course feed-sack material.

"Ya from around here?" the woman asked.

"Darke County. My sister moved here to Garland and I came to get a job."

"Don't know whereabouts that is. I'm Tina Rose Barnes. My Josh and I are from Kentucky. Somerset."

"Rachel Morgan is my name".

"I been here three months, doing some house cleaning. It

don't pay enough to feed a flea. My Josh is a house painter. Other folks ain't got money for paintin', though. Seems like nobody's painted for years in this here town. Grit from the mills covers everthing. Maybe it ain't no use to paint."

"Some places near the mill look bad, all right."

"Ya married? Have younguns?"

"Not even going out with anybody," Rachel admitted.

"Well, watch out for them steel men. At least I heard that. They drink it all up, and you got nothin'. I don't have children neither."

Their attention was caught by movement on the chest-high loading platform in front of them. The mass of bodies surged forward as a rust-fringed metal door slowly slid upwards. A heavy, sweet tobacco aroma and clanking machinery sounds flowed from the building to mingle with street sounds and rising hum of voices of impatient job seekers.

A man with a ring of gray hair framing his glistening bald head stepped under the door before it was fully raised. He clasped a clipboard against his blue uniform. His indifferent eyes scanned the undulating masses.

"We got two jobs today," he shouted above the machinery noise and people's groans. "This is gonna be quick."

Rachel and the woman were shoved forward, Rachel sliding against the Ford, as some men made platforms of the cars, scrambling onto fenders and hoods.

"Here, here!" they shouted at the man, waving their arms to attract attention.

"Take me!," another shouted, "I gotta have work. Ain't had none in six weeks. My kids is hungry."

Women in the crowd were no less polite in the shoving match - jabbing men beside them in the ribs, shouting at them, and smiling at the official as their female way to capture awareness.

"I pick this woman right there," the company man said, reaching down and grabbing the hand of a woman in a Navy blue dress and hair cropped in a brazen short style. She scrambled on her knees onto the platform and stood erect, a smile of relief on her face.

"And that little lady back there," the man said. Rachel saw the finger pointing toward her, swallowed, wondered how she could get through the crowd. She began to move forward.

Douglas Hodge also thought Rachel had been selected and began describing her on his pad. "Average height, shoulder-length hair parted in the middle, more like a shop girl than a factory worker..." Then he stopped writing.

"No. No. The pink," the factory man shouted, indicating Tina Rose beside Rachel.

That seed-sack dress did it, and those blond curls, Rachel thought. I would pick her, too, for looks, but she's sure awful little to do much factory work. Tina Rose glanced up at Rachel, confused, also thinking Rachel was the man's choice.

A flush swept over Tina Rose's face when she realize a good thing was happening to her. Nothing much good ever came her way. Now this. She was slow to react.

"Let's hurry it up," the man shouted. He pulled a red bandanna from his hip pocked. Mopped his head. "Help her out there. Get her up here."

Although disgruntled from not being chosen, the men lifted Tina Rose under her arms and passed her up through the crowd. She clutched her handbag even tighter. Two men finally lifted her onto the platform.

"I hope you got a lot of mouths to feed, lady," one man who refused to help snarled at her. "Cause you're keeping food out a my family's mouths."

The crowd broke up slowly. Men and women turned from the tobacco factory and began a mechanical pace to other mills in their continuing search for work.

Rachel hung back. Still new at job-hunting, she decided to get a newspaper and go back to her sister's place. Maybe she should concentrate on making herself a new pink and blue dress out of a feed sack, she thought, suddenly smiling. It helps to joke when you feel let down, she thought.

Douglas reluctantly scribbled out Rachel's description on his pad, and jotted down words about the "pink" woman being selected for a job. He was not conscious of searching for a final glimpse of the dark-haired woman in the crowd. But he did.

He sensed her disappointment and wished it could have been different. He felt sorry for all of then, as his narrowed eyes scanned the crowd before he headed for the newspaper office to write his story.

Tina Rose and the first woman who had been hired waited on the platform.

"Congratulations," Rachel said in a loud whisper to Tina Rose.

Tina Rose leaned down toward her. "Looks like I had the luck today," she said. "I sure needed it, kid, I tell ya."

"I'm happy for you," Rachel said, offering a small wave as she took a step backwards, then another. Where would she go now, what to do to fill the hours until she returned to wait at the plant again the next day? She dreaded going back to Alice without work.

"You keep trying," said Tina Rose, turning away to join the other new employee in following the company man through the raised door. It creaked noisily down to enclose them in the hot, odorous, production-line intestines of the tobacco plant.

* * *

CHAPTER THREE

It was a slow news day at Garland's Beacon Journal Newspaper. Douglas had met his morning deadline, the story about the continuing unemployment lines at the tobacco factory, and filled the remaining time until lunch by going over his copy for a story on safety in the steel mill.

He was not optimistic it would ever be published. The editor and publisher feared angry retaliation of the city's largest employer and the industrial "Big Daddy" that was the major force in the community.

"People are getting hurt. They're dying," Douglas repeatedly told the news editor and publisher in a continued push for them to consider his story.

"It's a steel mill, for Christ sake, not a bakery," he had been told. "If the mill closes or moves out, think what will happen to this town."

Douglas knew the community's background well, and weighed the potential of losing the steel plant. It was doubtful that Garland, a town of 15,000 people nestled in hills embracing a bend of the Great Miami River, would survive without the steel-making jobs.

The tobacco company was carrying the city now, keeping wives and daughters working while husbands and fathers were laid off at the mill.

Douglas knew that if unemployment continued much longer, a migration to larger nearby cities would deplete Garland's job force. He had written that in stories. The threat was near, but had not yet occurred. The benefit was diversified employment in the city, such as tobacco and paper plants.

Farming was the community's original livelihood, followed by pig farms, then subsequently paper mills, the tobacco plant and finally the large steel mill. Life was good, despite the fact some towns people reviled the multitude of saloons that mushroomed near the mill. They also wanted better speed controls for the wildly-driven motorcars or motorcycles.

It was good, until the depression hit. Unemployment was not unique to Garland. It was an epidemic throughout the country. That was the theme that dominated many of Douglas's newspaper articles, but he also was pushing for awareness of better safety standards at the steel mill.

Company officials, he was extremely aware, tried to do their part. They had established a safety committee and awarded various departments for their outstanding efforts. It was the workers who often lacked caution in the hazards they faced.

Sometimes they were just ignorant, often they were careless or indifferent, but some of them always were a constantly threat to themselves and others. Job hazards were a fact of life that plant officials stressed daily.

Sounds from the plant alone made the community aware, such as when blasts reverberated and the ground quaked in winter months when red-glowing slag from the blast furnace was emptied at frozen dump sites. The force from the steaming-hot slag meeting the icy landscape was an ugly reminder of the mill's power to mutilate and kill.

Douglas had spent months compiling statistics on mill accidents, and his work had received tentative editor approval, but the publication date was still in the future somewhere. He was going over the paragraphs again, polishing the words, as a copy boy passed by his desk.

"Jim said to give you this," said the youngster, handing Douglas a teletype story that had been passed along by the news editor, Jim Porter. Douglas glanced down the room at Porter, a raggedy-collared, churlish loud-mouth who had absorbed the gossips and scandals of the city for nearly thirty years. Nobody crossed him, he knew too much.

Douglas laid aside the pages of his own story, and skimmed the wire story about bloody industrial strikes hitting major corporations throughout the country. What if it happened here, he wondered. Unemployment, safety conditions and now potential strikes.

Hell, is there anything else we may have to deal with, he wondered.

Douglas personally did not think a strike was a threat. Not at this plant. Company and employee relations were good. The company wanted a good product and workers wanted a well-paid job.

Workers in other parts of the country, according to the teletype story, were on strike for better wages and working conditions.

It could spread to us, he reflected, realizing that human nature can be infected with dissatisfaction if people think others are getting more. Although Douglas wanted to awaken local citizens to the need for safer working conditions, he knew Garland was not cursed with the sweat-shop working conditions described in the wire story.

Some of his past newspaper articles had stressed how the local MVS steel company and its independent union had a cooperative agreement on resolving grievances.

The document, re-evaluated and re-endorsed every year, had been touted as a ground-breaker in the nation's industry. Douglas reflected on that agreement now, and realized if it were upheld in the future, it could be the major factor in preventing a potential local strike.

"Douglas," Porter roared from the front of the news room, interrupting the reporter's thoughts. "I'm sending back another wire story." He shoved the paper into a copy boy's hand.

"Cut it to four inches for me. Some crap about two New Orleans doctors saying smoking causes lung cancer. Didn't the shits ever hear of consumption?"

Lighting up a "Lucky" and adding to the blue smoke hovering near the high ceiling of the room, Porter searched through a pile of other sheets of paper torn from the teletype. He was checking for other last minute news items worthy to serve as fillers for the day's page layout.

Quickly scanning one story, he raised his voice to reach the society editor in a cubical at the end of the room. "Kathy", he bellowed.

Katherine Courtney, a slender widow hunched over her desk, glanced up under the brim of her brown feathered hat. She wore hats to hide her hair's dark roots on days before her regularly-scheduled beauty salon appointments for hair sets. This was one of them.

"Story here," Porter's heavy voice rumbled down through the room, "about Disney throwing a big bash in Hollywood for his first feature-length cartoon, `Snow White and the Seven Dwarfs'."

"So?" Courtney yelled back.

"Can you take 10 inches?"

Reporters' heads turned, knowingly. Porter realized, too late, from Courtney's long pause, that he had set her up once again for her traditional response.

"I'll try," Courtney cooed in her sexiest Mae West imitation.

"Shit," Porter cursed, tired of being the cause of the staff's chortles and guffaws that followed. Yet he realized the too-often repeated dialogue served as a tension breaker, such as now, at deadline.

After the last story was shot off to the typesetters via the inter-office tubes, Porter headed down the news room toward Douglas. Other reporters pushed back from their desks, several made bathroom trips, and a few left to keep appointments for stories the next day.

"Did you see that wire story about Hitler?" Porter asked Douglas in passing, aware that the young reporter read most wire stories daily in his drive to increase both his journalism talents and his awareness of world events.

"Haven't seen the story yet," Douglas answered, his eyes locking with Porter's. The younger man's gaze often made people uncomfortable. It was intense, made people feel as if he were seeing inside them. It didn't affect Porter. He had been around, experienced too much. Nothing fazed him.

Porter relied on his ability to size up people, and he knew he had Douglas pegged. He was aware the younger guy liked his job, but was ambitious and would move on to something bigger in the future.

Just now, Porter knew Douglas would ask for a raise if he thought the newspaper could afford it. He needed the money to buy household luxuries and other goodies his young "porcelain-like" wife was increasingly impatient to have.

His gut feeling was that Douglas could never provide everything the blond rich-bitch's parents had prepared her to expect in life.

"Guess I tore it off the teletype and left it on my desk," Porter said of the Hitler wire story. "It's about Neville Chamberlain meeting the Fuhrer at Berchesgaden. I decided to hold it, at least for today."

"I don't think it's something we can ignore," Douglas said, standing. "A lot's going on in Europe just now, Italy withdrawing from the League of Nations, Chiang Kai-shek's war on Japan...."

"The story didn't say what the hell the meeting's about, but, we can throw it in the paper tomorrow to cover our ass if something comes from it," Porter said, turning to saunter away.

"Any particular reason why you didn't use the story about industrial strikes throughout the country?" Douglas asked.

"What's the use of printing that crap?" Porter barked over his shoulder. "Doesn't apply here. Besides, why give some unhappy bastards ideas?"

* * *

CHAPTER FOUR

Rachel realized she was greedy in life. She suspected part of it was because she was spoiled by watching depression-era motion pictures in Garland. A twenty-five cent ticket allow her to share the lives of heroines who swept through life in satin dresses and pearls. Although the elegant women agonized many crises, they always ended the films living happily in their mansions on the hill.

It was escapism. Rachel did not expect to be rich, although the thought was lovely. Still, she had the urge of every woman for someone to love and to have a family of her own.

Sometimes, dreams were suffocated with longing for just the basic necessities of life, a job and place of her own. Each daily rejection at the tobacco factory left her with a hardening resolve to grasp from life these two simple compulsive demands. Many other people, with children, were without homes and jobs, she realized, but that did not lessen her drive to achieve them.

In the five weeks she had been in Garland with Alice and Tim, her simple cotton clothes had begun to hang on her slender body. It was not that they lacked enough to eat, it was that the ache in her stomach and tightness of her throat forced her to just nibble at her food. The triggers were fear and dread, she realized, and the uncertainty of what was going to happen to her.

Rachel knew she would move out of her sister's place as soon as possible. She had to do that. The living conditions were not what she had expected when she had become determined to leave her parents' home and move to Garland.

In this agonizing time of joblessness and indecision, she often lay awake late at night in her offensive quarters at Alice's place and recalled her efforts to break free and get to the city. Her mother had not made it easy.

* * *

"I'm going".

Rachel stood defiantly in the center of the farmhouse kitchen. She and her mother had hurled words viciously back and forth for nearly a half hour. The argument had escalated over the previous weeks.

"Alice is coming for me Saturday and I'm going to the city with her and Tim," Rachel said, her eyelids narrowed angrily until her deep-blue eyes resembled slivers of marble.

"Talk's cheap. You can say anythin' you want to, and you probably said most of it a hundred times, but you're stayin' here. The city is no place for a girl."

"Alice moved there when she was seventeen."

"She was married and had a man to take care of her. Always been like that, always will for women. Alice is better able to take care of herself, too. She was always better able. This nonsense is stoppin', Rachel. I'm not spendin' more time on it."

Nan Morgan turned from facing her daughter to pull a rocker away from the wood-burning cook stove and closer to the window. She plopped down as if dismissing their quarrel. The window was filled with pots of flowers, lush with late summer growth. Nan gently began pulling out dead leaves and breaking off dried stems. Her fingers seemed to caress the delicate plants.

Rachel had no memories of her mother just sitting still and doing nothing. Nan was never inactive, and she never backed off from any challenge in her life. She was not about to now.

"I tell you, Ma, nothing's going to happen to me. I'll live with Alice and Tim, and get a job. They'll look after me."

"I know nothin' will happen, cause you're staying here with

19

your family," Nan said. "No more talk."

"Why you so stubborn? I should have know you'd be like this," snapped Rachel, too angry to cry. " You make your mind up the way it's to be, and nothing and nobody can change it, even when it's wrong."

"All you're thinkin' about is yourself. What about us here? There's a lot of work and you're the last youngin' at home. You're just now beginnin' to pull your share".

Nan gathered her apron up with one hand, and tenderly dropped a handful of crunched leaves and stems into the pocket she had created.

"I could send money home like Ted."

Nan's raised her voice until it echoed in the room. "Your brother was always the providing one. What kind of job you think you can get? We want you here, helpin'. Not going off to some drinkin', gamblin' town where you'll lose your reputation and no one'll ever marry ya."

"That's what you think, huh? Lot of faith you have."

Rachel had never known warmth toward her mother, who was not a person with praising words or pats of affection. She could not remember seeing her mother show tenderness to her father, hugging him or touching him as he passed. She did not offer that gentleness to anyone, although the girls in the family thought their mother favored the boys.

"Then there's nothing for me to do but just go," Rachel said, losing her anger with the realization that they would never resolve the rift between them. "I'll just pack my things and be ready when Alice and Tim arrive Saturday."

Nan, clutching her apron full of plant debris as she stood, pushed her daughter aside and headed for the trash pile outside.

* * *

20

Saturday arrived. The last of Rachel's parcels was stacked in the back seat of the Model T Ford that Tim and Alice had borrowed to come after her.

Rachel checked several times to make certain her three prized books were packed carefully in her large, cloth travel bag. She owned little, but all her possessions crowded in the back of the car left scant space for her.

Tim was puffing and red-faced from the exertion of his overweight body helping her lift some of the items into the car. She could have done it easily herself, but he insisted on sharing.

"Isn't Mom gonna come to say good-bye?" Alice asked, almost mockingly, as she glanced toward the stooped, bonneted figure in the garden patch beyond the house.

Tall and thin, Alice stood as ramrod straight as an officer overseeing troops. Like her mother, she wore a severe hair style, stretched tight in thick braids that were wound into a crown on her head. When other women switched to rolls at the back of their neck and hair puffed softly over their ears, Alice still held to the stretched, taut style she felt suited her.

Unlike some siblings, Rachel had never yearned to be like her older sister. Alice was too unyielding for her. She had to be the one giving orders, acting the part of the school teacher in their games or the queen ruling over the land. Rachel would like to have taken turns in being "the leader", but that generosity was not one of Alice's character traits. Still, she could not complain about her sister now. Alice was willing to take her into her own home in Garland over their mother's objections.

"She's just ignoring us," Rachel said, shielding her eyes with her hands to see her mother's figure huddling in the garden like a plant drooping in the sun. But Rachel knew her mother was not soft or weakening. "She hasn't talked to me for two days, so I can't expect she's suddenly going to change. She told me never to come back."

"You know Ma. She'll hold out awhile to make her point." Alice glanced back toward the house as Tim walked out the front door with their father. The screen door was not allowed to slam. Her father was careful. Ma always scolded, otherwise, saying, "Fred Morgan, were ya raised in a barn?"

Rachel walked to her father and put her arms around his neck, aware of the sweaty but not unpleasant smell of him. She had to stretch. He leaned down to pull her against his chest.

"Why's she acting like this, Pa? She knows I'd leave sometime."

"It hurts parents to see kids go. Everything changes."

Her father patted her on the back before releasing her. He took a red bandanna handkerchief out of his back coverall's pocket and wiped his brow, still damp from his labor in harvesting the back forty acres. His forehead was vivid white, marked where his straw hat provided protection from the summer sun.

Dad was the one Rachel always turned to with her problems, the one person she would miss most. He was the one who got up in the middle of the night to rub her feet when they ached or put a cold cloth on her head to cool a fever.

He knew how to remain silent in the evenings when her mother harangued over something or other, usually not important. Rachel had watched Alice do the same with Tim. That was one thing she decided she would never do with her husband, whoever he might be.

Rachel wondered what the city would hold for her. It had to be better than the farm. She wanted the emotions of love she had read about in books. She fantasized about sitting with her husband at sunset and watching the clouds exchange colors. She longed for moments of kissing children's sweet-smelling foreheads at bedtime.

I've read too many books, she often thought. I don't know anybody who really has all that I'm wanting, but I'm willing to work hard a lifetime to get it all. Now as she looked back at the figure in the garden, she realized the challenge was beginning.

Cupping her hands around her mouth, she shouted, "Good-bye, Mom. I'll write to you."

The bonnet did not turn toward her. The face remained hidden. Hands from the figure continued moving, half hidden in the plants.

22

"Tell her good-bye for me, Pa. I don't know if she's going to forgive me or not. But I have to go." She hugged him again, squeezed tightly, then let go to step up into the back seat of the car.

"Alice, you and Tim look after her," Fred Morgan said. "She's a little pine knot. The toughest part of the tree, but we all need a little lookin' after now and again."

"We'll take care of her. I'm still the big sis," Alice said, wondering somewhat jealously if her father's eyes had looked as moist when she left home. She could not remember. She, too, had been anxious to get away.

"Scoot your boxes over in the corner so you'll have more room," Alice ordered Rachel, who considered her possessions already packed as tight as possible.

"Sit behind my seat so Tim'll have better view out the back."

Rachel, rearranging, resented just slightly the dictating tone Alice used in settling into the car. She had to accept it now, but sometime soon she would have to let Alice know in a nice way that being a grown up woman was the main reason she was moving to the city.

Rachel's spirits lifted when she was out of sight of the farmhouse. It was actually happening. She was leaving.

"You said in your letter there's not many jobs. Do you think I can find work?" Rachel asked as they drove along the pike toward the small village where her parents did their weekly shopping on Saturday afternoon.

"There's some jobs," answered Tim, his eyes never moving from the roadway. "They're hard to come by. Most of the work for women is at the tobacco plant where Alice works."

"It's good clean work, too, and pays well," Alice added smugly. "I'd say we women workin' at the tobacco plant are luckiest in the city, even more than men at the steel mill. They're always having layoffs there, ya know."

"I want to get something soon so I can start paying you board," Rachel answered, trying to visualize herself handling tobacco in a factory. She did not welcome the idea, but the work would be a beginning step toward getting a place of her own. She also wanted some time to get some books at the library, study and improve herself.

Momentarily distracted by passing through the little town she was leaving behind and the school where English teacher Amy Hudson had introduced her to books, Rachel felt an ache. The books had awakened such a thirst to know more, to see more, surround herself with lovely things in her own private place. She felt no sadness at leaving.

Goodbye, Little Town. I won't be seeing you again for awhile, she thought gleefully. Rachel settled into her seat as they rode through farm lands where each homestead had it own patch of woods. After a time, she asked how Tim's barbering business was doing.

When he didn't answer, Rachel thought he was considering the question until Alice blurted in a loud voice, "She asked how your barbering business is doing."

Rachel had forgotten Tim had partial deafness since childhood.

"Seems like people still need haircuts. We'd like to raise the price over a quarter, but times are tough. We're hanging in," said Tim, both hands gripping the steering wheel as if lacking confidence in his ability to drive a borrowed car.

Alice often bragged about Tim that he had a steady job, did not drink and was considerate. Rachel doubted that those qualifications really compensated for living with a man who overflowed chairs, had thinning hair and a large nose. But that was not her decision, it was Alice's.

"You're lucky you were able to go to barber school and have something steady," Rachel said, striving to find kind words for Tim after her negative thoughts.

"My Tim's a hard worker, too," Alice said proudly, reaching over to pat his hand on the steering wheel. "He doesn't just close the door at five o'clock if someone comes in late and wants a haircut. He's what I call dedicated."

"It's more than that. It's money," he said, pleased at his wife's fawning comments. "You can't just walk away from a quarter or fifty cents in the 1930s."

It was obvious Alice never lost an opportunity to brag on

Tim, or to hold him up to Rachel as a model for the man Rachel should marry. Her litany was always the same: "He has to be hard working, neat and punctual, never use bad language or drink, and most of all not be a steelworker. You don't want a grimy steel man who brings filth into the house, and who faces a layoff and unemployment almost any day."

Alice always pledged to help Rachel meet some of the right kind of men in the city. The time was ripe, Rachel felt. Conversation slowed and the flat fields of west central Ohio gradually swelled into rolling hills over the next two hours as the car traveled south toward Garland.

"We're almost there," Alice announced as she saw larger hills in the distance. "Wait till you see the mountain we're going down. Tell her about it, Tim."

"It's not a mountain," said Tim, having no problem in hearing Alice's booming voice. "But it's the biggest hill around, and they still use it to test and see if cars can climb it."

Rachel grew more excited. She had grown up with level fields that stretched to the horizon, never realizing land could be so majestic.

"You don't have to be scared with Tim driving," Alice assured. "He knows what he's doing. He's a foundation person, like Jesus building on Peter the rock."

Rachel was not listening. She was gripping the handle of the door and pushing back into the soft seat, away from the massive drop off on the side of the roadway ahead. Then she saw the city spread out below.

"Oh, I already love this city," Rachel said, gripping her hands together in awe.

You don't even know it," chided Tim, finally releasing one of his hands from the steering wheel as they reached the bottom of the hill. He flexed his fingers, getting some feeling back into them.

"I don't care. I love this city anyway. It's going to be my home, forever," Rachel declared.

Downtown Garland had more wealth in stores and conveniences than Rachel had ever seen. Both Alice and Tim pointed out businesses and government buildings as they passed through the downtown district. She memorized locations of Garland City Hall, the Beacon Newspaper building, Johnson's Department Store, the three downtown theaters, drug stores and churches.

"Be sure to be careful if you're walking down Clifford Street near the mill, in fact, don't walk down Clifford," warned Alice. "There's about thirty saloons there and steel men are falling out the doors all the time."

Rachel was impressed by the number of people she was seeing. "Are there this many people here everyday?" she asked, wondering where everyone was going in such a hurry. Autos were going in both directions, horns honking, brakes screeching, people were talking to each other, or waving as they went in or out of buildings.

"It's not so busy during the week. They're off today and trying to get everything done," said Tim, sticking his arm out the window to signal a turn.

"You'll never go back to the farm again," Alice predicted.

After a couple of blocks of one-story houses, auto garages and empty lots, Tim slowed the car to a stop in front of a long building with four store entrances across the front.

"We're here," Alice said, gathering her purse and some of Rachel's packages.

"Where?" Rachel asked.

"Home. This is where we live."

"It's a store", Rachel said, confused. White drapes covered the large front window, preventing her from seeing inside the building.

"It ain't a store now." Alice explained, her voice tightening in defense, as it would many more times in coming weeks. "Tim and me needed more than just a rented room in someone's house. And who can afford to rent a whole house, even if you can find an empty one. These stores are all converted into apartments now. They're fine. You'll see."

Rachel, arms loaded with her packages, walked through the door Tim opened into the "store". She would always consider it that.

"You've made it look nice", she said, feeling her tone of

voice was unconvincing.

A maroon mohair sofa, the material worn thin, was on the left side of the opening, along with a matching chair and a tall lamp. The lamp shade wasn't straight. Behind the sofa was a gray-color, six-foot-high room-divider screen on legs about a foot high. The store area, long and narrow, was divided with several of the screens. They served as walls.

It was dim at the end of the building, where Rachel was led to her "bedroom". It was a sectioned-off area. Hooks lined the wall for her clothes. A night stand was beside the narrow day bed. Light reflected into the area, both above and below the screens, from three single light bulbs suspended from the ceiling. They were equally spaced from the front to the back of the building.

"We'll get a bed lamp as soon as we can," Alice said as she smoothed a wrinkle from the cover on the cot. "I hope it sleeps all right for ya."

"It'll be fine," said Rachel, suddenly feeling as if she were shrinking into herself. "You and Tim are great to take me in. I won't make you sorry."

"We'll get along all right," said Alice, who then began a list of dictates about eating times, laundry, not playing the radio very loud, not leaving food to spoil in her "room", and other instructions fit for a child, not a seventeen-year-old woman.

To herself, Rachel cried, I hope it's not going to be like this. It's as though Ma followed me here. Alice might as well be Ma. When her sister walked away, her shoes clicking on the worn linoleum floor, Rachel sat on the day bed to the screech of rusty springs.

I won't live like this, she vowed. I'm going to have a home of my own. A REAL home. And my sister will not make the rules for me.

* * *

27

The tobacco factory job continued to elude Rachel for weeks to come, despite Alice's efforts in putting in a word for her with the boss.

Finally, after weeks of no income and board costs escalating with Alice, Rachel was hired for an assembly line job.

Her eight-hour shifts at the Richards Bag Co. had her grabbing brown paper bags from a conveyor belt, counting and stacking them, and then shoving them into another machine to be tied with string. It was a mindless job that required lifting the heavy bundles of sacks and standing on her feet for long shifts.

She couldn't sleep the first couple of work days. String and paper cuts on her hands became infected. The calves of her legs ached from her conveyor-belt vigils. But young and determined, she soon adjusted.

With a little money now, being able to pay Alice and starting to save a little, Rachel turned to thoughts of entertainment.

The city was filled with activities that she soon was discovering. There were fall concerts in the park with some new girl friends, occasional square dances at the community hall, church activities, library visits, and the favorite pastime of most city dwellers - attending movies about twice a week.

Young men, in starched collars and summer cotton suits regularly asked her to events, but she generally turned them down. They were not the ones she secretively glanced at in gatherings.

She wondered over and over, *Why can't I look good to the ones that look good to me?* One young man she did notice at Sunday church services turned out to be a steelworker, or so a friend said in steering her away from him.

He had dark hair and eyebrows that nearly grew together over intense brown eyes. Rachel had seen him watch her also, but she was determined to avoid steel workers.

She was constantly barraged with Alice's words and common knowledge in the city about steel men, described as "a slovenly bunch that hung out in saloons after work hours and staggered home to boarding-house rooms to sleep in beds still damp from their sweat of the previous night."

I'll know the right man for me when I meet him, Rachel

reassured herself. There's no doubt about that.

Still, the vision of the dark-haired man in church, steel man or no steel man, lingered with her.

* * *

CHAPTER FIVE

March, 1935

Marty had dated some real lookers. He prided himself on that. But this one, this beauty he kept seeing in church, made him doubt himself. Made him feel that not even his good looks, his willingness to spend money or his easy teasing manner would make her tumble for him.

This was a special-looking and acting girl that would expect more. She was like one of the really pretty ones on the cover of the Silver Screen magazines. Blue eyes and black hair, a nifty combination. Marty sensed his Kentucky hill-farmer background and his experience in hiking girls' skirts behind tobacco barns would not get him far in wooing this girl.

Marty determined one evening to ask old-time steel hand Steve, when Steve took his break in working the overhead crane, for advice on words to say to the girl that would help him get a date with her. Perhaps Steve would laugh. But Marty felt strongly enough about wanting to date the girl to chance it.

How would he put it to Steve? That he had seen this beauty at church, and he wanted to get to know her? Yeah. Steve was going to laugh. Marty had to do something, though. He feared his grimy hands - he had been scrubbing them a lot lately - or his coarse way of talking would turn her away. Not that Marty wanted to get serious and get tied down, or anything. God, No!

Perhaps Steve wasn't the greatest guy to give advice, but he didn't swear every other word like most of the other mill guys Marty knew. Steve was married, had three kids, and a dog. He did not go catting on Friday and Saturday nights when the gang had a few beers

30

after work at Barney's First Base Saloon. Yes, he was the sensible one to ask.

Since his trip up to Ohio eight months before from Kentucky, Marty had lived a limited existence. Rotating on different night-and-day shifts meant he spent several days just getting used to sleeping in the daytime or then in the nighttime at his rented room on Reily Street. He lived close enough to the plant to walk to work, like many of the men. The lucky ones had motorcycles or, rarely, a car.

Mostly Marty's life was working, playing some baseball with a company team on weekends, dating girls when he needed release from the pressure of his twenty-two-year-old maleness, fishing, and going to church on Sundays.

It was at church, the West Street Congregational Church, that he had seen the girl, although he had not yet learned her name. He could not decide what made her different. He watched her sometimes during songs, especially when she turned the pages and was not aware of his glances.

Her features at a distance all went together well, a strong profile with a nose just the right size. And her chin didn't slant away. He liked that. Dark hair, heavy and thick, and vivid blue eyes.

All that made her seem so beautiful and special of all the people filling the pews on Sunday morning. It was like she was the prettiest blooming apple tree in the whole orchard, Marty thought. He suddenly felt foolish. His general idea of beauty was the fur pelts of animals he trapped along creeks back home, and that attitude was for the money they brought.

He definitely needed help if he was getting soft in the head about the girl, Marty realized. He determined to talk to Steve that night.

But the break seemed a long time away, more heats were coming up. Marty was pulling on his gloves and joining Pig in the pit when a shadow caught his side vision, causing an instinctive reflex of wanting to throw up an arm in protection from the sudden movement. He froze, cursing his own fear, until he realized the shadow was just a figure approaching across the raw earth floor of the open hearth pit.

"Another new nigger", Pig said, not recognizing the light-

31

brown face moving nearer.

The youngster, probably not more than sixteen, walked briskly, keeping his distance from the red glow of the hearth to his left. He had the thick shoulders and solid thighs of a potential steel man.

"You the new helper?" Marty asked in a raised voice when the kid was in hearing range.

"Yeah. I'm assigned on the other side for a time. Shoveling stuff. I'm Brian Young, sometimes called Hooper", he said, the whites of his eyes vivid in his brown face as he eyed the brilliant furnace.

"Why's that?" Marty asked.

"High school basketball, making hoop shots," the youngster said, turning his face away from the heat.

"A lot of 'em, huh?"

Hooper offered a broad, white grin in response.

"I'm Marty, and this here's Pig. This is not basketball, and the first thing to learn until you're experienced is to keep someone between you and the furnace all the time."

The time for talking was over, Marty knew. Now it was a matter of keeping from being hurt and staying alive.

"We're gonna pour the heat now," he explained to the kid. "You can stick around if they don't need you on the other side, but stay back there out of the way." Marty motioned to the outside platform and railing where he had stood.

"Why you friendin him up?" Pig asked as he and Marty walked toward the approaching drag. "All we get new around here is niggers. The company must be fartin' niggers."

Marty punched Pig in the ribs with his elbow. "Shut up.Pay attention, now."

They prepared to deal with the drag, a line of small buggies moving along a track and carrying single-file ingot molds. They were like massive Jello molds, except when the molten red steel was poured into them and cooled, they turn out metal ingots fifty-eight inches wide, eight to ten-feet high and forty inches across.

Marty, as pitman, waited while Steve moved into place in the overhead crane. He and Pig positioned themselves as "Billie-Boy"

Morrissey, the ladle man, approached along side the drag.

They gathered around the empty containers with the intensity of blackened, unsanitary doctors ready to deliver a baby. Like midwives, they prepared for a heat of steel from the furnace's glowing womb.

It was a job, a dangerous job, but they got paid. That's all they thought about - not about the fact they worked alongside six primitive furnaces in a building with sides open to snow blasts in the winter or heat waves in the summer. They never thought about the need for steel to meet the demands for new automobiles and ice boxes in the 1930s.

The job just challenged them to escape at the end of each day unharmed. The roof of the nearly ten-storied high steel mill was pocked with holes and bulges from missiles of steel hurled by explosions. Almost every worker, despite layers of clothing, had scars from splattered steel.

Marty, only too aware that he was one of the rare steelworkers still unmarked, watched the slow start of steel flowing like lava from the furnace into the massive ladle. When the furnace was finished tapping, or emptying, Steve maneuvered the crane over the ladle and picked it up with two huge hooks that resembled upside-down question marks.

The crane, with it's heavy cargo, moved slowly across the earthen pit to position over the molds.

Marty, pulling the red bandanna up over his nose and biting it with his teeth so he could breathe through it, moved closer when Billie-Boy, as ladle man, pulled down the stopper-rod handle. With the rod pulled from the ladle, like a stopper out of a bathtub, the red molten steel started to flow out of the nozzle into the first mold.

As Billie-Boy controlled the flow with the rod, Marty and Pig made quick inspections of the molds as they rolled on the narrow-gauge tracks. If they had been outside overnight and rained on, or picked up traces of moisture for some reason, the dampness would be highly explosive when it came in contact with the molten steel.

Even a minor blow-up could crack a mold, splatter steel like rice, put more holes in the ceiling and, most important, injure or kill workers.

Workers knew that every "heat", with a temperature of 2,800 to 2,900 degrees, was a killer.

Sometimes the stopper rod could not control the flow, if it got hung up on top of the nozzle or was sheared off. The murderous stream would be unleashed, and the ladle man would bellow to the crane operator overhead the dreaded words, "Running stopper".

Bodies would dive out of the way, and the crane operator would try to move the streaming ladle to the next mold as smoothly as possible, then to the next and the next leaving red spills along the way as the giant ladle emptied.

Some workers could panic. Marty knew of crane operators jerking loads in frightened reaction, starting a pendulum effect. The mass of glowing steel rolled from side to side with greater increasing force until the ladle couldn't prevent the heat from splattering and finally dumping on the pit floor below with a Fourth of July-fireworks effect.

Marty's crew tensed now as a team. They knew if one got hurt, they all could get hurt. They looked after each other, even if they could not stand each other.

The ladle positioned over the first mold. Steel started flowing in a scarlet jet. Billie-Boy watched the level and started to slow it down when it was about eighteen inches from the top, cutting it off when it was twelve inches from the top. He judged from experience.

As Billie-Boy controlled the flow into each successive mold, Marty guided a funnel that directed aluminum shot into the stream. Then, flinching as he neared the molds and bracing himself to not let his hands shake, he began laying four to six 1/8-inch-thick sheet metal plates across the top of the molds. Their purpose was gradually to melt into the mold, and prevent crusty surfaces. But they could not melt too quickly.

Pig followed along with a water spike, spraying water over the plates to delay the meltdown.

Marty forced himself to move steadily. If one plate wasn't placed squarely, it could drop down into the mold, and melt, destroying the purity. Marty also was careful not to let fingertips of his clumsy gloves dip into the bubbling, churning molds.

He bit tighter into the red bandanna, squinted his eyes against the heat, and took short breaths through his mouth.

Marty visually measured to make sure one plate was not higher than another. He made certain there were no gaps between the plates and liquid steel where water that Pig was spraying could be trapped. If water were caught between plate and still-scarlet steel, it escaped in some form of explosion. It could be a little puff of air, like a mini-steam engine allowing a mini blast of hot air to escape.

But if a lot of water were encased in boiling steel, it had to find an escape, and that was to blow, explode, and sometimes violently.

Workers were alert to begin. One by one the crew carefully filled the molds, topped them with steel plates and sprayed them with hot water until the drag of buggies and molds was completed.

The crew's job done, Steve waved from overhead and backed the crane away to await the next heat. Sweat-soaked bandannas dropped from mouths as gloves and coats came off.

Marty, walking toward the lunch room for his half hour break, could not understand the indifference of the other men in just turning away from this red horror they had just experienced in the pit. His knees could barely carry him.

The chant that seemed to haunt him every day returned now - I'm going to die if I keep working here. This place is going to get me.

* * *

It doesn't really matter about the girl, Marty realized when he saw Steve in the lunch room, which was just a sectioned off area of the mill. He remembered he wanted to talk about the girl at church. It would be hopeless to go after a girl like that, he thought.

Before eating his pork chop and biscuit sandwich, Marty followed the workers' routine of changing clothes. They each had

35

three sets of clothing and were assigned a three-prong hook on a chain.

Workers stripped off damp trousers and shirts, attached them to one of the hook prongs, took another set of clothes off the hook and donned them. They gave the chain a yank, pulling the damp clothes toward the ceiling to dry. They seldom were totally dry in the summer humidity. They smelled, but the men would wear them until they washed up at the end of the shift and hung them up again.

Steve, seated on a bench at a wooden table, had a drumstick in his hand and his lunch box open before him.

"Your wife must be a good cook, but then I think I said that before," Marty said, opening the wax paper on his sandwich.

"Yeah, she is. Chicken and beef stew are her best, and her pies. I've shared her pies with ya, haven't I?"

"Sure, they're great, too." Martin said. "You been married what, about fifteen years?"

"Sixteen. Two kids are fifteen and twelve now. I'm already talkin' to the foreman about the oldest, for when he's ready for a job. It's gonna be a tradition in this family," Steve said proudly.

Pig entered the eating area. Marty was concerned he would join them. But Pig changed clothes, pulled the wet ones up on the hook, and headed toward the other side of the furnace where he would join other workers in grabbing a few minutes of sleep. Time wasted. It was common practice.

"Watch out for him," Steve cautioned when Pig was out of hearing range. "I been watching him. He's not called Pig for nothin'. He's gettin' sloppy and careless."

"I watch him."

" I wouldn't want to be with him in the pit. Guard your ass, is all I can say."

"Yeah, I will," Marty said, not wanting to waste his time on Pig. "I been wanting to ask you, how did you meet your wife?"

"You hot for somebody?"'

Marty didn't like Steve talking like that. Not about this girl. Maybe he'd made a mistake doing this. "I thought maybe you could give me some tips," Marty explained. "I don't know if the girl I've seen will even talk to me. Not that I want to get serious or nothing."

36

"You sound like everybody else who ever saw a pretty face. You'll change your mind and marry like the rest of us. It's expected," said Steve, gently wrapping the chicken bone in a piece of wax paper, and laying it in his lunchbox.

"This girl at church is the prettiest I seen so far," Marty volunteered. "She's got eyes that when they look at you, it's like she's touching you. She looks away quick."

"Don't just look for pretty. They're the hardest to please," Steve cautioned.

"Maybe it makes ya want to please 'em more. But I need to know some things to say. I want to go over to her and say somethin', but I just freeze up."

For the next few minutes Steve guided Marty on how to talk to the girl and suggested topics - the church stain glass window, the minister's sermon, children playing around if there are any. Women like children, he said.

"If she answers back when you speak to her, ask to walk her home, that's always a good beginning", the older man said.

Marty made sure Steve knew he never had any problems getting girls, they were always after him, but this one was different.

"That's what we all think sometime or other." Steve smiled. He slammed his fist against Marty's shoulder in a knowing gesture and winked. He closed his lunch box and returned it to the shelf.

"This is the one I'm gonna marry, that is if I ever think about marrying," Marty blurted. "Marrying seems awful far away, but I don't want anybody else to have her."

* * *

Pig was anxious to get the last drag filled in the steel mill and meet his pals at the saloon. It was late in the Saturday night three-to-eleven shift. The gang would be several beers ahead.

He scratched his two-day stubble of beard with grubby

fingers, then wiped the pending drip from his nose on the back of his hand. Pig liked Saturdays, not having to get up early the next day and staying up late to drink as much as he wanted. It was his happiest time, just as long as someone was left at the bar to help him stagger home.

The four-man crew of Marty, Billie Boy, Pig and Steve on the crane already had poured three molds in this last drag of their shift.

Billie was controlling the flow of molten steel into the massive square containers. Marty followed along, laying plates across the tops.

Pig controlled the long water pipe some feet behind, spraying molds. But he was hustling.

"Let's speed it up there, Buddy, you're gettin' behind", he shouted at Marty in a mock growl, while stretching the red bandanna across his face. But he was dead serious about getting the job done.

"Knock it off, Pig," Marty shouted back, paying attention not only to Pig's spraying of molds but his own job of laying plates. The scolding didn't phase Pig. It flowed over him and disappeared as quickly as the water he sprayed on the fiery molds.

"You want slow," he bellowed, deliberately delaying his spraying motions until he appeared to react in slow motion. He waited for the plates to turn even more cherry red before directing the stream of water on them.

Billy shifted his eyes from the steel flow to lock glances with Marty, the whites of their eyes appearing large and prominent in contract to their dark red and black-shadowed surroundings. Both were on guard.

Don't let any gaps occur between the steel and plates, Marty methodically repeated to himself. Don't leave any place for water to get trapped.

Some small entrapments always occur. Just watch out for the big ones, Marty thought, always keeping his mind directly on the actions he was taking on the job so his mind could not wander.

With growing irritation that his antics didn't make the guys laugh, Pig grew more daring. He began to pick up sprinkling speed again. He moved the nozzle down toward his crouch, directing the stream spray into the air and giving the appearance from the side that he was spewing a massive stream of urine.

Heads swiveled at the sound of his attention-getting hoots, but the crew did not give Pig the satisfaction of reacting.

They just watched with apprehension, while giving the appearance of ignoring him. Marty and the others tried to appear to be looking the other way from Pig's next play acting of sweeping the spray back and forth as if watering a summer lawn.

Billy Boy had enough. "Stop it, Pig," he bellowed, "or we'll see how you look with that spout up your ass."

Pig's eyes flashed at him. He didn't answer. He also ignored the sweat that was flowing down his temples and into his brows.

"Shitty bastard," Pig mouthed to himself as he turned the water spray on the next mold. He moved on to the next one more quickly, unaware that the strong stream had shifted one plate a fraction of an inch out of line.

The spraying water began striking the center of the mold, forcing the plate to tilt as the cooling liquid began collecting below it in a hidden pool.

The undermining of the water pool, creating a soft bed on the already slippery molten steel, allowed one end of the plate to slip silently and unnoticed into the mold.

More water flooded around the already melting end of the plate and followed it down into the depths. It was swallowed with bubbles and gurgles. All heads were turned away, with the crew falsely believing that Pig had returning to being the competent steel man he had proven to be in the past.

The men failed to see the ignited fuse. There was nothing they could do now to stop the blast that was to come from water entrapped in the steel.

Martin and Billy Boy were about forty feet ahead of Pig when they felt the concussion.

Their ears rang, the back of their heads burned. Martin was knocked to the ground by the impact. Steve, in the overhead crane cage, activated an alarm siren. With a surge of mechanical power, he began sliding the enormous crane toward the end of the line to dump its ladle of roiling steel.

"Where are ya, Buddy," Martin screamed as he stood unsteadily and turned toward where he had last seen Pig. The stooped, twisted silhouette of Billie Boy was to the left, scurrying through the steamy pit toward the platform and safety.

Marty yelled for Pig, but no sound. Was he deaf? What was the matter with his hearing, Marty wondered. Again he shouted, "Where are ya". Marty heard nothing, not his own voice nor a response from Pig. It was like a slow-motion silent motion picture in which he could feel the devastating heat, see the fiery, steaming spills around him, but the silence made it unreal and separated from him.

Strength drained from his legs as he stood near pools of spattered steel that darkened as it cooled. Marty dropped to his knees, started to crawl toward the steam where he had last seen Pig. He snaked along the hot earthen pit, struggled to avoid larger pools of cooling metal.

The first few moments, Marty knew, could be critical for Pig in getting grease on his burns and keeping oxygen away from them.

"Where are ya, Buddy," he kept screaming. He was desperate to find Pig alive.

Billie's screams at a distance, unheard by Marty, added to the clamor of the alarm bell and hissing of the steel as it spilled along ridges in the pit's earthen floor. There was no screaming coming from the concealing steam where Pig had stood.

Marty crawled, finding his left leg difficult to maneuver - until he saw Pig, face down. He wasn't moving, patches of blackening steel covered his steaming upper body. Pig's back was coated almost solidly from the waist up, transforming him into a seemingly carved, grotesque statue.

Reaching out a hand, Marty gripped and pulled on a clean patch of Pig's heavy pit coat, tugging at his body until his chest pulled loose with a sucking sound.

Part of Pig's face was uncovered. One eye was open, staring wide with dread. The lower half of his face was covered with a dark hardening crust as if it were a beard.

Martin pushed his gloved hand to wipe it away. He rubbed Pig's cheek, shoving the cooked flesh aside, exposing white bone to contrast with the black. Bile forced up from his stomach. Martin could not fight it down. He didn't hear the continuous clanging alarm, the voices of workers racing to help them, or his own screams.

* * *

CHAPTER SIX

March, 1935

The explosion rattled the screen door and windows in Douglas Hodge's rented cottage in east Garland. His wife had just stomped off to their bedroom after another argument about needing more space. That was a goal of his, too, both to have a more impressive home and to bring a smile back to his wife's beautiful face, but he could not convince her they should not go deeper in debt on his newspaper salary.

Despite the low pay, Douglas eagerly leaped to his job, as he did now, when he was certain a major accident had occurred at the mill. He first called the police department to confirm what he inwardly knew. Details were slim, police said.

Douglas grabbed a jacket, note pad and pencil in anticipation he would be able to get near enough to the plant to talk to some workers. He suspected officials would not say anything for the record, at least for a couple of days.

"I'm heading to the mill. There's been an accident," Douglas said to his wife outside the closed bedroom door. No answer.

At the guardhouse at the entrance of the fenced plant, where a growing crowd of frantic family members and spectators was stirring, Douglas watched across the 60-foot compound where police and firemen milled around among vehicles and equipment. He could not detect what they were doing, if anything. There was no sign of a fire, or activities to fight one. It appeared to be a scene of confusion, and waiting.

"Are they going to let me in?" he asked again of the security guard.

"Not likely, not unless you're wearing one of them uniforms," the guard said, referring to the police and firemen. "Somebody'll be along pretty soon to talk to you."

Douglas was not convinced, but he knew for certain he was not going to get any information waiting where he was. Employees at the end of the shift probably had been cautioned not to leave by the main gate, and Douglas suspected they were avoiding the public by leaving through a rear gate. He raced to that area and waited in shadows until he saw several workmen shuffling slowly past the gate attendant.

Startled at seeing him, the men did not want to talk at first. People in tragedies are initially stunned. But if the right questions are asked, Douglas knew, they could open up. It was not that Douglas faked an empathy with people to make them trust him, it was that he had a sincere interest in their welfare and they sensed he wanted to help.

"Were you hurt?" he asked, approaching one worker who as about to unchain a small motorcycle from a metal bar.

"No, I was clear down at the other end of the mill," answered the man, who appeared no more than a moving shadow in the darkness.

"Was anyone else hurt?"

"You a reporter?"

When Douglas admitted he was, the man moved away. "I'm not telling you my name."

"I'm not asking you to. But families are waiting to hear something, and you know the company won't tell anything until tomorrow, and maybe even the next day. Families deserve to know something." That made the worker think of his own wife and children.

"They carried four of them out. I heard one of them got it bad, died. I guess it was instant. We haven't had anything this bad for a long time."

After asking the worker a couple of more questions, and talking to two other men briefly, Douglas went back to the front gate and waited. A company representative finally came to the gate with prepared statement that an accident had occurred, with the details yet unknown.

Douglas took the statement with him to the small, community hospital, where he confirmed three men had suffered severe burns, and one, who the coroner identified, had died.

When his story broke on the front page of the Beacon newspaper the next day, a company official was irate and complained to the news editor on the telephone that Douglas had not followed proper corporate procedures.

Jordan, appearing contrite in light of the steel company's influence in the city, told a company representative he would chastise the offending reporter.

"I should have told him to go fuck himself," he told Douglas. "Good work".

* * *

Martin Bradford seemed to Rachel to be transformed into a different man after the fatal accident at the mill. Her softening regard for him was more then the bandages he wore the day he returned to church the first time. It was the hurt look about him, although she would have denied to anyone that just sympathy altered her perception.

Originally he had been just another rugged steelworker, but she had noticed him because his eyes kept turning in her direction. Her reaction was to show no reaction at all.

Now, everyone in the congregation was aware of his presence as a sensitive hero who tried to save a friend's life and risked his own. Rachel also was aware.

Glancing over her hymnal, Rachel watched the man, who she now had learned was Martin Bradford. He was seated two pews ahead, to the left. Bandages still covered part of his hands that held his song book. Part of his black, course hair had been cut away on the back of his head for a bandage. There also was a white patch on his neck. It disappeared down into the collar of his tan jacket.

Marty did not seek her out, as his eyes had in the past. He hardly moved. Once, when she saw him in profile, it appeared to Rachel that his eyes were circled with red as if he had not slept for several nights.

Forgetting to follow the words of the song, Rachel was startled to see what might have been a bright glint of a tear on his dark eyelashes until, with a strong blink of his eyes and furrowing of his brow, it vanished.

I have to talk to him, I must say something to him, she thought to herself. He is such a gentle man, but is afraid someone will know that. It touched her.

She watched his mouth move with words of the song. Suddenly she suspected he was not singing, just mouthing the words so no one would guess how choked up he was. All these emotions she gave him, without knowing him, without ever having spoken a word with him. She wished she were close enough to touch an unbandaged part of his hand, to stroke it tenderly in compassion and understanding. She wanted to comfort him.

Rachel's thoughts of Marty in the past had been that of an unsavory steelworker. An image based mostly on Alice's warnings, but partly because of his sometimes dirty fingernails or appearance of needing a shave. She could not have known that he had shaved an hour or so before, but his heavy beard denied that.

She liked his eyes, the few times they had contacted. She admired the way his hair curled near his collar and how the front part flopped over his heavy brow until his hand whipped up to comb it back with splayed fingers. The hair didn't stay in place long.

Emotions increased in Rachel as the service neared an end. Her thoughts were overwhelming compassion toward the strong, sensitive, hurting man who sat with bowed head two rows ahead.

If he asked again to walk her home from church, she would not refuse.

The sermon was not getting through to Marty. He wished he had not come. His hands, neck and leg burns were throbbing, and he did not want people staring. Images of the mill accident still were vivid in his mind, and he was experiencing a growing fear of his

45

bandages being removed and having to go back into the mill.

Marty had to force himself to remain in his seat, not get up and walk out of the church. He longed to escape, but did not want to be noticed. He kept having mental pictures of Pig sprawled in the steaming, melted steel. He saw himself there, instead. It was his own mortality he cared about. He almost died. It could happen again, any night of the week. He escaped once, maybe not the next time.

I don't want to go back, Marty thought to himself. Damn, I don't want to go back in that God-damn mill. Don't swear in church, he thought, you may have to pay for it. But, damn, damn, damn, I don't want to go back.

Marty stood when the congregation stood. He lowered his chin, stepped quickly when other shuffling feet started moving slowly up the aisle. He felt gentle pats on his shoulders from sympathizers. He kept his head down. His purpose was to get to his room at the boarding house, shut the door, shut the world out.

Waiting in the line of people, Rachel watched the young man's stiff legged stride away from the church and down the street. She personally could feel the pain in the man. She wanted to touch him, draw out the agony he was suffering.

* * *

Marty no longer seemed interested in Rachel or anything other than his inner agony. He was caught up in thoughts of death and dying, fighting the fear verging on nausea each midnight shift when he returned to the mill's black depths.

His dark moods only began to lift, but not disappear, weeks later when tree leaves were turning color in the cooling fall. That was when Rachel reached to touch his hand one morning after church and he responded.

They talked briefly, Rachel's emotions swelling at his nearness. He was about a head taller, causing her to look up into his brown eyes. His stiff, dark hair flopped forward. He shoved it back with his right hand, still pink with puckered scars.

"Wanna go for a walk this afternoon?" he asked tentatively, his dark-shadowed chin drawing downward, fearing her rejection.

That walk was the season of change for them. They began meeting at the corner soda fountain, attending Saturday evening movies, and spending weekends at band concerts or softball games in city parks.

Rachel was apprehensive at their first band concert together because most people sat on blankets or quilts on the ground. She didn't want to be seen sitting on bedding with Marty, particularly since Alice and Tim might be in the crowd. She was becoming more and more uncomfortable living with them in the store-front building, and she didn't want unnecessary friction in their relationship.

She had suggested to Marty that they go early to the concert, so they could occupy one of the few park benches as they listened to the throb of the tuba and the drum beat of the Miami Valley Steel Co. band. Marty's hand reached for her hand, and she allowed it. It was almost dark, and maybe no one would see. She was beginning to recognize the feel of holding his hand, gritty and rough, reminding her of a cat's tongue when it licked you. It was not unpleasant. His hands were like the rest of him, she realized, a rough exterior, but actually sensitive and gentle inside.

Since their first walk, Rachel had looked for signs of his tenderness. Through their talks in the past several weeks, Rachel learned a lot about Marty, including his unhappiness about working at the mill. That made her more caring toward him, knowing he didn't like the crude and dangerous work he performed to earn a living.

Marty never mentioned it, but she suspected he was ashamed of his lack of schooling. Her own education was limited to high school, but she constantly read books and listened to how people talked or acted so she could copy them and improve herself.

When their conversations verged uncomfortably close to Marty's schooling background, he changed the subject to activities that gave him pleasure, such as rabbit or coon hunting in the hills of Kentucky, or fishing secluded streams.

Tonight his thoughts were on none of those recreations he had enjoyed at home. He was aware only of the sweetness of the night, and the girl sitting beside him in the park.

Walking home over a period of weeks, he had developed a pattern of stopping a short distance from her place to say goodnight under a massive, drooping-limbed oak tree. Marty generally kissed her lightly, stepped away, then hung behind protectively the last few yards to safeguard Rachel to her door.

Tonight he gripped her elbow and guided her under the shadowy protection of the tree. As his face neared, she glimpsed his narrowed eyes and could barely see his lips in the darkness. She closed her eyes and felt them press heavily against hers. Her body was pulled against him.

"No", she said, pushing back, pushing her hands against his chest.

Marty sounded offended. "You don't want me to kiss ya?" His voice was raw with emotions and questions.

She was still held tightly, could feel his pounding chest.

"This is not a very good place," she said to stall.

"What then? Where? A place you say. We don't have any good place."

Rachel pulled away, fearful he would feel her trembling. She looked at the ground, embarrassed.

Marty held her by the arms, turned her to face him in an attempt to see her eyes. He pulled her close again, gently, wrapped his arms around her. His breathing was hot on her temple.

"It's okay, Babe. I want you, but we won't rush it too much." Marty patted her softly on the back to calm her trembling, which had stirred him more than he realized. Although he wanted to grab her and love her, he felt protective also.

"We don't have a place, Hon. But I promise ya, we will, soon."

* * *

48

"Our people are creating their own problems", Daniel, a brown, shriveled man with a cap of wiry white hair, warned his grandson Hooper as they sat on the front porch of his two-bedroom, brick house in the south end of Garland.

"Seems like people want all the benefits of a job, but they don't want to work at it," said the older man.

The teen-ager was caught in the dilemma of most young colored men in Garland in the mid 1930s - make a career decision to work in the mill or spend a lifetime in service jobs, like custodian or kitchen helper. He didn't like any of the choices.

Brian had grown up watching his father and grandfather head off each day to work in the mill, and he was aware they had used their pull to get him his job in the open hearth. It was like that in mill families. He should be grateful, he knew, but he hated the expectation laid on him to continue the tradition.

He'd often heard from his grandfather how he'd been recruited for a mill job from Atlanta, along with others of his race from Arkansas, Alabama and Georgia. He became a "charger", a worker who put slabs of steel back in the furnace to reheat, so they would be soft enough to be rolled. It was a good job for a colored man.

"We started out good, but somehow our young men got ideas about how they wanted to work, they didn't wanta work weekends," Daniel repeated again to his grandson as they chatted on the porch when Hooper visited one fall evening. "Where'd they get that, they didn't wanna work no weekends? We worked, and your daddy still does, whenever they want us to, weekends or no."

Daniel lit up his pipe and settled back into the scarred and weathered wooden rocker that had been in his family as long as Hooper could remember. The grandfather never let the rocker remain on the porch overnight, but always dragged it inside for protection. He mostly spent his summer retirement time now rocking on the porch with the pipe in one hand and a fly swatter in the other.

"I donno that I wanna work in the mill," Hooper said, finally blurting out what he knew could hurt his grandfather. "I really don't see none of us getting anywhere doing that."

"What ya mean gettin' anywhere?" Daniel exploded. "We have clothes to wear, and more'n we need to eat and I own this place. We're doing better than most of' them down south, where we lived before. I can tell ya that."

"The steel company built these row houses just for colored families," Hooper blurted back.

"And I was lucky to rent one and finally to buy it," Daniel snapped. "Don't you put down our home."

Hooper hoped his grandfather would not repeat again how he and other colored workers first lived in temporary, all-male barracks. Then to keep them on the job, the steel company built houses so the workers could have wives and children with them.

But just as Hooper suspected he would, the older man began reviving memories of the by-gone days of living in the barracks and the pride of moving into a newly-built house.

"White workers didn't fare as well," he recalled. "They rented rooms in boarding houses, couldn't afford to get married."

"I wasn't putting us down, grandpa. I didn't mean to do that. It's just the mill I'm thinkin about. It's hell."

"Shaddup. We don't talk like that in this family. There's enough words to say what we want without swearin'," warned the older man, his rocker stopping on a forward peak.

"Wasn't really swearing, Grandpa. Ya' know Hell's in the Bible. And the mill's what ya think hell is like, hot and never gonna stop burning. And ya can't say life's been easy for Grandma and Mom. They've cooked and cleaned in almost all those big houses up and down Center Street."

Daniel's voice shot up a notch in his anger. "Ya wantin' it easy? It ain't gonna be, son. Maybe you gotta change your thinkin'. Maybe you gettin' like them that don't wanna work weekends, either."

Hooper was defensive, but stood his ground. "It's not like that with me."

"Hope not," the rocker returned to its full roll. "We just gotta be more grateful for what we do have."

Hooper had heard that before, too. He knew the discussion

was ending. It always ended on the "being more grateful" part.

"Company people think we're not responsible no more," the older man continued. "They're not giving us responsible jobs. Your generations gotta do better, son. Just gotta."

The talk with his grandfather did not lift Hopper's spirits as he left the porch and headed down the street to his home. Maybe he was just reacting to his pending graduation from high school, where things really had not been so bad, Hooper realized.

He had entered the public high school - which was attended by children both from the town's elite and colored families - with a reputation from middle school as an outstanding basketball athlete. His talents were long shots, which gave him the nickname 'Hooper', in recognition of his hoop shots.

Although the predominately-white student body had a quota of not more one or two colored players on any one sports team at a time, a daring coach had put three colored players on a hot 1934 basketball team. That included Hooper, who was more surprised than anyone when he was elected team captain.

The team won regional championships and made a good showing at the state level in the next three years. An athletic scholarship was a strong hope for Hooper at one time, but it didn't come though. He tried not to complain, but it hurt. The scholarship would have been his door to the future. He mentally fought having to compromise, but he took the mill job his father and grandfather had arranged.

But I'm not going to stay in it, Hooper swore to himself as he neared his house. I'm going to be looking for something better until I find it.

* * *

It had been months since Rachel savored Marty's first serious kiss. Now they were routine. Marty borrowed a friend's car several times in the spring so they could park under the trees by a lake in an old stone quarry. Marty's increasing deep sighs and insistent kisses told her he wanted more, far more. What surprised her most was that part of her did too. Yet she felt uneasy, not sure how much to respond.

"It's okay, Babe. We're gonna git married. I just get carried away and can't hardly wait I guess. When ya gonna tell your sister about us?"

"I been waitin' for the proper time," said Rachel, buttoning her blouse.

"Seems like you should have had that many times." Marty's voice sounded strained as he pulled away from her slightly. "You're not bein' fair to keep us waitin' this long."

"I know, but we need to find a place to live. Okay. I promise, I'll tell her," said Rachel, dreading the moment when her sister would know she was marrying a steel man.

* * *

CHAPTER SEVEN

July, 1936

Rachel's dread of talking to Alice about her marriage to Marty kept her silent for long periods as she and her sister seeded cherries in the steamy kitchen of the store-front apartment.

The steam from the kettles swirled cloud-like near her , but so intent was Rachel in her thoughts that she was unaware of the warm discomfort of the room or of the routine pattern of her fingers rolling the cherries around in her hands like red marbles.

Only a bubbling sound was heard as Alice placed filled and sealed jars into the canning pot on the old gas stove. The large kettle covered two of the burners, and wedged against the gas oven at the side.

"We're lucky we got this many before the birds got'em," said Alice. Rachel was silent. She sat with a pan of the brilliant-color fruit on her lap and a bowl for the seeded cherries on the table in front of her. Her hands were red and slippery as she dug her thumbnail into each cherry to remove the seed.

Rachel deliberately picked canning time to talk about Marty. She had lived in her own room in a boarding house for weeks now, but she returned to Alice's store-front quarters to reveal her marriage plans under the disguise of the canning process activities.

"You're awful quiet," Alice said. "Cat got your tongue?"

"I guess I've just been intent on what I'm doing."

"You can still use your hands and talk, can't you."

Rachel had to smile, despite her growing discomfort.

"Well, I've been wanting to tell you something, and didn't know how," she said in a quiet voice that had to compete with the bubbling sound from the stove.

"Best way to begin is jist to spit it out."

"It's that... Martin Bradford and I are going to get married," said Rachel in a rush of words, hoping she had picked the right time. She was wrong, there wasn't a good time.

"Whose Martin Bradford?"

"You've seen him at church."

"He's not that steel man that got hurt."

"Yes"

"Haven't you heard nothin' I said about steel men?" Alice bellowed, the force of her breath cutting a swath through the steam. "You're still a kid, not old enough to get married, specially to one of those drunken no accounts who can't even hold a job most of the time."

Talking back would have no effect on Alice, Rachel knew, no more than it ever did with Ma. She waited while Alice spewed more anger.

"You haven't even been out on your own very long. You don't know what it's like not to have grocery money at the end of the month." Alice banged another pan of seeded cherries down on the kitchen table. A few plopped out onto the yellow oil-cloth covering.

"You're just not gonna do it. I'm not gonna let you. I told Ma and Pa when I let you come here I would look after you and by gum, I'm gonna do it." Alice's shrill voice bounced off the ceiling and hard linoleum floor.

"You really don't have much say about it , Alice," Rachel countered, deliberately keeping her voice low, her words slow. "You don't know Marty or what he's like."

"I don't have to. They're all alike. You'll just keep on having babies, and you won't have money cause he'll drink it up at them bars. I've watched enough since I've been here."

"I won't let that happen."

"Sure, as if you'll have any say." Alice stomped to the sink to rinse the cherry juice from her hands. Rachel resisted the thought that the juice looked like blood.

"You should marry a man like mine. I knew what I wanted, and waited for him." Alice wiped her hands on a dish towel she grabbed off a rack by the sink, and slapped it over her shoulder.

"We went out of our way to take you in here, gave you a place while you got started," Alice reminded.

"I've told you every time you bring it up that I'm grateful," Rachel said soothingly, despite the fact she hated the store-front apartment. It had lacked any privacy for her. Muffled whispers and movements late at night from Alice and Tim's sleeping area had been offensive to Rachel, plus the fact that Tim's bloated and ponderous body had more and more frequently passed by her room partition when she changed clothes. She had not complained to Alice.

"You can save money on your job at the paper mill if you give up this silly notion of marryin' somebody you just met, and a steel man at that."

"I didn't just meet him. I've known him for months."

"An you're just now tellin' me. Figures," Alice snarled. "You should stop this nonsense and start thinkin' about meetin' a man at church."

"I did meet Marty at church."

"Oh, Marty Smarty, I don't wanna hear no more about him." Alice's voice grew in intensity as Ma's did in giving an ultimatum. She grabbed the tea-towel from her shoulder and began mopping up the table. "What you're gonna do now is concentrate on your job and save your money."

Rachel took a deep breath. "What I'm gonna do now, Alice, is marry Marty. My name is going to be Rachel Bradford. And the wedding is going to be in about a month. I would like you to be there."

"You ignorant, stupid child. You're really going to do it then? No matter what I say?"

"No matter what you say." Rachel responded with a tone new to her, one of authority and decision. She liked the feeling. Alice froze. Small twitches in Alice's fingers shook the damp towel in her hand.

"You think you know so much. You're gonna cry like you never knew you could."

* * *

Alice is just like Ma, trying to control me, Rachel thought as she lay awake that night in her small boarding house room.

I have to make my own decisions, and not let anybody force me to do something I don't want to do - like the kittens, she thought, the horror of the kittens sweeping down over her after all this time. She hasn't thought of them for many years. Whenever Rachel felt ordered about, or controlled against her will, she remembered the kittens.

* * *

Rachel had been nine years old when her mother told her to get a feed sack out of the barn and drown the new litter of kittens.

"Why don't you tell the boys to do it, or Alice, she's older. Why do ya always make me do the ugly things?" She had pleaded with her mother.

Ma sat on the summer porch, breaking green beans in her apron with hands heavy with blue veins almost as big as the beans.

"Get the kits from the back barn and take'em to the creek," her mother repeated without emotion.

"The creek?"

"Too many cats in the barn now. Have to get rid of 'em."

"We don't wanta do that, Ma." Rachel's voice seem to be back in her throat, didn't want to come out. "We can find homes for 'em. People will take 'em."

"Do as I say and don't argue." The snapping sound of the beans continued. "Get a feed sack out of the tackle shed. Put in a rock and throw'em in the middle of the creek. Leave the sack by the barn and Pa will bury 'em."

"Don't make me. Please I don't want to."

"Do as you're told."

Rachel remembered turning and heading for the barn.

Then she was with the little ones. The three gray kittens, barely three days old and struggling to open their eyes, crawled and tumbled over each other as they meowed in the sandy bank by Rachel's knees.

The sun was hot on her neck. She shoved her dark hair off her shoulders. Ma always said her hair was too heavy and wild for a nine-year-old girl.

"What does it feel like to drown?" she wondered, picking up one of the little squirming bodies. It lifted its heavy head and felt around her hand with a searching mouth, as if to nurse.

She put it back down on the sand with the other two. They nestled together. It was important for them to be together, close together, to comfort each other, she realized. Their heads bobbed and bumped. Their little mouths meowed, their weak feet and legs struggled to lift their slight furry bodies in the unsteady sand.

"Stay together now. You need each other", she whispered.

The sun burned. She sat and watched the little ones until her toes accidentally dipped into the cool spring water of the creek. Her feet sprang back. The water suddenly was ugly and threatening. It would take the kittens.

"I'm not going to do it. She can't make me." But even as the words left her mouth, her eyes searched the upper part of the creek bank for a suitable rock. She would do it. She knew she would. Always, what Ma said. But never like this before.

Put the rock in first, or the kittens? Probably didn't matter. She sat down again, scooting closer to the little ones.

She picked them up one at a time, brushed off the sand and laid them tenderly in her lap.

"No, don't look at me," she said, her voice catching at the pain of seeing the little victim squirming in her hand.

She closed one palm over the little face, and reached for the feed sack beside her.

She froze suddenly. "You need names," Rachel said.

"Nothing should die without a name. What shall I call you?" It wasn't easy. The names had to be unusual, but similar, so one would not be slighted. Then it came to her. This would be their last day. She would name them after the parts of the day.

"You are Dawn," Rachel said as she kissed one small head and put the kitten tenderly into the sack. She reached for another, kissed it, and named it "Noon". "Dusk" received the final kiss and was laid in the bag.

Standing, Rachel searched the rocks with her eyes, looking for the right one. It has to be a stone that was shaped like in cemeteries. A monument, because it's going to be their monument. She selected one, washed it in the creek, shook the water off so it wouldn't be cold and strange to the kittens.

She laid it tenderly in the bottom of the sack, moving little legs and feet out of the way. Meowing grew louder as Rachel tied the bag with a piece of twine from the barn. Did they know? Their tiny, soft claws were piercing the feed bag as she moved with it in one hand to the creek's edge.

Say something about then, she reminded herself, wading to the center of the stream.

"Take care of these little creatures, God. They never had a chance on this earth. They never even got to see it."

She dropped the sack, plop, in the center pool, tried not to watch. But she didn't want to abandon them. She had to watch, comfort them by her presence. Movement. Bubbles came up. Yes, bubbles. Then they stopped, or so she thought.

Yes, no more. Over so quickly.

No one will make me do anything like this again, Rachel vowed, as she waded to the center of the stream, lifted the floating top of the bag until it sucked clear of the water. Never.

* * *

That same rebellion and determination strengthened Rachel now as she lay on her narrow bed and planned her wedding with Marty.

* * *

58

The almost impersonal marriage ceremony on a rainy summer morning was performed in an empty church. Only the minister was present, along with his wife who served as organist and witness.

Rachel invited some relatives, but they had listened to Alice and stayed away. Marty's family could not travel up from Kentucky. He shunned asking fellow steel workers. He wanted to distance himself from the mill

The honeymoon was a train ride to Cincinnati and dinner at a historic inn. The ride back that evening in the rain, and a quick run along wet sidewalks, left them drenched by the time they reached Marty's boarding house room. They had to move into his quarters because Rachel's boarding house forbid male visitors.

"It'll only be temporary, until we can rent an apartment with a kitchen," Marty, his damp, stiff hair matted to his head, explained again as he hung their dripping coats on door hooks.

"You keep your room neat," Rachel said, searching for some words, as she sat down on the one straight-back chair. Her cloth suitcase was on the floor inside the room where Marty had dropped it off before the ceremony.

"Not much to get messed. But I did try to straighten a little for ya. I cleaned space for your things in the chest of drawers," he said, gesturing in a jerky motion toward the four-drawer chest between two windows. A quilt-covered double bed, a floor lamp, and a table were the only other furnishings in the room.

Rachel studied some wood-carved figurines on the table between the radio and clock, then asked, "I bet you've had those a long time?"

"My grandpa made them. He used to take his carvings to county fairs." Smiling with pride, Marty walked to the table and picked up the carved figure of a young boy with a fishing pole in his hands.

"This is supposed to be me." He looked shyly at Rachel as he held it closer for her to admire. "He taught me a little about carving, when he wasn't tending to his tobacco crops, but I wasn't too good."

Rachel took the figurine in her hand, ran her fingers over the smooth, age-darkened wood. "You should start working at it again.

I bet it's a talent that keeps improving."

"Never good as grandpa, though. He left me some of his knives. I still have'em packed away here, but I bet they're all rusty now. Say, do you want to hear some music?"

Still standing beside Rachel, Marty turn to switch on the table radio, spinning the knob quickly and catching a station playing waltz music.

I like that, how romantic, thought Rachel, gently setting the wooden statue back on the table. He's picked soft, sensitive music. I'm right about him. I knew it. I just knew it.

Marty was not aware of the music. He was tense. His gesture and the selection were just for sound to break the silence and awkwardness he felt.

"I suppose you want to get changed. I have a towel and wash cloth ready for ya." His quick steps took him to the chest of drawers where he earlier had laid them folded neatly on top.

"The bathroom's the second door on the left."

Rachel stood to accept the faded blue towels. She laid them on the chair, then went to her suitcase and took out a new white cotton gown and a matching robe. They both had small pink rosebuds as trim. The prettiest, softest, most romantic gown set possible, she had thought when buying it, what memories will I have when wearing it?

She turned to Marty, in anticipation of changing in the bathroom down the hall. "I think I'll take my coat, too, to wear over top," she said, reaching for her still-damp coat off the hook. Marty opened the door for her, pointed to another door at the end of the ivy-leaf wall-papered hallway.

"The light switch is just inside." His eyes watched her intently as she walked away from him.

Rachel would have liked soft lighting when she returned from the bathroom, maybe candle light, but there was no way to soften the one bedside lamp in the room.

Marty was wearing maroon pajamas and sitting on the edge of the bed.

Seeing him in the obviously new garment, Rachel suspected he was not a pajama-wearing man at all. Maybe it was because the fabric stretched tightly across his muscular back, or that he seemed too rugged to wear shiny maroon cotton. It didn't matter, Rachel was delighted he had gone to the trouble to make this evening special.

She found herself anticipating that same special masculine quality in the love making.

Nice, she thought, when Marty was exceptionally gentle as he took her in his arms and leaned her back on the bed. But his body felt bristly with coarse hairs when they shed their clothing. She didn't mind, even when his rough hands rubbed tenderly along her back and hips.

Her senses soon became muted with the pleasing things he whispered to her.

"You're so soft and smell so nice. I could just hold you like this forever." His voice was low and husky, too, reassuring. His stroking increased, his body pressed stronger against her, and his eagerness left him unaware her passion had not yet matched his when he started to enter her.

"I can't wait, Hon." The tone of his voice mounted in intensity.

Her flesh pulled. It hurt. She almost felt separated from the love making, as if she were watching from somewhere else in the room.

It was over soon. Marty rolled off her.

"That sure was powerful for me," he said, curling beside her. "Did you make it?"

"Uh huh" She wondered what he meant.

His head was on her left shoulder, and his large hand spread over her stomach. It was only minutes before his breathing deepened into sleep.

Rachel lay awake a long time. She had so much love to give. Marty was the one she had chosen, Rachel told herself. It didn't matter that she was not all filled up with love the way she expected to be. It would be all right. It will grow.

Rachel didn't cry. Much later as she felt approaching sleep muffle her senses, it was almost as if she were back in her old room at the farm house. Tears had come often to her there late at night as she had watched twisted shadows of the grape-vine leaves flutter outside her window. Sometimes just the thought of the undulating leaves brought a sense of sorrow. But she would have no more tears. She would not allow it.

It was a time for building a new life. This was going to be a bright period of her life, Rachel told herself. A time to start planning to get a house and have children. No weak tears from now on.

* * *

That beginning, starting a family, occurred when they were living in a rented three-room apartment over a bakery in the summer of 1937. Rachel became pregnant.

Marty was disgusted when she began begging off from making love. To her, it had become an activity much like doing the Monday laundry or getting in groceries on Saturdays. Once in a while she experienced - during his hot, panting sex - the building sensations in her body, followed by the emotional release in her shuttering and racking. But she couldn't fathom why it happened sometimes and most often not. She learned to settle for just being kissed and held by him.

"You're just using the baby as an excuse," Marty accused as her body became larger. He began stopping off at the corner bar more often after his mill shift, and staying late.

* * *

Rachel could not stand one more day in the small apartment after her confinement following the birth of Martin Allen Bradford on a snowy day in March. He weighed in at seven and a half pounds, and at twenty-three inches long.

She was bursting with energy on this fairest, warm spring day, and needed to be out and about with people. After all, the baby, she called him "Sonny", was old enough for his first outing and the warm day was just sucking her out of the second-floor apartment.

We're a family now, she thought enthusiastically, we have to plan for a home of our own now. I have to get back to work and we have our lives ahead.

She placed little Sonny in the buggy a neighbor had loaned to Marty, puffed up now in his role as a father, and wheeled it out the living room door of the apartment to the top of the stairway.

Bouncing the buggy gently down the steps of the apartment, Rachel felt a lightness of body and spirit that surprised her. It was good to move outside, fun to push the buggy in front of her, bumping it easily over cracks in the sidewalk.

Rachel headed for the downtown, a few blocks away. She wanted to see a lot of people again, look into store windows. She gazed headily, with starved eyes and a retentive memory at what people were wearing, new furniture in windows, and people sitting in the ice cream parlor. She was starved for all these sights.

Saturated after several blocks of window gazing, Rachel decided to stop by the butcher shop for a couple of pork chops for their dinner. Marty had been carrying in groceries, and this would be special for him, Rachel thought. She would even buy an extra one for him to take in his lunch bucket, a treat after the bologna sandwiches he had been taking to work.

The pork chops looked good, thick and just enough marbled fat in them, but not too much to Rachel's now experienced eye.

"Anything else for you today?" the butcher asked, handing her the wrapped package. She thanked him took the package, and laid it at Sonny's feet in the buggy.

Struggling to hold the shop's door open with her left foot and push the buggy through, Rachel saw a woman holding a child in her arms grab the door from outside and pull it back for her.

"Rachel?"

How does she know my name, Rachel's thought flashed. Oh, she suddenly recognized the woman from the tobacco plant and the pink dress.

"I ain't seen you forever," gushed Tina Rose as if they were lifetime buddies. "An you got a baby, too."

"Looks like yours is older than mine," said Rachel as she swung the buggy around to park it parallel with the meat shop window.

"This is Teddy. He's nearly a year now," said Tina Rose patting the large, pudgy baby that lay listlessly on her shoulder.

"He's pretty heavy for you to be carrying, isn't he?" Rachel noticed the baby's legs hung almost to the petite Tina Rose's knees.

"He's a big boy, all right, like his daddy," cooed the little blond, patting her baby's back in time to her words. "An he's a little slow getting started. He ain't walking yet, and sometimes I think he's jist too lazy to feed hisself, but he's a dear little thing."

Tina Rose shifted the heavy load to her other slim shoulder, and leaned down to the buggy. "What's your baby's name? It's a boy, too, ain't it, from the blue blanket?"

"Martin Allen, but I started calling him Sonny. He's a month old and it's his first outing. Mine, too." Rachel proudly pulled the little coverlet away from Sonny's face, which puckered against the bright light of the spring day. It was one of the few times she had shown him off. She had wanted Alice to come to the apartment to see him, but that had not happened.

"I can see you in him. He has full lips like your, and your dark hair," Tina Rose said, making cooing noises as she stood erect again to balance the burden of her son.

Rachel looked closer at the drowsy toddler Tina Rose held. His heavy-lidded eyes were in her direction, but there was no connection, no baby twinkle. They were just hollow eyes, covered with lids that seemed to take great effort to raise again.

When they parted, pledging to meet soon again, Rachel watched the flopping arms and legs of little Teddy as he was carried away.

Something's bad wrong with the child, Rachel thought, grateful for her own healthy "Sonny" and that she had not accidentally said anything about Tina Rose's baby to alarm her. The baby's not right, though, she was convinced.

The pork chop dinner was cooked and re-warned several times that evening, when Marty was late getting home from the 11 a.m. to 7 p.m. shift. Rachel puzzled over any perceived hurt he may have felt that could have sent him to the bar after work. They had not argued that day, and life should have been pleasant.

Things had been going pretty smoothly since Sonny's arrival and Rachel was feeling content after her afternoon venture out in the world. Now Marty's late arrival blotted some of her enjoyment.

It was late evening when she heard the living room door opened and closed. Rachel listened to the floor squeak from his footsteps as he apparently headed for the bathroom at the rear of the apartment, but she failed to catch a glimpse of him. That was not like Marty.

He generally thundered into the living room or bedroom after work and picked up Sonny.

"Anything wrong, dear," she asked outside the closed bathroom door.

"Nothing, I'll be out in a minute."

She waited. When he stayed in the bathroom for a lengthening time, she became apprehensive that he was ill. She knocked on the door gently.

"Marty, you all right?"

"Yeah, out in a minute," he answered in a familiar, but strained voice that she had learned to recognize when he was in one of his moods. She could hear water running.

"I'm coming in," she said after several more minutes, unable to stand the suspense

"Ah, don't …"

She opened the door anyway, and stared at his nakedness as he stood in front of the sink in partial shadow from the single light bulb from the ceiling. A black crust covered his genitals and his legs halfway to his knees.

Marty tried to cover himself with the dirty washcloth he held in his hands.

"My Lord, Marty, what happened to you?" she asked, reaching out to touch him. He jerked away.

"Are you hurt?"

"Just from trying to get this God-damn stuff off," he said, twisting away to hide the shame of his condition. The struggling to control his emotions, verging on violence, caused Marty to blink repeatedly as if fighting off tears.

"I was greased," he finally blurted.

"What on earth is that?"

"The guys do it. They just grab a handful of this greasy graphite, jerk your pants down and whip it between your legs."

"That's so stupid. I can't imagine grown up men..."

"I doubt they're grown up," Marty said, jabbing the washcloth under the hot, running water and wringing it out before putting it back between his legs.

"How do you get it off?"

"Like this, how do you think?" he snapped. "It dries and cakes, so you can only get it off a little at a time. And the hairs hurt like hell."

She took the washcloth from his reluctant hand, turned the water hotter in preparation for the long task of removing the black mask of graphite. With the stiff consistency of carbon mixed with water, the offensive mask almost seemed as if it would require a scrub pad to get it off.

"I can do it myself," he growled, jerking the cloth from her hand. "I don't need nobody to wash my balls."

"I'm just trying to help," she said, staring in stunned rejection as he began wiping at his encrusted penis.

"Why did they do this to you?"

"I got a promotion, that's the bloody hell why."

"What...?"

"Yeah, the foreman told me tonight. I'm moving up to a ladle man. This is the guys' way of congratulating me."

"You're promoted to a better job and the men do this.....?"

"Greasing is sort of a way the guys have of showing they're proud of ya and ya've done a good job. Yeah, sure.....I gotta get the hell outa there," said Marty. His voice dropped to a moaning whisper. "It's not human to spend your life in a place like that."

Over the next several hours Rachel stayed with Marty as he cleaned himself. She refused to leave. Without realizing her presence gave him an outlet to berate all things he hated about the mill, Marty talked non-stop about what had become to him the horrors of the mill.

He blamed the money, the opportunity to earn sixty to seventy dollars a week, as the reason he and other workers were willing to risk their lives daily in the plant.

"It's not jist the scary, dirty, backbreakin' work, that's gonna kill me," he moaned, "it's also the crazy guys that do things like this as practical jokes."

His angry mood deepened. He told of how mill hands put dead rats, some as big as cats, into workers' lunch boxes before meal times. He described how they put dirty grease in helmets and threw buckets of mud laced with graphite at workers in showers.

"Talk's randy, work's randy and food's randy," Marty said, groaning. "For a guy to whip his cock out of his pants and lay it on the table as a gag is nothing."

For the first time Rachel understood part of what had been haunting her husband in the mill. She longed to comfort him, which she did later when she held him, cleaned and soothed, as they lay in bed.

"I mean it, Rachel, I have to get out of there."

Marty's voice was muffled against her breast. "I like the promotion and the better pay it will mean but the mill's gonna get me if I stay."

* * *

CHAPTER EIGHT

December, 1941

Douglas Hodge, enjoying the Sunday afternoon quiet in the absence of his wife and daughters, was only vaguely aware of the march tune playing on the radio in the small study of his home.

Sandra had left abruptly in a temper that morning to visit her parents. His puzzlement was how to keep her happy. No matter how generous he felt he was being in providing whatever she wanted, Sandra always seemed to discover something new that was more important. Now it was horseback riding lessons for the girls he still considered infants, in addition to their ballet lessons. His wife had no answer when he had asked how they could stretch his newspaper salary to cover that new expenditure.

The late afternoon found him engrossed in sorting through old newspaper clippings to select the top story of 1941. Only a few more weeks remained in December. In his new role as features editor, he regretfully was using some of his free weekend time to help select the year's top story.

President Roosevelt's mandate to end discrimination was a major move for mankind, Douglas recognized, skimming the first few paragraphs of the story. But he wryly suspected an article about DiMaggio's hit record in fifty-six consecutive games would reflected the country's stronger reaction to the "important" news.

Douglas hoped to be finished before his wife and daughters returned from Columbus. When he heard the back door open, he quickly sorted the clippings into piles for a later review and decision.

"Halloooo", he called to whomever might respond. It brought his daughters, petite replicas of their blond mother, thumping into the room with the wiggling enthusiasm of puppies and little-girl squeals of "Daddy".

"Did you have a nice visit with Nanny and Papaw?" He hugged their small bodies to him, one in each arm as he sat in the faded leather chair at his make-shift desk.

"We wanted to ice skate, but the pond wasn't frozen hard," said Barbara, the four-year-old who always took the lead over her younger sister, Connie, three. "Papaw said even the snow was mushy".

"Can we have ice skates for Christmas?" pleaded the youngest of the family in her baby lisp. She began shedding her snowsuit and boots.

"We'll see what Santa Claus decides, but you have to ask him," Douglas answered, surprised that Sandra had not insisted the girls remove their winter clothing at the back door. That was the house rule.

"Where's Mother?" He swooped Connie into his arms and carried her to the rear of the house.

"She went upstairs... she was crying talking to Papaw." Barbara's words came in spurts as she plopped on the floor by her sister and struggled to remove the rubber boots from her shoes. Douglas stooped to help.

"Why was Mother crying?" Douglas already knew. He was familiar with the on-going family conversations - Sandra longing for the lifestyle she had before marriage and her father eager to provide it.

Barbara looked puzzled in remembering. "Donno. Schools and trips and things."

"Was it a nice ride home?" Douglas hung their snowsuits on hangers inside a small closet.

"Long. It's a long ride," Barbara sighed. "Connie fell asleep."

"Did not".

Douglas, leaving the girls to their toys, knew what to expect when he climbed the stairs. Each time he considered their life together resolved, Sandra's dissatisfaction re-surfaced like poison ivy in Eden. Six years of this, he thought, six years since she agreed we would live on my wages and the life I could provide.

His hand slid up the smooth stair railing as his slender, muscular body climbed the stairs with reluctance. He had stripped the old varnish from the railing and re-finished it. He felt pride. It was one of many projects he had tackled in buying an old house and restoring it. It's looking good, he thought, we are not deprived.

Douglas would not allow himself to resent the gifts of clothing, toys or household items Sandra's parents generously offered. But he was adamant that it was his responsibility to provide a home for his family and furnish it, and make installment payments on their car.

True, they could not afford country club life yet, which his parents-in-laws could not understand. But that was one of the luxuries he felt would come in time. They had argued over it so many times that he tried to shove it from his mind now as he opened their bedroom door.

Sandra, still dressed in her beige suit with the golden mink collar that matched her blond hair, lay face down and silent on the bed.

"I understand you had another chat with your father," Douglas began, sitting uneasily on the edge of the bed to comfort her, if she would allow that.

A long silence. Finally she rolled over on her side, her head on her arm and faced him. Her beauty, as always, awed him. Delicate features, each pleasing. Blue-green eyes that stared at him coldly now. A wisp of hair was tangled in her long eyelashes. She stroked it away with a scarlet fingernail.

"I keep trying, but I don't know for how much longer," she whispered in an unsteady voice. "Daddy wonders why I put up with it."

"Sandra, I can't help it that you didn't like this town when we moved here. You said at the time that you did." He had searched for words in the past to convince her. There was little left to say. "Some pretty important people live here."

"Nobody I care to know." She turned away from him, put her hand to her temple, signaling one of her headaches again.

Douglas stood. "I'll get the girls something to eat." He left

70

the room, descended the stairs with heavy steps. He should have realized when he first met the fragile beauty at a sorority dance in Columbus that she would never be happy as the wife of a struggling journalist in a steel town, he thought.

Her life had been cushioned with long-time family money so that she had no concept of what it would be like to live on a budget. But she had been just as determined at the time to marry him, a literary-minded student with noble goals of helping people and bettering mankind.

The newspaper job seemed the avenue to do that, communicating with those same people he wanted to reach. And he had not been sorry, well, except the salary, even as a news editor, limited him in giving Sandra all she expected.

I don't plan to work at the newspaper all my life, Douglas reassured himself, struggling to reaffirm his pride that his work had value.

After preparing the girls a treat and re-occupying them with some toys, Douglas returned to his study. He tried to free his mind of the on-going dispute over money by listening to music on the radio and sorting through the newspaper clippings to select the top story of the year.

The task and daily strife in general faded in importance when the radio blared an announcement that the Japanese had attacked Pearl Harbor.

* * *

Marty was divided with emotions at the outbreak of war.

"Doesn't look like the mill will get me after all," he told Rachel. His dread was stronger, now that he faced two potential enemies.

When production accelerated with the war demand for more steel, journeymen such as Marty were deferred from the draft for a time so they could turn out materials for weapons and tanks.

"I see guys leaving every day, and I'll have to go, too," he said resigned, uneasy that each day could bring his draft notice closer. His work load at the mill increased. The double shifts, the six and seven-day work weeks, left him with sunken eyes and inability to sleep when he had time off.

"We're lucky to all be together," Rachel encouraged. She kept her paper-mill job, leaving four-year-old Sonny with a neighbor lady, and spending some of her free hours rolling bandages with the Salvation Army or collecting tin foil and balls of string for the war effort.

When Marty's turn came for the draft, deferments no longer counting, he was relieved to be assigned to army shore patrol duty on the west coast. "It's a snap", he wrote home to Rachel.

Marty was gone only a year and a half before the war ended and he was discharged. He felt some guilt when he returned home that he had enjoyed army duties while other soldiers lost their lives. He never mentioned it, or the dread with which he returned to his mill job that was waiting for him.

Rachel had a miscarriage for an unexplained reason shortly after she and Marty settled back into their married life. Failing to conceive again, she resigned herself to having only one child.

"I guess you should be like your big sis," Alice chided after producing her second daughter. " I guess Tim and me are just fertile."

Tim's ruptured eardrum kept him out of service. His barbering business remained fairly steady, although fewer men were around needing haircuts. He raised prices to compensate.

Hooper served on Wake Island until the end of the war.

Douglas became a drill sergeant and later won a battlefield promotion to lieutenant in the march to Berlin. The scars he brought home were memories of the frozen bodies of young American soldiers stacked like cords of firewood. "Our country's most precious asset," he had written in what served as his journal, consisting of scraps of paper jammed into a small food tin to keep dry.

The war experiences transformed Douglas into a more mentally-reclusive person when he returned home. He never mentioned the hunger, cold, or the discomfort of sleeping on the ground in clothes unwashed for weeks. Outwardly he became a smiling, competent and compassionate leader who attracted others to him, but few realized that he was a seriously concentrated individual determined to correct every faulty situation he encountered.

"Your jobs been waiting for you," the newspaper publisher told him. "We've been really short handed, even brought some women into the news room."

Douglas glanced around at the familiar cluttered desks, stacks of newspapers turning yellow and wastebaskets overflowing.

"I need a few days to move my family back from Columbus," he responded. A lot of changes had occurred, faces were different, two reporters had not returned from the war. Yet the atmosphere was familiar, the paper smell, stains of ink, half-empty coffee cups.

Later recalling the publisher's favorable comments about how he had performed his previous job, Douglas felt a rush of excitement at being alive and stepping back into the communications role he had created for himself. He was home. This community and his newspaper were his life, although he did not plan to stay in journalism permanently.

Douglas felt expansive, mentally hugging to himself a broader perception of the world and the need to build a peaceful future for mankind.

Yet reality set in. Would Sandra be willing to come back to Garland, he wondered, after she and the girls had been living with her parents for three years?

* * *

Douglas had never seen his wife more beautiful than when Sandra flowed gracefully down the curved staircase of her family's Columbus home in a pale yellow dress that matched highlights of her hair.

He almost feared destroying the illusion as he took her in his arms, kissed her in a greeting without passion, and held her momentarily. It had become their pattern on past furloughs.

"I've thought about this for a long time," he said, which was true, but his reason was not just the longing to see her, but to test her reaction. It was predictable.

"I just can't believe you've been gone so long this time."

Sandra freed herself, carefully to protect her manicured fingernails, and led the way into the living room. She was anxious to call her parents in from the sun room for emotional support, but she delayed temporarily in a show of wanting to spend a few minutes alone.

"You won't believe how the girls have grown," said Sandra, slithering down into one of a matched pair of chairs instead of sitting on the couch where he could join her.

"I thought they'd be here with you, but I guess they're still at their school," said Douglas, thinking that someone must have taught his wife to sit down like that. He wondered if his girls were being tutored in the same studies gestures and actions in their private school.

"We'll pick them up this afternoon," Sandra explained. "I made arrangements for them to be home this weekend so you could spend time with them. You'll love them in their little uniforms."

Sandra had described the decision on the private school in overseas letters, saying, "Daddy thinks it's the best at this time." She told of their classes in social graces, from piano to soiree etiquette. Sandra said she personally was overwhelmed with war-time activities in Columbus from Beaux Arts fund raisers to charity dances for wounded veterans.

"I think I've had enough of uniforms, and I can't particularly see them on our daughters," Douglas said in delayed reaction to Sandra's remark.

"Oh, but it's not the same. You'll see."

"I don't think they'll have any difficulty adjusting to Garland schools."

Douglas's words abruptly were interrupted when Sandra began, "That's what I want to talk to you about." She sat up rigidly on the soft chair, and launched into a negative account of their previous life in a increasingly shrill voice that brought her parents

74

from the adjoining room.

Her father, sitting down in a fireside chair with his legs spread to accommodate his massive stomach, soon dominated the conversation.

"What kind of financial investments have you made, Son?"

Douglas sensed where it was going. He no longer had the will to compete against what money alone could provide.

When the family conference ended, in time to pick up the girls at their school, Douglas's and Sandra's future was outlined in an abhorrent plan he reluctantly accepted.

They would be a sometime family - Douglas living in Garland, continuing in his role as an editor until he decided to move to Columbus, while Sandra and the girls would stay under the parents' wings. Douglas could establish his own home in Garland, with his family condescending to visit on weekends, summer vacations and other to-be-scheduled times.

"It's not much of a life to build on," Douglas said, finally consenting to the rapid fire arguments of his wife and in-laws. A battling life in Garland was not one he would inflict on the girls. He felt that even if he accepted a job in Columbus, such as a banking job offered repeatedly over the years by his father-in-law, Sandra still would want her parents' lifestyle. Even banking would take years to reach that goal, he recognized.

"Columbus and Garland are not that far apart," Sandra reassured, taking strength from her parents at her side.

"You know, son," began Douglas's pompous father-in-law, laying down the final condition in the arrangement, "our Catholic background and my status in the banking community can not recognize a divorce in the family. This is a reasonable solution that serves the best interest of everyone."

"That conclusion can only be determined sometime in the future," countered Douglas stiffly, holding his temper to avoid having his wife and children vanish from his life permanently. Even a semblance of a marriage is a link that maybe can pull us all back together in the future, he thought, although realizing the concept's weakness.

Douglas held to that goal in the following years while his

family lived in two locations. As time passed, he spent more and more time alone in Garland.

* * *

April, 1945

The heavy spring downpours of several days had taken an afternoon break. Bulging black clouds still hovered on the horizon as Rachel's eight-year-old Sonny hurried anxiously after Tina Rose's son, Teddy, who was racing unsteadily on a path that led downward to the river.

Sonny understood and accepted the fact that his friend, even though a year older, had something the matter with him. He could not catch a ball very well and he usually stumbled when he attempted to run. But now Teddy's pudgy, unwieldy legs were propelling him wildly down the path with Sonny in pursuit.

"Wait, Teddy, it's muddy.....it's not safe for you," Sonny called.

Teddy was silent. He did not talk much, and teachers had given up on keeping him in school.

"You're not being good," Sonny scolded angrily, keeping his eyes on the billowing red jacket of his friend and not realizing the noisy river below was muffling his words.

It was not uncommon for the boys to be together, but it was unusual for Teddy to be the leader and race ahead like this. He liked to be with Sonny and periodically slipped away to meet him after school, as he had today. That always made the lady mad who cared for Teddy while his mother, Tina Rose, was working at the tobacco plant.

Sonny knew the lady would be angry, and usually tried to get Teddy back home as soon as possible. Today, however, when he left the school building, he had seen Teddy at a distance and had not yet caught up with him.

"I don't think we should go down here," Sonny shouted as he eyed the swollen river. It usually was peaceful, but no boats were out today. The water was brown, churning and rumbling.

"Teddy, wait......."

* * *

Rachel glanced at the kitchen wall clock in their apartment above the bakery, realizing Sonny was late getting home from school. She was not worried, suspecting Teddy had joined him again.

She and Tina Rose decided in their talks about the boys that there was no real harm in their outings. Sonny was consciences about taking Teddy on short walks, escorting him home, then coming home himself.

Her son's arrival stretched later and later today, Rachel realized. The ticking of the clock grew louder the longer she watched it. Rachel was grabbing up a jacket when she heard a rapid knock on the door and opened it to a frowning Tina Rose.

"Are they here?"

"I suspect they're out together again," reassured Rachel, who was motionless, waiting in the open doorway for a decision on what they were going to do.

"But it's gonna flood." Tina Rose's voice mounted to shrillness as her small hand reached out to grip the sleeve of Rachel's jacket in a tugging motion. "We gotta find'em".

"Flood?"

"It's on the radio. An they sent us home from the factory. Some workers have to git across the river to their homes." Tina Rose lead the way down the apartment stairway.

"They're afraid the bridge is gonna go. Where do we look?"

"We'll head back toward the school," Rachel urged.

* * *

77

"Teddy, you'd better stop." Sonny was breathless as he scrambled down the path in a humped, bent-over position to keep his balance.

Strangely, Teddy's red jacket was visible one moment, then was gone when Sonny looked again. No, he couldn't have fallen in the water, the boy thought, I would see him going down. So where is he?

When Sonny reached the spot where he had last seen his friend, his foot slipped in the stream of water gushing from a round, metal drain culvert to his left. He noticed the water was flowing on down the hillside to the river, which seemed to be getting higher and wilder.

"Teddy, where are you? You'd better answer me".

There was no place for Teddy to hide except the culvert. He wouldn't do that! He wouldn't go in there, Sonny thought, cringing at the thought. He couldn't even *get* in there. *Could he?*

Slipping on the wet ground, Sonny moved toward the pipe and gripped the metal edges. It was slightly wider than his shoulders.

"Teddy, are you hiding in there?"

No answer.

Then, "Sonny". The muffled voice came from the darkness of the tube.

"Are you really in there?" Sonny questioned in a panic rush. "Why did you do that? Get out here right now."

No answer.

"I said get out here." No answer.

The muffled, echoing sound again. "I'm scared."

"Then you gotta get out. Try crawling backwards."

No answer.

"Can you crawl backwards?"

"Sonny, help me, I'm stuck....an I'm wet...the water......"

Oh, golly, oh golly-ned, Sonny's thoughts raced as he realized not as much water now was flowing out of the pipe. He's gotta get out.

Sonny looked around for someone to help. No one. He's gotta get out...

"Help me, Sonny...." the voice sounding farther away, breaking off amid gurgling sounds.

Sonny peered into the dark pipe. How far back is he, he wondered. Terrified by the blackness, Sonny froze momentarily, then recovered to inch forward and move his shoulders inside the culvert.

The water on his hands and stomach was frigid. He closed his eyes, struggled forward, kept stretching his arms ahead to make contact with Teddy.

The stomach crawl seemed endless, but finally, the feel of Teddy's shoe. Sonny gave a tug. No movement, then another tug, and Sonny felt Teddy's shoe slip off his foot. Another reach forward, water getting higher, the feel of Teddy's wet sock, then a lunge to reach his ankle. Sonny tugged again, tightening his grip. No movement. He dug his elbow and knees against the cold metal of the culvert and put all his energy into his strongest jerking motion.

He felt Teddy's body break loose. More water gushed out around him.

"Ya, all right, Teddy," Sonny mouthed as water rose to his chin.

"Unhuh. Cold...."

Sonny wiggled backwards, pulling Teddy with him, easier now as the water flow smoothed the way.

"Push backwards with your elbows", Sonny encouraged as he felt his own feet tipping down over the opening edge of the pipe.

"We're almost out."

Scooting out of the pipe and balancing on the slippery ground, Sonny gave a final tug to free Teddy. The youngster's face almost matched the color of his soggy red jacket that was bunched up around his shoulders. Teddy was crying silently.

"I was scared."

"So was I," said Sonny, pretending to adjust the red jacket, but putting his arms around his friend in the process.

The mounting dark clouds, low and swift in the sky, began dumping their load of raindrops as the boys started their ascent up the muddy path.

Holding to each other for balance, they inched upwards,

sometimes grasping at rocks or clumps of grass for support. The river was not visible in the pelting rain as they struggled to the summit. It was still afternoon, but the storm blanketed the world in darkness that not even street lights would have relieved.

Buffeted in the gusting rain, Sonny led Teddy toward the quickest place of safety, his own home, picking the way by searching out landmarks disguised by the weather.

They were plodding slowly homeward, Teddy lagging more with each step, when Sonny thought he heard his mother scream his name. He turned, saw a watery vision through squinted eyes, and felt her arms around him.

Teddy, too, was curled into the safety of his mother's arms.

* * *

There was no scolding when the boys were taken home, bathed, fed and put to bed. The parents and neighborhood searchers were too grateful that they were found unharmed.

Other victims in Garland and elsewhere along the Great Miami River valley were not so lucky in the devastating flood that mounted in another three-day downpour. The muddy maelstrom overflowed its banks, surged through wheat and corn fields, and overturned trees in virgin timber land.

Turbulent waters that had amassed upstream gushed into Garland in a flood tide that inundated the first floors of downtown building and spread four blocks to the library steps on the east side of town.

People were evacuated from the modest row homes on a low bank along the river, while other residents took refuge on the second floor of their houses.

Douglas became one of the rescue workers when he and a reporter borrowed a rowboat to tour the flooded downtown area and found themselves evacuating a doctor from his office. Douglas had recognized the white-jacketed older man as he leaned out of his office window in the flooded downtown area.

The doctor's escape was blocked by the three-foot-deep roiling water.

"Hey, Doc, hold it a minute, we'll get there", Douglas shouted to the gray-haired man. "Why the hell's he still in his office?" he said aloud, not expecting an answer. He knew many people had delayed seeking safety.

The reporter, Sam Johnston, had allowed the ten-years younger and about forty-pounds lighter Douglas to man the oars. Sam actually had relinquished after nearly capsizing the boat twice.

After spotting his rescue team, the doctor disappeared from the window momentarily, then returned with hands filled with his black bag and sacks of medical supplies.

"I'm going to swing the boat around so the bow heads into the current", Douglas told Sam in a steady but slightly raised voice to be heard above the rushing water. "Grab the window sill when we get near."

"Don't know what I would have done if you men hadn't come along," the doctor shouted when the boat steadied beside the window. He handed out the supplies, then started to turn away. "Let me get one more bag of medicine."

Returning, he climbed through the window holding a pillow case bulging with various sized boxes.

"We could have a ton of diseases after this and we don't know what's happening to the pharmacies," the older man said, explaining his delay.

"What were you still doing in your office?" Douglas asked. "Didn't you hear the warnings?"

"I thought my office was where I could do the most good, where people could reach me. How did I know the water would get so high?"

After delivering the doctor and his supplies to the downtown McIntire Stag Bar and Restaurant, which was being used as the center for flood victims, Douglas and Sam helped two firefighters rescue a mother and child.

Douglas guessed they had escaped from one of the flooded

homes along the low river bank and had been swept to an abandoned train depot, where they had climbed onto the roof. It was a dangerous place for a rescue. Abandoned train tracks, paralleling the river and hidden under churning water, served as a funnel to increase the violent flow.

Each time the firemen tried to grab the roof, they were swept away. In a desperate attempt to battle the increasingly strong current, one of the men hooked his legs under the seat of the boat, and grabbed the roof's edge. The pull was too strong. He could not hold the grip.

Douglas maneuvered his craft until the two boats were linked. The combined strength of paddling to control the boats allowed the fireman again to grab at the roof and maintain a hold.

The tearful mother and child slid down into the boat, then were taken to join others at the rescue center.

Six lives were lost in the first day of the flood, but most humans were lucky. Many animals were not as fortunate. Dogs and cats could be heard yelping or meowing as they were swept away clinging to logs or branches, but more often simply fighting the powerful currents until they disappeared from sight.

The newspaper devoted several pages a day to the flood disaster. Some stories included minor human interest incidents such as a piano floating in the downtown hotel and breaking a chandelier. A pan of dough floated in one house and as it bobbed, it left patches of sticky dough on the kitchen ceiling.

One woman described watching a house float down the river from up stream and seeing a light glowing from one of the windows.

"I watched a long time. The light went out, either a lamp or a candle," she stated. "I never heard what happened to the owner or where the house came from."

Rachel, grateful the boys were safe and that her own residence above the bakery was spared the destruction Tina Rose's rented house had suffered, felt compelled to help feed the flood victims at the McIntire restaurant shelter.

She and other volunteers ignored the fact the building had a history as a stag bar that only men frequented. It was more than that now, a refuge.

Sonny went with Rachel, playing games quietly with Teddy and other children as she helped serve meals that were prepared on a massive wood-burning stove on the third floor of the restaurant building. People donated old blankets and quilts as sleeping pads.

Rachel, Tina Rose and other women carried plates of stew and large chunks of bread to temporary tables constructed of large panels of wood propped up on wooden horses. Chairs and bar stools were hauled up from the restaurant.

"This stove will go down in history," declared Rachel, holding two plates being filled from a massive kettle on the black, cast iron and steel wood-burning stove.

"It's already gone down in history. It's a treasure," said Glen McIntire, third generation bar owner and manager.

"My grandfather immigrated from Ireland and one of the first things he did in setting up a bar-restaurant business was to buy this stove. It was shipped by barge from the east coast."

Over the next few days, Rachel grew to appreciate the sandy-hair and freckled Glenn talking about his family. She learned the tavern business survived the depression by selling soup, sandwiches and "near" beer.

"My father said over the years we've served everyone from bank and steel mill presidents to winos on the street, and we have," Glenn bragged. "We've been a gathering place for most of Garland."

Glenn delighted in telling how his father convinced Grandfather McIntire to invest in the first juke box in the city and introduce music at the tavern.

"Grandfather finally agreed Dad had been right. One night he said he heard music blaring. He looked up and saw five couples, all guys, up dancing. We didn't allow ladies in the stag bar, but they were having a grand old time anyway. That juke box was a big hit," Glen recalled.

The tales were a learning experience about Garland for Rachel, giving her insight into the pioneers families of the community.

"The atmosphere is good here, and we're a tradition," Glenn told her, appreciating her attention during food breaks. "I'm going to keep it up, because I'm the next generation to take over."

* * *

Hooper became active in the flood clean-up by organizing men and youngsters of the Southside Colored Community Society to collect debris as the waters receded. They separated into teams to collect soaked debris that would go to the city dump.

Every downtown business had boxes or tubs of waste set out on the street to sell as damaged goods or simply as worthless trash to be hauled away.

Members of the collection teams, like other money-conscious citizens, sometimes slowed in their tasks to rummage through such sale items as slightly muddy socks for twenty-five cents a pair.

But Hooper hustled them along. He had developed a way of leading people, convincing them to do what he felt they should with a gentle manner, a smile and the right words.

The talent had taken seed and sprouted in the mill, where he knew he had to move up or move out, and taken root back home in the community when he returned from military service.

Hooper had pushed for promotions in the mill.

"So whatta ya think ya can do, Son? Maybe ya jist don't like your job here," said the foreman, a fifteen-year company man, who didn't like coloreds much, but recognized Hooper was one of the best on his crew.

"How about the boiler house?" Hooper was bold in making the request. The job of ash man was the only one open to coloreds in the boiler plant. He won that "step-up" job, but pushed himself to learn the equipment with the aim of being the first of his race to work as a boiler tender.

"I never got that job in the boiler plant," Hooper told years later. "But they saw that I was colored, aggressive, and progressive. They found another job for me."

His new role was with the mill's independent union when it still was in its infancy. Colored employees in his department lacked representation in their grievances. They turned to Hooper.

He was challenged one day when asked by a company man to step into a controversial case and represent employee Jamie Gus

Rogers in another department. Rogers was one of the well-known drinkers, brawlers, womanizers and petty thieves in the city's south end.

Rogers grinned at Hooper with ragged teeth and the insolent look of "you and me are different from them and you're gonna get me outa this."

Backing out of the hearing range of Jamie Gus, Hopper muttered through tight lips to the company negotiator, "This is impossible. He's colored and everything he says is gonna be a lie."

The company man at first couldn't believe what he had heard - the straight-forward impartiality of Hooper's words. But he soon learned that the new union representative for coloreds told it like it was. As Hooper's reputation grew, he was appointed to a full-time negotiator position, relieving him of mill work permanently.

Hooper always contended in his community dealings that a lot of segregation was forced on the colored population, but that they created a lot of it on their own.

"We sent our girls off to school to become teachers," he said, which included his future wife, "But when they came home, they had no place to teach in the white public schools."

The steel mill built a school for the colored students and they were satisfied, he said. Then the Southside Colored Community Society demanded that steel company officials provide a recreation center for them to substitute for the white populations' golf course clubhouse.

A Southside Center was built. A park of their own was the next goal, Hooper recalled. They got that.

"The philosophy was, 'We want our own', and that was segregation," he contended.

As Hooper and his flood clean-up teams now passed through the slowly drying downtown commercial district, he was surprised at how many of the white merchants and other volunteer citizens recognized him. They called to him, "Hey, Hooper", or waved from a distance.

They know me outside the colored community, he thought, a pleased shiver crossing his back.

* * *

"Marty, we've got to consider buying one of them," Rachel said to her husband over supper one evening after hearing about three flood-damaged houses being offered for sale by a bank. Owners had abandoned them and the houses would be sold to pay off mortgages.

"What do ya want to think about that for?" he asked, already discounting the idea with the tone of his voice. "Hell, we already live this side of the tracks. Why do ya want to move into Hunkie Town?"

"It would be owning something," she explained. "We could fix it up, sell it, and maybe buy something better."

"As if I have any time to fix it up."

"Then I'll do it, and Sonny will help me." Rachel looked encouragingly at her son. His eyes widened.

"Sure," Marty growled. "A kid doin something like that."

"He'll be a big help. You wait and see," she encouraged, smiling at he boy. " At least I'll ask some questions about the houses. They may sell pretty cheap. People just walked away, leaving the doors flapping. Oh, Marty, maybe it's a way to get a home of our own."

* * *

CHAPTER NINE

June, 1945

The one-story house Rachel favored of the three offered for sale by the bank was a long, narrow structure known as a "shot-gun" house.

The design - a living room in front, followed by a dining room, two bedrooms off a hall, and a kitchen at the rear - would allow a shot fired from a gun at the front door to go through the house in a straight line and out the back door.

The house was on a narrow lot. It had a porch across the front and the once white paint was now a russet brown from the mill's airborne coke dust over the years. Muddy flood waters had added more stain to the wood.

Despite her longing for the house, Rachel barely refrained from holding her breath against the souring odor as she walked through it the first time with a bank agent. He kept twitching his bulbous nose as if to dislodge an offensive fly on the end of it. But he kept smiling.

They were reacting not only to the rancid stagnant-water smell, but to mounds of discarded trash in the basement that reeked of rotting garbage. Somebody had kept a filthy house.

Flood water had nearly reached the ceilings in the rooms, leaving stains and swollen wood. But Rachel saw them as they would be when she finished painting and wallpapering. A quick movement in the silent, empty kitchen caught Rachel's attention, causing her to jump. A small cricket had leaped from a windowsill and disappeared in a crack under a baseboard.

"Ah, a cricket on the hearth," Rachel said elated.

"Then there you are," the agent said. "It's meant to be your house, if you call that a sign."

Watching the agent lock the front door of the pitifully disfigured house, Rachel became resolved.

"I want us to buy it," Rachel told Marty that evening. She was sitting up in bed, having waited for him to get off the midnight shift and stop for his drinks with the guys.

"It'll cost fifteen hundred dollars, but in the long run it'll be cheaper than rent. And it can be fixed up."

"You're crazy. I been talking to fellows at work, and they think the same thing," said Marty, shucking out of his blue work shirt and trousers. He had turned bitter at picking up his old job after the war. "Those are shacks, and a lot of foreigners live in that part of town."

Marty disputed all her reasoning as he crawled into bed to sleep.

"That's all we're going to talk about it. Hush."

Rachel kept up a barrage of reasoning over the next two days, as she gathered a supply of buckets and spare rags in clean-up preparation. Marty stayed away even more. She always waited up, building her resolve to hold her anger and offer calm reasoning.

"It's movin' down, not up," Marty objected. "You're a crazy woman. Guys at work are laughin' at us, just knowing you're thinkin' about it."

It was as if he just got tired of the discussion after a while. Finally he gave in, binding her to a pledge to, "Take all the responsibility for the cleaning and making it a fit place to live."

Rachel noticed he didn't say "proud place to live".

She knew it would not be that for him. But ownership would be the pride for her.

* * *

Rachel and Sonny arrived at the house early one Saturday morning with cleaning supplies, a change of work clothes, and a sack lunch in heavy cardboard boxes they had carried with them on a bus.

"It stinks," said Sonny, driven back out of the house by the ripe odor. "I don't wanna go in there. It's a shack, like Daddy said."

"There are things we have to do sometimes, and cleaning up this house is important, because we're gonna live here."

"I don't want to."

"It'll be all right. Come on, now. Help me get some of these windows open and air this place out."

Rachel had suspected it would be bad, but she hadn't counted on how difficult it would be to clear the basement of trash. They had to start there. Strong odors on the first floor would never disappear until the dirt and debris were shoveled out below.

The previous owners obviously thought the way to get rid of trash was to shove it into the basement. It was all there, from bags of hardened potatoes to stacks of moldy newspapers, empty food cans, rotting socks and shoes, and unidentifiable items encrusted in filth and dirt.

"Tie this rag around your nose," she said to Sonny, handing him one of the cleaning cloths. "Maybe it'll help. I'll start shoveling into these buckets, and we'll carry them upstairs and dump them out back. Later we'll think of a way to get rid of it after it dries up and stops stinking."

The shoveling seemed endless. Her back, arms and legs ached. Each jab of the shovel into the ripe, moldy mass sent stabs of pain through her, but they loosened the clogged pile so that the crusty, black debris plunked onto the muddy basement floor. She laid a few wooden boards as a walkway. Her stained shoes slipped on them.

The stairs were being layered with sticky, gray paste as they made trip after trip to the back door. Another jab brought down more trash, but it was packed so tightly the loosening effort only seemed to increase the bulk of the mounds. The small bucket loads, two each trip upstairs, made very little difference.

Rachel guessed it was about noon when they stopped for lunch. After washing up and drying their hands on clean rags, they crossed the gummy kitchen linoleum again and went to sit on the grass for their lunch.

"It gags me," Sonny said of the hard boiled egg, held in his black-fingernail hand. He dumped the egg back in the sack.

"Take a couple of bites. You'll get weak, otherwise," Rachel urged.

"I can't. I feel sick."

She put her hand on his head to feel for fever, then brushed his thick, brown hair back from his dirty forehead.

"Don't do that", he said, jerking his head back. "Leave me be." He swallowed deeply to keep the bile down, fighting the nausea that finally forced him to struggle to his feet and walk in halting steps around the yard.

Rachel found herself swallowing, too, to control her own stomach that was in sympathy with her son. It passed in time, for both of them. They sat quietly the next half hour.

"You can stay out here, if you want," she said, not looking back at him. She had barely picked up the shovel again, when she heard his light footsteps on the stairs as he returned to help her.

Sonny went back to school on Monday, leaving Rachel to tackle the job alone after her work day at the paper bag company. A dent had been made in the debris during their weekend work, however, and she could handle the disgust now. She knew what to expect.

The noise of her shovel jabbing into the trash and clanging against the metal buckets prevented Rachel from hearing the knocking at first.

She stopped, listened, realized someone was at the open front door. A man's voice was calling, "Hello."

Douglas stood on the porch, straining to peer through the torn screen door into the house.

Emerging from the basement, Rachel, seeing him, tried to withdraw into shadows so he wouldn't see her filthy dress and tussled hair.

He cupped his hands around his eyes for a better view, and spotted her. "Hello." He smiled.

"Hello." She kept her hands behind her.

"I'm a writer for the newspaper here in Garland. I've been trying to reach the new owner of this house for a story. Are you the owner?"

As his hands came down from his eyes, Rachel could see his dark eyes under heavy brows looking at her and holding her gaze. He was so crisp and clean looking as he stood on her worn porch.

"Yes, we bought it", she answered simply, ashamed to be seen.

"Would it be all right if we write something about your efforts here? May I come in and talk a minute?" His manner was gentle, he didn't appear to be judging her.

"I don't know what there is to say," she responded, putting out a grubby hand to push the squeaking screen door open a couple of inches.

He reached out, grabbed the door handle and suddenly his strong, masculine presence was towering over her about a foot away. She shrank back.

Something about her made Douglas feel he had met her before. When the light shown on her face, despite the grimy layer she wore and the plain, soiled clothes, he was certain of it. But he could not remember where. Her appearance in the flood-damaged, insignificant cottage gave him no memory link to the dark-haired woman he had seen in the crowd at the tobacco factory.

"I'm Douglas Hodge," he said, reaching out his hand to take hers. She recoiled. He put his hand on her elbow, slid it down to her palm so that her hand then was gripped solidly in both of his. He squeezed it gently, then released her. She noticed he did not wipe off his hands.

"Just the fact you bought this house and plan to renovate it is a strong human interest story," he encouraged, wanting her to consent to a story.

"It ain't much of a house," she said, suddenly aware of the "ain't". She hated it and wished she hadn't said it. She had been working on improving her speech. "I mean it's not very good, and I'm not sure how it's going look when I'm finished."

"You mean you are doing it, the clean-up and fix-up?"

"My husband and I bought it." She hesitated. "Right now I'm doing the cleaning."

"That must be quite a job." He held her gaze again, then turned to glance around the room. "Mind if I look around a bit? I've

91

been wondering what it's like in here."

"You'll get dirty."

"I've been dirty before".

She noticed that he watched where he stepped, avoiding clumps of mud or still-damp patches on the floor. She studied his attention to the room. He's not avoiding being here, but he'll take precautions, she thought, watching him closely. He reached into his shirt pocket and took out a small note pad and pencil.

"What's your name?"

"Rachel Bradford."

"Do you mind if I write about you, Rachel?" He turned and walked into the dining room, not waiting for an answer.

Trailing after him, instead of leading the way, she became less defensive and admired him in secretive glances as he assessed the house. He took it all in, they way she had hoped Marty would if he had ever come to the house. She liked the studied way Douglas looked at the walls, windows and floors. He missed nothing, but appeared puzzled when he turned back to her.

She guessed what he was thinking - why couldn't he see any evidence of cleanup to account for her grimy appearance.

"I'm working in the basement," she explained. "The other owners just shoved all their trash down there. I've been spending all my time getting rid of that first."

He swiveled, looked for the basement door, walked over and pulled it open.

"Mind if I look?" he asked.

She waited for him to comment on the odor coming from the open basement door. He didn't.

"It's a mess," she apologized, following him down the encrusted steps.

"You doing this yourself?" He studied the partly reduced mass of debris under the stairs. One bucket was half filled, another empty.

"It's been slow."

"And heavy work." He turned, looked to the one window in the basement. "No one's helping you?"

"My husband is a worker at the mill." That's no answer, she

realized.

"There has to be a better way to get that stuff out of here," he said, sizing up the beams in the basement ceiling and looking again toward the window. "Are you working here late afternoons? No one's been here when I stopped before in the daytime."

"I work during the day. Actually, I have a full-time job at a paper bag plant, but work is slow right now. They let me have time off."

"Let's go back upstairs," he suggested. "I'd like to ask you a few questions about buying the house. I won't keep you long."

After cautioning that she would have to get her husband's approval before he wrote a story, she told him about Marty and Sonny, where they were living, and why she felt it important to own the house.

"I'll hold these notes until I talk to you again. I'd like to interview your husband, too," Douglas said, putting the pencil and paper back in his shirt pocket. "Would it be all right if I stop by another afternoon this week?"

"Sure, if you want."

Douglas stopped with his hand on the screen door as he was leaving. "I want you to know, I admire what you're doing, all alone."

She smiled. Rachel didn't want to return to the basement, carrying with her the pristine image of Douglas walking off the porch, but she headed down.

The next day she was ready to quit hauling when she again heard a knock, and was surprised to see Douglas standing outside the screen door with his hands full of bags.

"Handyman," he said, grinning in response to her puzzled expression. "I brought some things to help you get that mess out of your basement."

Dressed in worn cotton trousers and a plaid-cotton shirt, he didn't wait for her to open the door, but opened it and entered.

"What did your husband say?" He led the way through the house toward the basement. She followed.

"He didn't tell me yet."

"He'll come around." Douglas set the packages on the basement floor, took out a pulley, some rope and two larger buckets.

"I've been thinking about this. The simple solution is to take it out the window, otherwise, there's no way to avoid climbing the stairs with heavy loads. I'm going to erect a pulley system that will take a bucket of trash up to the window, then you just shove it out in the yard."

As he worked hanging the pulley from a ceiling beam and adding a hook to the rope, Douglas explained it would operate like a well - putting a bucket down into the water, turning a handle and pulling it back up.

"In this case, it will be this rope you pull. You will need something to stand on at the window, so when the bucket is at the necessary height, you can just shove it out."

It would not be elaborate, he explained, but it would use two or three pulleys so the loaded buckets would not be heavy to raise. The system would involve pushing full buckets out the window, walking up the stairs empty and then carrying the outside buckets to the trash pile out back.

"Why are you doing this?" she asked, suddenly emotional at this caring gesture by a stranger.

"This is a pretty big job for you. If this little system works, that'll please me." He adjusted the pulleys, ropes and hooks until she was able to maneuver the buckets easily out the window.

"It'll go a lot faster like this," she said in gratitude. "I don't know how I can thank you."

"No thanks needed." He patted her gently on the back in parting, encouraging her to accomplish her job now that it was made easier for her.

Rachel found herself anxious for his next visit, since Douglas said he would return again to learn if her husband favored the newspaper story.

When he arrived two days later, she was aware she looked just as grimy as before, but she felt oddly feminine under his steady gaze and proud to show him the cleared basement. It was as if they were sharing the project and he understood that it was impossible for her not to get dirty in the task.

"A milestone," he said, sharing her smile. "So, can we write about it?"

"At first my husband didn't want the story. He's gotten a lot of ribbing from men at the mill," Rachel explained, leading the way back up the clean stairs. "But he says if the newspaper thinks it's good, maybe the guys wouldn't make so much fun."

"We'll convince them," Douglas said, lingering, although the purpose of his visit was accomplished. "We'll write about it now, then do a follow-up story when you're finished and living here. Sound all right? Mind if I return later?"

"I'd like that," answered Rachel, a little uncomfortable in sensing he detected the eagerness in her voice.

* * *

In the following weeks, Rachel whitewashed the basement, stripped wallpaper in the ground floor rooms and scrubbed everything with disinfectants.

When the woodwork was painted a vivid white, and other rooms a rich cream color, she covered the living room with a beige stripe wallpaper.

That's all the papering I can do now with the money we have, Rachel realized. She did make one final decorating decision, to add white Dotted-Swiss curtains.

The time came when Rachel, pounds lighter and muscles tighter, called a house showing for Marty and Sonny.

"Well, it looks pretty clean," Marty said, his footsteps squeaking on a floor board. He glanced down, to direct her attention to the obvious flaw.

"Older houses have squeaks," she excused, shrugging her shoulders.

"It's still not a great part of town." Marty strolled along the hall to the kitchen, glancing into the two bedrooms as he passed. He seemed to be testing the floors.

"I'll get some of the guys to help us move in Saturday, if

that's what you want," he said reluctantly. "But it's not a place I'd choose."

"We won't always live here, Marty. But it's a good investment. We can rent it later."

Sonny returned from wandering around the house, including spending a long time in the basement.

"What do you think, Sonny?"

"It's all right, I guess. You cleaned up the basement nice."

* * *

The pride Rachel felt in the house after they had moved in prompted her to ask Alice and Tim for dinner as a gesture to smooth the long-time rift over her marriage

She was pleased both that they agreed and that Alice was not critical. Actually, her sister paid little attention to their new home. A few nods, "uh huhs" and noticing the Dotted-Swiss curtains, was all Alice offered.

The fried chicken meal was up to Rachel's standards, but Alice's only topic was how a new employees' union was going to improve conditions at the tobacco company.

Tim was silent most of the time, commenting only that more mothers were cutting their youngsters hair. He could not compete against Alice's continuously running mouth.

"The company thinks it can walk on us as it's done in the past," she said, her face muscles animated by her tightly stretched hair.

"We're going to show them," she said, thumping her fork on the table as if cadence for a battle march. "If they don't listen to our negotiators, we're gonna strike."

Alice paused to allow her last word to have impact.

"Can't you imagine what'll happen in this town when all four hundred or five hundred female employees go on strike at that plant? Don't you just love it?"

* * *

96

CHAPTER TEN

November, 1945

"They're not gonna give us any more money. We're just wasting our time," moaned Shirley Gibbins, a tobacco company worker who had complained the past hour about the cold the women were suffering in an informational picket line.

"Why don't we wait until we go on strike before we freeze like this?"

Her breath misted around her face like a white-lace scarf. Sparks exploded from wood fires in oil barrels on the sidewalk outside the plant's main entrance and lit the frigid November evening.

Fragile warmth from the barrels held Shirley and other bundled females in a huddled mass around them.

"Get your sign and get back out here," Alice bellowed at the slackers. She approached the barrels, leading a block-long, straggling procession of females carrying signs that demanded representation by a strong national union.

"You can't do nothing for the cause hanging over barrels," Alice said in a tone sharper than the icicle spears hanging from the tobacco plant eaves.

Shirley, with only her red nose and puffy lips visible in her swathing of sweaters, coats and scarves, jabbed her cotton-gloved hands closer to the flames to store up heat before leaving.

"We're just going through this for nothing," she whined.

"If we don't stick together and become a stronger organization to get more money, whose gonna feed your kids. Those steel guys sure ain't," screeched Alice, apparently oblivious to the cold despite holes in her mismatched gloves. She grabbed Shirley's sign from the ground and shoved it at her.

"Either work with us, or get off this tobacco block."

Shirley stomped back in line to take a position in the column just in front of Tina Rose, who longed to stop, to sit down somewhere.

Tina Rose doubted if she could walk much longer. It was her feet, swollen and numb. Unsteady, she reached up and brushed aside little wisps of blond hair that escaped from her wool scarf. She had not stopped and warmed as often as the other women, mainly because she did not want to make anyone angry and get yelled at.

Her plodding steps went on and on. She would try to stand it a little longer, Tina Rose told herself, because she had a lot to be thankful for despite all that was going on with the tobacco company.

Her husband Josh was getting more painting jobs and they had not been late on a rent payment in three months. And it looked like Teddy was finally able to look after himself a little more. Right now, though, Tina Rose just longed to be warm at home with her beloved Josh and Teddy.

The union business just confused Tina Rose. She realized the American Amalgamation of Labor union had long represented about four hundred of the female tobacco company employees. She had been one of them. She didn't object, just coasted along, when organizers for the National Conference for Industrial Organizations (NCIO) came in and signed up about one hundred and fifty workers.

Those hotheads, which included Alice, now were heading up a battle for an employee vote on a National Conference take-over. Tina Rose had heard the speeches about better pay and safer working conditions, but all she wanted was to keep doing her old job and getting paid.

Instead, she tramped along with other union protesters on numb, unsteady stumps that were her legs.

* * *

Company officials called an outdoor meeting of employees after the 4 p.m. shift change later that week. It was the day before the union representation vote, and apparently scheduled to threaten future consequences if the vote was to put the NCIO into power.

Employees, huddled in the late afternoon chill, had an immediate reaction to the announcement and it froze resolve.

They were disgusted that company bosses were stupid enough to send Personnel Director Billy Rogers, a familiar womanizer and flirt, as the spokesman who stepped out on the crusted loading platform to speak for the company.

He was known to misuse his job-hiring and job-assignment powers by forcing secret trysts. They did not stay secret. That knowledge prompted sneers and frowns of contempt across the faces of the workers as Rogers attempted to convince them to support the company's long-trusted union.

"If the union vote forces a strike, or a shutdown comes because you think you can get higher wages, the company will either have to close up or move south." Rogers shouted in an effort to be heard by all the huddled, shivering crowd. "We don't want to do that. This plant's been here thirty years," Rogers yelled, his voice getting rough.

"Keep in mind, you're not going to receive those Friday paychecks if we close up here," he threatened.

"It not worth waiting in line for 'em, as little as you pay," shouted a strong female voice in the rear of the crowd. Heads turned. No one acknowledged being the heckler, but other catcalls followed.

It was a short session, ending with jeers and hoots from the employees that convinced Rogers they were even more fired up for a union vote. Frustration that his own job could be on the line mounted in him, along with realization that he could not convince the silly bitches to stick with the company.

Vote results the next day were not surprising. The NCIO led by a wide majority, an outcome that prompted spontaneous cheering and some impromptu dancing at cigarette rolling machines.

"Now comes the good part," gloated Alice to a small group in the pipe-tobacco department. A few females celebrated the victory by tossing pinches of tobacco back over their shoulders in a good-luck gestures.

"We're going for more pay now that we're backed by a large union with a big bank account and lots of power," Alice predicted.

* * *

Alice was not as vocal during the next ten days. She and other workers did not anticipate the impasse that resulted during that time under the new bargaining organization. The national union representatives' belligerent attitude and company officials' determination to hold the line on benefits left no middle ground to negotiate a labor contract.

A strike vote loomed, but meetings were scheduled on both sides to prevent it.

Anger and threats erupted on both sides. Cigarette machines whined to a halt when belts were severed, and carpet tacks were found for unexplained reasons in sensitive shredding devices.

Other vandalism acts occurred at many job stations.

"Somebody's gotta let'em know who their dealing with, even though I don't approve of the damage," Alice told other employees in the lunch room one day.

Puffing up under a new leadership attitude, Alice relished the way employees came to her now with questions. Her opinions were important to them, she increasingly realized.

She made certain her little sister knew the status of her role. "It's like they can't even think about the future," Alice said one day after stopping by Rachel's house. It was a busy time for Rachel, because Tina Rose's husband Josh was scampering up and down an outside ladder as he covered the grimy exterior of the recently purchased flood-damaged house with a coat of white paint.

"Some of these women don't realize they're just gonna be in the same place years from now unless they take a stand," Alice said.

100

"They're just being hardheads."

Rachel secretly was concerned about the outcome, but she hesitated to dampen Alice's enthusiasm with doubt. She did tentatively raise the subject by commenting, "Tina Rose said she's afraid there won't be any jobs left when this is over."

"Well then, she's one of the chicken-shits scared to come out of the hen house," huffed Alice. "We're gonna show'em. We'll show'em good."

* * *

Garland residents failed to understand the conflict at the tobacco plant, the block-long employment-machine that had provided steady jobs even during the depression.

Everyone knew it's reputation was so wide spread that when trains pulled into the local train station, conductors called out the name of the plant's main tobacco product, "Brown Grizzly" chewing tobacco, instead of the city's name of Garland.

Females employees were secure in their jobs over the years. They processed as much as ten million pounds of tobacco annually, mostly scrap and plug chewing products, but also some pipe and cigarette tobaccos.

But plant workers had recognized it was time for a change when even veteran employee June Clark decided to favor the national union. June had the reputation as the best humidor packer in the plant. Standing on stubby legs that looked like corner-fence posts, June could fill, weigh and seal up to eighteen hundred humidors in an eight-hour day. But she wanted better pay for her work than the $16.25 cents-a-day paycheck she received.

June never hesitated to remind other workers that as many as fifteen hundred people worked at the plant in the 1920s when she started.

"Where are all those people now?" she asked. "They're gone,

just like other jobs could be gone, yours and mine. We'd better make our big money now when we can."

In the days while negotiations lagged, Alice tried to stiff up her confidence that the company would buckle under the pressure of the determined workers. Just in case, she and other employee leaders prepared for a strike.

The impasse held. Finally, no more meetings were planned. It surprised no one when the workers, including Tina Rose, reluctant to call attention to herself, voted to strike.

Insecure and feeling lost at not reporting to work, she was one of the first to volunteer at the strike headquarters, set up in a dilapidated two-car garage across the street from the tobacco plant.

Both Tina Rose and Alice encouraged Rachel to join them at the garage headquarters in her spare time.

"You had experience feeding a lot of people, after the flood," Alice said convincingly, "And I know you're helping out with feeding people at the church. You're good at it."

Rachel was aware her sister was trying to flatter her into being a kitchen volunteer. Although telling herself she would not be manipulated, Rachel did volunteer. She liked helping people, and she felt sympathy for the strikers. Those emotions increased in her when the women began their second week without a pay check.

One of the two coffee makers needed refilling again one evening when Rachel was volunteering in the strike kitchen at her sister's request. She was measuring coffee into the metal basket when she saw Douglas Hodge standing just inside the garage doorway.

Wearing a dark-brown top coat and stuffing his gloves into a pocket, Douglas was talking to a couple of women when he suddenly turned his head and caught Rachel looking at him. She glanced away quickly after their eyes met, then felt childish and immature for having done so. She looked back, to see him still watching her. He smiled, returned to questioning the woman.

Rachel finished the coffee and started making ham and cheese sandwiches, wrapping them in waxed paper, when Douglas began moving in her direction. He had taken a notebook and pencil out of his pocket, and was jotting notes.

Her dark hair tumbled forward, but not enough to obscure her view of him as he stopped to talk to one striker, then another, but always was maneuvering closer to the table where she was working.

Feelings mounted in Rachel that she resisted. She wanted both to slip into another area of the kitchen and be out of sight, and yet be near him. Douglas had almost reached her when Alice stepped like a ramrod in his path.

Rachel could hear her sister spelling her own name, talking about how "dedicated the women are" and that they would "stay off the job as long as it took".

Douglas did not look in Rachel's direction, but the pull toward him was almost more powerful than if he were staring at her. She sensed she knew this man, but it was only the third, no fourth time, they had seen each other.

It wasn't that Rachel consciously wanted or would work at having anything happen between then. That wasn't part of her upbringing or nature. Still, she could not help feel the strength of his personality and appearance when he was near. It's just that I am fascinated by him because he's a pretty important person, working for the newspaper, she told herself. He seems special, she sensed, aware of the manner in which other people in the room were reacting to him.

Douglas even managed to evade Alice's aggressive encounter before moving to talk to other strikers and finally ending at the table where Rachel was working.

"We keep meeting, but I didn't expect to see you in the strike headquarters," he said, reaching out his hand to her. She took his hand and released it quickly, surprised at how warm it was since he had just come in from the winter evening.

"I'm helping out because my sister asked me to. She's one of the strikers," Rachel answered, studying his features, his dark eyes, the heavy brows above, and his lips. She would have to stretch up at least ten inches to kiss him. She quickly blotted the thought.

"You seem to get involved in a lot that goes on. Your husband told me when I interviewed you before about how you helped the flood victims, and now this," Douglas said.

She glanced at the gold wedding band on his left hand that

she had noticed when Douglas had interviewed them for the newspaper article.

"It's just because I have free time, and they have needs," she said weakly.

"In that case, I may be calling on you for a committee I'm working on," Douglas said. "We need people like you in the community. Look..."

"Would you like some hot coffee?" she interrupted.

"No, I'm fine. I haven't been out in the weather like some of those women out there", he said, opening his top coat and taking it off as if he were preparing to stay.

"Since you're here, I must assume you've sided with the strikers. They're not going to win, you know."

"You think not?" she asked, curious about what information he had.

He was silent. She thought for a moment he had not heard her question.

"Not from what I'm hearing from company officials," he said slowly, thinking about how much he could say and choosing his words.

She had noticed that about him, that he took time to say the right thing. She now was more aware of the impact of his gaze, as he glanced at her.

"I don't think they can fight the union, and the company can't pay more. That's my assessment. It's a stalemate. But, then," he said, returning to his smile, "I'm just an impartial writer who is not afraid to voice an independent opinion."

"What's going to happen to all these women? A lot of their families depend on them." Rachel noticed Alice was approaching and apparently had heard her last comment.

Douglas also was aware, but he continued the conversation by saying, "We can't know for sure what will happen, but it's certain that a long strike will not be good for the community."

"If you wanna know what's gonna happen, we can tell you," Alice interrupted in a strident voice. She took a couple of long, military-like steps and stood in front of Douglas. "We're gonna make company people crawl. We'll keep this plant shut down as long as it takes."

Douglas did not respond immediately. Then he said calmly in respond to Alice's tone, "Do you know how long it will take employees to make up for the pay they're loosing in this strike? I'm all for people sticking up for their rights, but you may be in a losing battle."

"Never. This company's making money, and we deserve some of it." Alice's voice was climbing in volume.

Rachel sensed more than saw Douglas move backwards imperceptibly, preparing to disengage the conversation, apparently realizing he was not talking to a rational person. He's not someone to waste effort or argue for the sake of making a point, she thought.

"I don't expect the company will wait much longer for a decision," Douglas concluded, abandoning the subject.

"They're gonna decide we are right. With more people smoking in this country every day, there's more than enough money to go around. Just put that in your paper," Alice said, snorting and whipping her head to one side as she turned and stalked off.

"Give people a taste of power, and it takes control of them," Douglas said when Alice was out of hearing range.

"She's my sister," Rachel said, unable to avoid a smile.

"Hey, I'm sorry." His eyes stayed linked with hers. "She doesn't seem anything like you. Again, forgive me."

"I understand. You couldn't know, and you're right."

"Look, I started to ask you a few minutes ago, I'm getting together a group of people to come up with ideas about community needs. How about joining us?"

"I wouldn't know anything about that?"

"Some people at the steel company asked me to do a little public relations for them, through the newspaper, and wanted me to get up this study group. You'd be a natural."

"I don't know what I could do." She shied away from the idea, afraid she would be intimidated by other people in such a group.

"None of us know what's to be done yet. It'll be a group of business people, elected officials, community leaders and residents like you," Douglas urged. "We'll probably talk about parks, buses, street lights, who knows."

"All those people know more about the city than I do."

"You'll be fine, and I'm going to count on you. So say you'll do it." He put his notebook and pencil in his jacket pocket, then began pulling on his topcoat.

He's leaving, she thought, regretfully.

"On the other hand, don't say anything yet," he urged. "I'll get word to you about when and where we'll meet the first time. It'll be after all this is over and the community settled down. And it will settle down," he added. "Eventually."

* * *

Alice's ire grew stronger in the next three weeks. She became more belligerent toward the company and spoke of getting even when the strikers returned to work.

"It's their way of making us suffer, but you wait and see. We're gonna have the last word," Alice said. Her words were becoming repetitious, like a needle stuck on a broken record. Alice wanted to hide the fact she had lost her excitement after weeks of walking picket lines, trying to keep warm and re-heating stale food in the strike kitchen. She also felt the loss of a weekly paycheck. Life with Tim was strained. Their finances depended on his hair cutting business.

Optimism flared one evening, however, when strikers were handed flyers from guards at the factory doors telling of a company announcement to be made at 10 a.m. the following day.

"We've won, we've won," some of the women cried, as their faces scrunched up to fight off tears of relief.

"We knew we could do it," Alice declared, suddenly elated, as she walked back to the kitchen to tell others.

"We don't know if they're givin' in," cautioned June, warming in the kitchen and wishing she'd stuck to her humidor packing.

"Sure we do," Alice countered, filling a cup with steaming coffee from a container on a hot plate. "They wouldn't call a meeting just to say the strike's going to continue."

But a meeting was not held the next morning. The flier had not stated a meeting, just an announcement.

That announcement, printed on sheets of paper handed out by guards at the plant entrance, stated the tobacco company would "officially close on January 1, and the production operation would be moved to the company's facilities in North Carolina."

The brief document also carried a threat, "Any trespassing on the property is prohibited. Violators will be prosecuted to the fullest extent of the law."

The stunning effect for employees at first was silence, followed by murmurs and then growing anger.

Throughout the day they continued to mill around the now ominously-empty plant waiting for answers, wanting a different answer from the one they had received.

Douglas interviewed company officials by telephone that morning, talked to strikers in the street and went to homes for comments by former tobacco-company workers who had distanced themselves from the picket lines.

He spoke to Rachel in the strike kitchen, but did not see Alice again until late afternoon when dusk cast a shadow of the tobacco building over the somber street scene where a few women hovered over the still-burning fires in the oil barrels.

"What are you doing here?" Alice moved out of the shadow and faced him.

"It's my job, working up features stories about the strike."

"Doesn't seem to be anything to strike against now, they're just walking off and leaving us." Alice turned her back on him and gave her attention to the other jobless women around her.

"Could you just tell our readers..."

"I'm not telling them or you anything," Alice blurted. "You're just a no-good bastard who's been hanging around here feedin' off our suffering. You been writin' about this stuff, but you ain't been livin' it."

Turning away, Douglas talked to other women standing off at a distance who were not reluctant to talk. They gave him a few, halting comments. They were shuffling and constantly moving about, still gathered as a team when there was no longer a game to fight and win.

Several of the woman, fidgeting and gesturing recklessly with gloved hands, said they needed to be together now, as they had in recent weeks. A few women began singing, as if to relieve the mounting nervousness.

Douglas could sense the tension building around him. Realizing his effort for calming words had little effect, he moved away from the employees who were no longer employees. Their voices and words were increasingly verging on the violent.

The crowd's emotions peaked about 9 p.m., when the women, so cold they knew they could not stay out much longer, were driven to make a final gesture as their anxiety erupted.

Grabbing up burning torches from the oil barrels, they threw them at the door of the tobacco building. They tossed empty bottles through first and second-floor windows. Some used ice picks from the strike kitchen to jab tires on cars parked nearby, not caring who the owners were.

The crowd's frenzy of destruction mounted, nothing else mattered. They injured each other, unintentionally.

Alice was caught in a rush of arm-swinging bodies, she lost her balance, her feet tangling with others. Falling, she swore at everyone as she went down. The skin of her knees tore open at the impact, leaving a red smear on the concrete sidewalk. No whimper left her lips. Her angry, accusing eyes lifted toward the top of the looming, empty tobacco plant.

* * *

CHAPTER ELEVEN

May, 1946

The minor scars on Alice's knees disappeared over the next few weeks. Scars in the lives of the women and their families who suffered through the tobacco strike festered for a long time.

They found other jobs and carried on. But tradition was gone. The massive red-brick building stood rigidly as before against the skyline, but lifestyles, friendly associations and salaries faded just as the environment around the plant lost its tobacco odors.

While many of the former tobacco plant workers were struggling to buy weekly grocery supplies, Rachel took action to expand her family's finances. She convinced Marty to let her invest in buying another of the still-vacant, flood-damaged homes. Although he resisted the idea, she argued that the rental income from the second house would help them pay off both mortgages.

"You're going to do what you want to do anyway," he conceded in relenting. "What do I care what you do?"

Rachel accepted that as consent and completed the purchase through the bank. She had nearly finished the clean-up and painting on a May Sunday when Alice and Tim stopped her to chat in the church corridor.

"I'm working at Harding Elementary School now," Alice began as she rearranged her feathered hat and jammed a hat pin to anchor it to her coil of braids. "I'm in the school cafeteria. It's not as good a pay, and it's only nine months a year. Job's ending in another month."

"You probably enjoy being around all the children. All that

energy."

"I hate the little snots", Alice snapped back. "They're always shoving each other and complaining about the portions. I just have to step up my nerve pills to cope. Don't know why parents don't give their kids discipline like Tim and me do our two girls."

Rachel, anxious to meet Sonny after church school, was uneasy in almost any conversation with Alice these days. If she mentioned the city was recovering from the strike, Alice started another tirade about what should have been done to lock the company into staying in Garland. Now, when Rachel commented favorably about the cafeteria work, Alice could only see what was wrong.

Alice always made positive comments, however, about how her girls "were well disciplined". Rachel thought it was more like they were suffocated with orders. She was turning away when Alice stopped her.

"How's work coming along on that second flood house you purchased? Can't understand why you'd do that?" Alice was probing. "Where'd you get all that money."

"The down payment was not that much." Rachel was not going to share more than that.

"But you can't live in two places. Do you think of maybe rentin' one of them?" Alice glanced at Tim.

"I already have. Tina Rose and her family are moving in as soon as it's finished."

"Well, huh. Shows what you think of family." Alice grabbed Tim by the arm and was stomping away.

"Alice, you mean you would consider living there?" Rachel was surprised, her tone of voice faded as she realized her words were being ignored.

"Listen", Rachel heard Tim saying to Alice as he treaded heavily down the hall with her. "I don't think I would want....."

"Then tell me what you do want," Alice snarled in a louder voice that carried back to Rachel. Tim, who was becoming more obese every year, did not answer as he struggled to keep pace with her. His belt circled below his belly, allowing his pants to drape in his crouch and the trouser legs to cover his shoes.

* * *

Rachel was determined not to let her sister's roller-coaster emotions disrupt her own life on a daily basis, and her outlook improved even more when she received a mailed notice from Douglas Hodge about an upcoming meeting of the new Garland Citizens Committee.

She has almost forgotten about being asked to serve, but he evidently still wanted her to be a member, she realized. The meeting could be interesting, and she would see him again.

When the day arrived, however, she was excited about both expectations, but became intimidated when entering the hotel where the gathering was scheduled. She was actually going to lunch with elected officials and community leaders to discuss what could be done to help residents. What did she know?

The historic brick hotel, with its elegant wood-paneled lobby and curved staircase, was the social hub of the city where dances, political banquets, weddings and anniversary parties were held. Rachel had never been invited to attend any of those events at the hotel, and had never before had lunch there. She wished for more sophistication now to play her role.

Smile, she told herself as she entered the private dining room, where about twenty table settings were waiting.

A few people were standing around, mostly men. Rachel was a little surprised to see a colored man there, but never having met Hooper, she was unaware that he rapidly was assuming a leadership role in the city's south side community.

Hooper was talking to an older gray-haired man at the far side of the room. Rachel surmised he was a little uncomfortable, too, as if he preferred to be in more comfortable clothes than the gray business suit he was wearing.

Her discomfort lasted only until she felt a hand touching her elbow and, turning, she looked up into Douglas's face.

"Sorry if I'm late," he said, glancing from her to scan the rest of the room. "Had to get some last minute facts together. Have you met everybody?"

111

Douglas walked her around for introductions, made certain others were greeted and made welcome. He is very at ease doing this, Rachel thought, impressed that he was able to remember all the people's names and knew them on a first-name basis. He does this a lot, she guessed. Rachel, reassured by her arm brushing against his coat jacket, wished she could stay comfortably by his side the entire meeting.

The tall colored man who faced them as they approached had one of the broadest, most pleasing smiles she had ever seen. And he was sincere in his warmth, she recognized.

"This is Hooper Young, a community leader," Douglas said in making the introduction. "He's a union negotiator for the mill and the person who showed the city how to play basketball."

"That community leader you're talking about," Hooper chided, "is that what I've done, or what I'm about to do?"

"What you've been doing for years," Douglas countered. "This is Rachel Bradford, one of the city's newest pioneers, almost single-handedly resurrected two of the flooded homes. You probably read about her. She's also been involved in human services, feeding flood victims and strikers."

Rachel was stunned by Douglas's words about her. Is that what I've been doing? Is that the way he sees me, she wondered modestly. But she caught herself, don't be deceived, she thought. It does not qualify you to be here with these leaders.

Her interest peaked when Douglas mentioned that Hooper had problems getting his own home.

"I didn't know what I was getting into," Hooper explained. "My wife and I lived in an apartment in the south end of the city, and I was born in a house on that street. We wanted to build a house on the next parallel street, but were told we couldn't. We could build on streets on either side, but that one had a deed restrictions saying whites only. It was just some rule put on in the past."

"It's illegal, they can't restrict today. But listen to this," Douglas added, leading Hooper back to his story.

"I got a lawyer, and we were ready to fight. But I decided I didn't want to do that", Hooper reflected. "My wife's in the school system, she's a teacher, and we have a young daughter. Sure, it

112

wasn't right, but we decided to try to change things, rather than get in a battle."

"And you were successful", said Rachel, grateful for her own uncomplicated experiences in home buying.

"We bought a lot on an unrestricted street, where we built the house we live in now," Hooper said proudly. "We're happy, and the city's relieved, but those restrictions are gone today."

"Those are the kinds of situations we want this committee to address, and the spirit we need," Douglas said, picking up on the fact it was an opportune time for the guests to move to the tables for lunch.

As she was selecting her own seat, away from Douglas and the speakers' table, Rachel was relieved to see a familiar face, Glenn McIntire, who arrived in time to claim the seat beside her.

"Don't know that I can stay the full time. Have the lunch crowd at the tavern to think about," Glenn said. "But I wanted to see what's happening here."

Rachel learned a lot about the city and particularly the steel mill during the meeting. The discussion was about needed services - better bus transportation, new equipment at the hospital, a future arts/music center, and ways to control the excess of liquor permits and bars in the city.

Rachel's perception changed that day. Her concept of the "mill", through Marty's reflections, had been as a dirty, life-threatening facility that was tolerated only because it was a necessity to put food on the table of workers.

Rachel felt surprisingly privileged to learn that it was steel company officials, with Douglas representing them as their unofficial spokesperson at the meeting, who were acting behind the scenes to improve the community.

The company's community-relations history, she soon discovered, was based on officials and department workers providing motivation, financial support and volunteer time to create a better city.

The results were many - good wages and benefits, a hospital years before cities of comparable size had one, a Community Chest program for the needy, updated roadways and lighting systems, a library, parks and a school system of a caliber to attract executive families.

Most top MVS officials were volunteers on at least one community project, Rachel learned, such as heading school levies, running campaigns for selected city commission candidates or organizing charity events.

"We already have a better community through involvement, but we don't want to stop here," Douglas said, calling for more suggestions during the meeting.

As Rachel listened to ideas proposed by others around her, such as an expanded jail at the suggestion of Police Chief Pendleton and an elevator in the city building, she felt her idea unworthy. But she recognized that she was not invited just to listen. She felt the necessity to share her concerns, even if they were perceived as frivolous.

She took a deep breath to begin, but not deep enough to leave her breathless and quivering of voice. "A lot of women work away from home, they have since the war, and many of them have no one to take care of their children," she said. "Not everybody has grandmothers or friends to look after their children.

"It seems like there could be some organized place to drop them off in the morning and pick them up after work."

Silenced followed. Rachel was sorry she said anything.

Douglas rescued her. "An excellent idea. That's why it's important to have women on the committee. They think of things the rest of us miss."

"We could turn the American Legion auditorium into a place for kids in the daytime," volunteered an older man across the table from Rachel. "We could bring in a few cots for their naps in the afternoon."

"I take it you're a grandfather who sometimes babysits", Douglas said, making rocking motions with his arms.

"You bet `ya."

Rachel was elated by his support.

"I bet some of the wives would be willing to work with that. They're always looking for projects," added another man. The few women in the room agreed.

"Would you be willing to help organize?" Douglas questioned Rachel, while making a memo on the pad in front of him.

She shrugged her shoulders, wondering what her contribution could be. "I'll help where I can."

"We'll count on you. And any other ideas?" Douglas turned to face the group.

"Do you think we can make any real change?" Hooper asked. "People tend to accept things the way they are, but gripe about them."

Douglas hesitated, selecting his words. "We should not accept things the way they are, or allow that to happen," he said, his eyes scanning the faces turned toward him.

"We should see things the way they are, and try to bring them to where they should be." He paused again. "That's one of the things we have to get across to our residents."

"I'm for giving it a try," said McIntire, speaking for the first time. "The city's been good to my family. I can't stay long now, it's the lunch hour. But I wanted to ask if you've heard anything about an interstate highway the federal government may build east of the city?"

Douglas called on the expertise of the city planning director, who admitted there were federal plans to that effect, but they were years in the future.

"I just hope something like that doesn't hurt our businesses, people just bypassing our town on an interstate highway," Glenn said.

When the meeting broke up, with many issues raised and some put on hold until the next session, Douglas stood at the door saying good-byes until Rachel stopped in front of him. She had hung back as one of the last to leave.

"I don't know how much help I will be on the day care committee," she said, beginning to distance herself from him toward the door.

"You've already come up with the idea," he said. "I knew you'd be an asset."

He waited, not walking toward the door with her, although she would have liked that. He's uneasy about it, she suddenly realized. It probably would not be good to leave together.

There was something so comfortable about him, though, she thought. It would be nice working on the committee and attending meetings with him. She reluctantly walked away, not realizing his eyes watched her while she passed through the hotel lobby and left through the brass-plated door.

* * *

Marty was indifferent about the purchase of the second house, and remained away while Rachel worked with Tina Rose and Josh to paint the second two-bedroom cottage inside and out.

She hung flower planters on the front porches of both the houses, and watched proudly when Tina Rose and Josh moved in to occupy the newest purchase next door to her own home.

"You sure made it something special," Tina Rose told Rachel, getting a nod of acknowledgment from her husband. Handing young Teddy and Sonny loads of towels to carry into the house, Tina Rose gently waved Rachel's hands away when she attempted to help Teddy with his load. His unsteady steps and slowness made Rachel ache with sympathy.

"We're doin' fine," assured Tina Rose, who since the tobacco company strike had been taking jobs caring for elderly patients in their homes. "We're gonna love it here. And one day we'll have our very own home, just like this."

Josh agreed. "We're moving that way, Honey Babe. A few more years of saving and we'll be there." As he talked, strong and good-natured Josh lifted a heavy chest of drawers from the bed of a pickup truck and marched with bouncy steps to the front porch, then into the house.

"I'm carrying this special," Tina Rose said of the hand-made quilt she carried folded over one arm. "My mother made it, and it's one of my prize possessions. It's going to have a special show place in the house. You're sure a lucky woman to have two houses,

116

Rachel, one to rent out to us."

"More than just lucky. It's been a lot of hard work." But Rachel hesitated to share with Tina Rose her growing compulsion to own property. Her appetite had only intensified with the second purchase. She had no idea yet what "enough" would be.

Owning property was becoming her security. Already she was planning to mention a third purchase to Marty, although he had trouble understanding the concept that rent money made the mortgage payments on more property.

* * *

Marty wasted most of his energy in fretting over job angers and fears, leaving him mostly indifferent to Rachel's still-embryo visions of real estate ownership and contributing something to the community.

The lack of unity and support between them made Rachel's life an endless yearning, for what, she was not quite certain. But the void left her convinced it was the need for more property, forcing her to devote more of her efforts toward that.

She ached for something more in her life, although she did not put words to the feelings of lack of companionship, tenderness and compassion. Those were not items on the need-to-have list, like buying a new car, repairing the roof on the second house and buying Sonny's Boy Scout equipment.

And it was not that Marty did not pay attention to her or that they did not make love. That was not the missing ingredient, although the love making had not grown into what she had anticipated as a girl.

Yet there was something, an unknown urgency that would not leave her in peace, despite her achievements, until she had achieved something else. She felt driven. But what was it? Find another house to buy? Be more secure?

One of Rachel's emotional releases was the monthly community meetings in which she shared ideas and continued to learn about the community.

She had helped organize the day care center, and was in the process of setting up a program of noon meals for shut- ins. It wasn't just her own projects that were providing discovery for her, however, it also was hearing other committee members sharing their involvement in road projects, park development and other city activities.

Rachel had a brief moment of panic after a committee meeting one day that it was all going to end. Douglas confided that he was changing jobs.

They generally found a moment or two at the end of each meeting to exchange a few words together. More and more often she would stand on the edge of the crowd to be among the last to leave and experience that brief parting.

"I'm changing jobs, but I haven't told many people yet," he told her abruptly one day. "The steel company offered me a job in public relations. I grabbed it. It just developed out of this community committee, I think. They like what we've been doing here."

Rachel felt privileged, special, that he shared the good news with her. Douglas explained how he would continue volunteer work with the committee, but now he would be paid for that as part of his role in community public relations.

"I'll continue with this citizens' group. It's one of the things I really enjoy."

Rachel felt her face flush as she caught his excitement. It almost was impossible for her to look away. She had increasing difficulty in concentrating on what he was saying. His eyes and the nearness of him were too much competition.

"Certainly it's going to be challenging," Douglas said enthusiastically. "Listen," he stopped suddenly. "I guess I'm wound up talking like this. Do you want to have a cup of coffee while I ramble on?"

She tried to remain calm. "I'd like to very much, but I don't have a lot of time."

"Right. We're both busy and we won't take long." Douglas grabbed her eagerly by the elbow and guided her out of the meeting room. In the lobby, he released her and they walked separately toward the hotel entrance and to the sidewalk outside.

"We'll go to the drug store. How's that?"

"Fine," she answered, moving beside him toward Garland's main intersection. Rachel had sensed from the beginning that the only reason she was asked to serve on the committee was because Douglas wanted her there. She was totally unaware of what the role would be when she first agreed to serve.

Yet, she had stayed on because she had an increasing interest in the city, volunteerism and, yes, in the man who got her involved.

Over the next hour as they sat in a booth at the drug store, Douglas described his new duties as a public relations man for the steel company. He had made many of the same comments to his wife over the telephone, but she broke off the conversation several times to give some instructions to their daughters.

He knew fully that Sandra was not impressed with his new job, since it was not in Columbus. None of his job explorations had turned up anything of interest to him there. Plus, he admitted, he probably was being a little stubborn, too. But he could not see a life controlled by the influence of his parents-in-law.

"I'll still be dealing with news releases," Douglas told Rachel eagerly as if ready to begin the job immediately. "But instead of receiving them for the newspaper, I'll be writing them and sending them to numerous newspapers and radio stations."

Rachel mostly listened as Douglas, losing his mannered hesitation and studied caution under her gaze, spilled out his excitement in joining the company. His duties mostly would be to write about the company, he explained, but still he would be involved behind the scenes with school boards and city commissions.

"I shouldn't take up your time with this," he said finally, slowing down and glancing at her as if seeking reassurance that he had not kept her too long.

"Working with the committee has been good for me," she

said, going on to explain that buying the houses had been her introduction to belonging to a community. Opening that topic led her to share some of her thoughts about more purchases, until her enthusiasm, encouraged by his understanding comments, elevated her to a pitch of eagerness that matched his new job anticipation.

Their rapid exchanges on real estate and his new public relations role carried them through two cups of coffee, and to the last treasured cold sips that were delayed far beyond a reasonable time.

Rachel shoved her cup back gently, signaling an ending.

"I just needed to let off some of this steam," Douglas said, his voice suddenly sounding husky. "Thanks for listening. There's nobody else around here to talk to ...right now my wife is in Columbus. Besides, talking is easy with you."

"We can talk any time," Rachel answered, realizing that really was not true. They both knew the other was married and he had re-emphasized that by the reference to his wife.

"We'll just do it", he said, but Rachel doubted that.

Although Rachel's perception of Douglas had been increasing since their first meeting - awareness of his compassion, ability to handle people, and knowledge of so many subjects - she realized the necessity of suppressing any emotions linked to him.

She left the drugstore first, with Douglas paying the bill and following shortly afterwards. They both carried away with them a sense of togetherness in the brief, sharing time together, a fragile closeness that was too delicate to unwrap and examine.

* * *

Over the next few months, as they continued to attend community group meetings, Rachel and Douglas did not meet for coffee again. She refused to dwell on any thoughts of him, particularly any speculation on physical contact.

"I'm not going to do anything that would hurt any of us," she vowed. "Nothing, nothing."

* * *

Marty surprised her in the spring of 1947 with the announcement that he had a new job. He rarely said much to her about his work anymore.

Rachel had gotten out of the habit of asking him since he returned to the mill after the war. It seemed her casual inquiries only triggered more awareness of his consuming fear of the blast furnaces' flames and heat. He would have denied that his job was responsible over the years for his growing sleeplessness, lack of appetite and increased consumption of beer.

Yet Marty seemed a different man the afternoon he was waiting for her at home after her day's work at the paper bag plant. He was smiling, a rare sight.

"You're lookin' at an MVS employee in the transportation department," he said, as she hung her light jacket on the hook beside the back door. "Now I drive trains."

Startled, Rachel could only blurt out, "Trains?"

"I don't actually drive'em, but I ride'em and switch the tracks and everything."

"How did that happen? Have you started yet? Why didn't you tell me?"

He walked past her into the hall. "Start Monday, an it's a hellava lot better than where I was, I can tell ya." He looked into their son's room then turned back to her. "Where's Sonny, I wanna tell him myself."

"He said he was going to stop by the library after school. I think the job is really great, Marty, if that's what you want." she said.

He ignored her, removed his own jacket from a hook and headed back through the door. "I'm gonna go meet Sonny at the library and tell him what his old man's doing. He'll love the fact I'm drivin' trains."

"I'm ready to start supper. Sonny will be home soon."

"I don't want to eat yet," Marty said, jerking open the back door. "I'll meet up with Sonny, then I'm goin' down to tell the guys over a beer. Boy, they're gonna shit their pants."

Rachel stood at the kitchen counter. We live here in the same house, but we're complete strangers, she realized anew. The sense of loneliness that swept over her crowded out any feelings of elation at Marty's announcement, but she was relieved he was getting out of the mill.

* * *

Marty's delight over riding trains lasted only a few days. He had grappled with his job fears for almost a decade, mostly keeping them bound tighter and tighter within his private thoughts, but now his dissatisfaction was directed at supervisors.

Although he did not voice his anger to Rachel, she felt the backlash of his mood when he was assigned a lower job than expected. Instead of riding in the train engines, his duties involved walking alongside the tracks, throwing switches and being outside in the weather at all times.

She only learned weeks later, when she overheard him talking to Josh next door, that he now had a lower job classification because his seniority in the blast furnace did not carry over to the transportation department.

Marty belonged to the company union, but he did not actively support the organization and refused to seek help. He was told it would not change anything, anyway.

Each additional week he spent with the railway department, the deeper his depression grew. He already had a sullen personality, but he turned more and more inward.

As winter deepened, Marty sat silently in the kitchen or in the basement whittling with his grandfather's carving knife he had brought from Kentucky. Sometimes with Sonny beside him, Marty cut bears, deer and birds from chunks of wood. They were reminders of his youth in rural Kentucky.

The carvings Rachel had first seen in his boarding-house room had always been displayed on a living-room shelf and they became models for his work, at least for a time.

Although Marty had only a fair talent, compared to the

carvings of his grandfather, Rachel bragged on his works and showed them to the rare friends who visited their home.

Marty was unfazed. He gave most of the wooden figures away. He isolated himself more and more from the family. He either was late getting home from work after stopping at a bar, or he escaped to his carving bench in the basement when he was home.

Long into the night, Rachel often could hear him sharpening, and re-sharpening his carving knives.

* * *

CHAPTER TWELVE

October, 1948

"I think Marty's right. You're spending a lot of time away from home," said Alice when she'd stopped by Rachel's house the second time in one week.

"I do go to several meetings a month, but usually it's when Marty's working and Sonny has something planned," Rachel said defensively. "I'm not neglecting them."

She always had to justify herself with her sister. Why do I let her do this to me, she wondered.

Alice's purpose for the visits was a selfish one, she revealed shortly when she asked about renting the second house Rachel had bought, even though Tina Rose's family was living there.

"You've fixed it up kinda cute, besides I expect the rent wouldn't be as much as I'm paying now," Alice said, the permanent whine in her voice revving up. It usually occurred when Alice spoke of Tim not getting much barbering business and the girls costing a lot for clothes.

"I couldn't just move Tina Rose out. She and Josh have been very faithful in paying rent," Rachel explained. "He also does a lot of work on the property at no cost. I can't, Alice."

"I guess you never heard the saying, `Bloods thicker than water'. Family should stick together in rough times," Alice, said, beginning one of the lectures Rachel had learned to avoid.

"Tina Rose wants them to get a house of their own. As soon as that happens..."

"Yeah, Tim and me'll be dead."

124

"Alice, I rented the place to Tina Rose when both you and Marty considered it another dump along the river. Those were your words," Rachel began to explain. "If you'd even given any indication you wanted..."

"Things change, even sisters." Alice said accusingly.

Rachel ran her fingers back through her shoulder-length hair, then lifted it off the back of her perspiring neck. "I didn't want to say anything yet, but we're thinking of buying another house, about two blocks away."

"Then you'll hold it for Tim and me and the girls," said Alice, controlling her excitement. "After you get it fixed up, of course?"

"Yes, Alice, if it happens, you can rent the place."

Rachel never seemed to find a good situation with Alice, and it was increasingly worse with Marty.

"You're jist getting too uppity to live in a little town like this", Marty said one evening. They were in the bedroom, where she sat on the bed sewing a button on one of his shirts.

"But you're not as special as you think. You're just like all women, a piece of tail. Wanna spread your legs right now. No, you don't like to do that, do you? Too much of a lady."

"You don't have to be like this, Marty."

"Like what?"

She laid the sewing aside, stood and headed for the kitchen.

"That's right. Walk away. You do that a lot. Don't wanna argue, do you. Just let me talk to myself."

I do, she thought to herself. I really do walk away when he gets like this. Taking his foul mouth without fighting back was the price she accepted. More and more she became subservient. As she became more giving in their daily life together - trying to ease the situation by preparing special meals or treats for him, accepting his lateness after work without complaint - he grew increasingly belligerent.

Marty relished his growing control through rough love making and put-down remarks. She tried to shield Sonny as much as possible, but he was a perceptive, maturing youngster who felt the stress between his parents.

"Why does he talks to you like he's angry all the time?" Sonny questioned his mother one evening when they were walking home from the corner grocery store.

"I think it's because of his job," she answered, trying to find a reason her son could understand. "He never did like working at the mill, but he thinks he lacks training to do anything else. And the train job isn't what he expected."

"Couldn't he get some special classes?"

"I think so. I want you to study hard, and prepare for a good job so you won't end up in a factory. Hang on to your thoughts of being a teacher and make it come true."

Rachel studied the face of her young son, noticing the soft fuzz becoming visible on his upper lip.

He's so young, but in a couple of years he will be living somewhere else, she thought. Rachel was resigned to accept that, realizing how fast time was passing.

It was a time in her life when she was coasting emotionally, struggling to cope with Marty's moods, Alice's harpiness and balancing her factory job with the real estate projects.

All that changed with a jangling telephone call from the steel mill early one rainy morning telling her Marty had been injured in a mill accident.

His worst fear has become reality, Rachel realized, trembling in her preparations to go to him.

* * *

Alone in the dimly-lit hospital waiting room for an update on Marty's condition, Rachel prayed over and over for his leg to be saved.

His foreman had met with her earlier at the hospital, explaining that Marty had slipped on wet railroad ties when grabbing hold of a train handle to pull himself aboard, and had fallen under a

126

moving wheel.

"He got out, but not before the wheel ran over his left ankle," the foreman said, shaking his head. "Doesn't look good to save it."

Both the hospital doctor on duty and the company doctor warned her the leg may have to be amputated. The wheel did not sever the ankle, but "the bones are crushed", they said.

She had sat beside Marty into the late morning hours, prepared to talk to him and ease his mind about the accident. But they'd given him drugs, the doctors had told her, so his body could begin recovering. He was medicated, they reluctantly admitted, because he became very violent, to the point of panic.

Rachel held the hand of her unconscious husband, gently brushed his stiff, black hair back off his forehead and adjusted the sheet folded across his chest. She glanced down at his sheet over his legs, one side raised over a support so it didn't touch his left ankle.

"I'm so sorry, so sorry," she whispered, her lips tasting salty. Was this punishment, she wondered. The dominant factor in Marty's life had been fear of the mill, she realized. The fear had won.

Her sorrow was for Marty, but the tears also were for herself when the doctors told her it was necessary to amputate his leg. The bones could never heal sufficiently to support his weight, they told her. The threat of infection was so great it could eventually claim his life.

* * *

The day was overcast, typical of Ohio in November. Marty sat on the day bed in the kitchen, peeling an apple with his whittling knife. His injured left leg was free for a brief rest from the new artificial prosthesis, but the stump throbbed with a life of its own even after weeks of healing. He hated it.

He rubbed the heel of his palm down the front of his thigh, trying to ease the pain. He stopped just below the knee, where the rest of his leg should have been.

Rachel, peeling potatoes at the sink, looked out the window at the light in the garage where Sonny was fixing a flat bicycle tire. She would call him in for supper shortly. He'd spent enough time in the cold garage, anyway.

Involved since the accident in helping Marty recover and carrying on with everyday life, Rachel thought now of how she had dropped out of the community committee meetings temporarily. She missed the different members and contacts especially with Glenn McIntire and Hooper. Douglas, who had written the accident news release for the newspaper, sent her a comforting note afterwards.

"Time has a way of passing our apprehensions of tomorrow into the dim memories of the past," he had written. "No matter how severe or painful the thought of tomorrow's problems might be, they will pass and become part of the past. So, no matter how bad things might be, time solves the problem in one way or the other. Courage."

Rachel treasured the note, tucked it into a bundle of family pictures out of sight in a drawer.

Thoughts of the note now brought a slight smile to Rachel as she stood at the kitchen sink, until she abruptly jerked back to reality. Marty had dropped the single long peel from his apple on the floor and slapped his carving knife down on the table beside him.

"You're going to spoil your dinner," she cautioned, trying to discourage him from eating just before dinner."

"Tell me about it," he answered in what was becoming his standard sneering tone of voice. His words also were slurred from a combination of pain medication and whiskey that he hoped Rachel did not know he had been sipping. His vision was a little fuzzy, but he had become accustomed to that.

Marty wished he were back in the bedroom, he didn't care about supper. He wanted a sip of whiskey from one of his hidden bottles. One was behind the day bed that he sat on, his leg propped on a pillow. She probably knew about it. There wasn't anything she didn't know, but she didn't say anything.

His buddies at the mill kept slipping him bottles and sneaking out the empties. He was going to owe then a lot of favors when he was on his feet again. Feet! Christ! He'd never be on his feet again.

He was hoping one of his friends would be by later that day with a new supply. He only had a partial bottle in his room and the one behind the day bed. Hell, it was a simple thing to want, after all that had happened, he thought, as his level of anger just below the surface mounted.

Why didn't anything happen to her? She just went about her business day after day. Always putting on her damn cheerful face. She acted like nothing happened to him, like they could live a happy life. God damn it, he wasn't happy before. What makes her think anything's worthwhile now?

Marty laid the remains of the apple beside him, reached for the carving knife with his right hand and slid off the day bed. He landed with a thud. He was weaker than he thought.

It's from lying around all these fuckin' days, he thought. His hand stretched over the knife blade to hide it as Rachel wheeled around at the sink to help him.

"Git back", he said when she reached out. It was his tone of voice that stopped her. She turned back to the sink and potatoes. She had learned that when he was hurting he didn't want to talk or have any attention. When he was ready to get back on the daybed, she would help him.

Marty flattened his free hand on the floor to stop the dizziness.

"You just going to sit there?" she asked, not looking at him. "Can I help you up?"

"I'll sit here as long as I want," he snapped. "Ya have any objections?"

"Supper won't be long. Let's get you back up on the day bed, and I'll get you a washcloth so you can wash up for dinner."

He didn't answer.

"I wish you'd at least try, Marty."

No answer. She glanced at him. He had shoved himself out from the daybed now, reclining on one elbow almost in the center of the kitchen floor, the other hand hidden beneath him.

"I'd be glad to help you," she offered.

Rachel finished slicing the last potato, and walked with the filled bowl to the stove by the window. She was preparing to light the gas jets to fry the potatoes, when she felt a sharp sting on the back of her leg.

When she reached to rub it and pulled her hand away, she saw both the blood on her fingers and Marty on the floor just behind her. She almost fell over him as she felt a sharper sting.

"What are you...." she started to ask when she saw a shiny flash from the blade of the knife in Marty's hand. He plopped on his stomach, grabbed her ankle, and she felt another slash and another.

Jerking away from his weakened, off-balance arms, she felt his hand pull off her shoe as she backed away.

"What's the matter with you?" she screamed, her eyes blurring with tears as she searched for an escape from the kitchen. His stretched out body, the knife in his hand reaching for her, blocked the way to the back door.

Marty was quick, too quick, on the linoleum floor. She slipped, but recovered, as she careened toward the dining room. Although he missed grabbing her leg a second time, he used one arm to propel himself across the floor and the other to swipe with the honed blade of the whittling knife in her wake.

Once in the dining room, her escape was quicker. He could not slide as fast on carpet. Crawling hurt more. Rachel kicked off her other shoe, and raced to the front door with blood from her wounds streaming down her legs and spotting the carpet.

Once outside, she screamed, screamed at the hurt she felt and at the horror of the dark-haired man she had left inside the house.

Josh came out of the house next door. Sonny stood in the open doorway of the garage.

"Come here," she said to her son, opening her arms to protect him. Turning to look at Josh's confused expression, Rachel said, "Call the police. We've got to call the police."

* * *

130

At the hospital, where the cuts on her legs were stitched, Rachel called Alice and Tim to come and take Sonny to their home for the night.

His eyes wide at both the sight of his mother's bandaged legs and the officers in uniform, Sonny argued to stay with her. He didn't want her to go home alone. Rachel, convincing him to leave, wanted to make certain their home was cleaned of blood before he returned.

"I'll be all right," she reassured her son. "They'll probably keep me here for hours yet, anyway."

One of the policemen told her when they were alone that Marty was in jail, but that he was not rational and probably would be admitted to the hospital also.

"He's not going to hurt you again," said the sympathetic officer, who had seen the criss-cross grids of cuts on her slender legs. "They're going to lock him up for good."

* * *

CHAPTER THIRTEEN

January, 1949

Rachel's first visit with Marty at the state mental hospital was an emotional agony that stripped away layers of her ability to cope.

She felt near panic at the uncertainty of their life, wondering how she would manage alone with a maturing son, questioning if Marty would recover, and fearing the prospects of being alone with him again in the future. The initial glimpse of him in the state hospital set the pattern for many more to come.

When she first arrived, she was led by a man in a gray uniform away from the main lobby, down a hall, and through a series of corridors and locked doors. The man's massive ring of keys jangled as he searched for each one to open the next door.

It was a sunny day. Rachel took every chance to glance out the tall, barred windows at the deep January snow cover and the blue sky. The warm blue sky. The outdoors became more important at each locked door. Inside, everything was a dirty beige or brown, peeling paint, dark benches and a medicinal smell.

"We're almost there," the man said as his first comment when they neared the end of another corridor and walked through a set of double doors into a large gymnasium-type room.

The only furniture was a row of wooden benches built into the four walls. They were filled with men of all ages and they had two things in common - they were all wearing loose gray shirts and pants, and no one was talking or moving at all.

They were silent statues.

The only sounds in the room were the rasping breathing of

some of the older men, occasional shuffling of feet and the buzz of one or two blow flies trapped in the tall sunny windows. A young male attendant, wearing thick glasses and a white uniform, approached Rachel and her guide as they entered the massive, silent room. The floor glistened, reflected the sun. No one squinted against the glare.

"She's here to see Martin Bradford," the guide said.

"Bradford's up there on the left, wheelchair in front of him," the attendant said, leading the way. Rachel's hard- sole shoes echoed on the slick wooden floors, despite her efforts to walk softly. No one turned to look.

Rachel realized she would have had trouble finding Marty by herself because she now stood in front of a gray-looking immobile man on the bench. It was Marty and he only had one leg, but she had to study him closely. It was Marty, but it wasn't. He did not look up at her. His sunken eyes were directed toward the floor, but she knew from his vacant stare that he wasn't seeing anything.

His face was much thinner, cheeks appeared to be sucked inward toward his teeth. He had a slight stubble of beard, and his hair was cropped into a war-time burr. The dark collar of his institutional shirt bunched out from his thin neck. The figure made her throat tighten and eyelashes flutter to hold back tears of sympathy.

Rachel reached down and took Marty's right hand in both of hers. There was no place to sit on the crowded bench. She could only bend over awkwardly to keep holding his hand.

"What's the matter with him?" Rachel asked, turning her head to look at the attendant and releasing Marty's hand.

Her guide had padded softly back across the room and exited by the double doors.

"He's in a state of depression. We have him on medication to treat that," the attendant said.

Rachel had heard the diagnosis from his doctor, but she did not expect this change in Marty's appearance. "Is he always like this?"

"Like what?"

"Not knowing anything."

"This is typical reaction for the treatment he's receiving. He gets a little violent without it. Really, he's doing all right. He'll get out of here sometime." The attendant's eyes swept the row of silent men in the room. "That's not something you can say for most of them."

"It's as if no one in this room is really living," Rachel observed. She leaned over, clutched Marty's hand again, She had to do something to try to comfort this man, despite what he had done to her.

Another attendant entered a door at the end of the room, walked to one of the patients, checked him, looked around and walked out again.

"Would it be all right if I sat here in the wheelchair with my husband for a minute?"

"Sure. If that's what you want. Coming here gets to a lot of people. They're not used to dealing with mental illness." He peered at her through the thick glasses that magnified his eyes. His hands were on his hips, and he shifted from foot to foot, as if he, too, would like a comfortable seat.

"I'd just like to sit here with him a few minutes."

"Stay as long as you want, up to a half hour. But I can't leave you alone. These guys are all passive, and wouldn't hurt anybody, but if one suddenly gets irritated or emotional, it could affect some of the others. I'll just stay nearby."

During the next several minutes that Rachel sat in the wheelchair and held Marty's hand, she talked to him softly about Sonny, described how well he was doing in school and that he had decided to be a teacher.

Rachel told him she wanted to leave her job at the paper bag company and maybe invest in a downtown hat shop. The third house purchase had gone through, she told him, and she was considering yet another.

Rachel could not detect if Marty heard the words she said in a low voice, or if he understood. He made no reaction. Rachel continued just to talk to him.

Occasionally there were slight interruptions in the room, such as when one of the old men started trembling as if he were having a nightmare while awake. The attendant went to him, and patted his back. He also took a handkerchief from his pocket and wiped the man's eyes which had suddenly flooded with tears.

Rachel, turning back to Marty, studied his features. She tried to remember a familiar smile, twinkle in the eyes, brows raised in humor, an expression of passion in love making. She found little to recall.

I don't really know you, she thought. I never really did. We came together at a time when we both needed somebody. We never had time to really get to know each other before we married. We cared, but we weren't in love.

As she watched Marty, secretly hoping he would suddenly awaken, she hardened her resolve to put everything behind her and go on to whatever future was left for her alone.

She became aware of her surroundings, suddenly aware the silence and separation of the men in the room had cocooned her, too. She had been staring into space, not communicating with anyone.

The attendant was watching her, but not with concern.

"Are they always this quiet?" she asked as he approached. "They don't even seem to be of this world." She took one last aching look at Marty, laid his hand, damp from the perspiration of her own hand, back on his left leg above the stump. She stood, prepared to leave with the attendant.

"They're living all right," corrected the attendant. "They're loving, fighting, crying and hurting, but they're doing it all in their own worlds inside their heads," he said, leading her toward the double doors.

* * *

Rachel only considered going to a controversial city-called meeting the next spring to keep active and overcome on-going worries over Marty. Glenn McIntire had called and asked that she attend, seeking some citizen support for downtown merchants in his dispute with city officials over the loss of local businesses.

She had more time on her hands now, even though she kept busy with her job and real estate. Sonny was adjusting to his initial feelings and confusion about his father, and was becoming extremely active in school, but he increasingly avoided going to the state hospital with her.

Marty was not responding to treatment, resulting in his doctors even suggesting that Rachel delay her visits for a time. That added to her guilt and feeling of uselessness. She turned to the business meeting for an emotional lift.

Owners of downtown businesses were in a dilemma over financial losses. The six-lane interstate highway was being built east of the city, as Glenn McIntire had questioned years before, and shoppers would be bypassing Garland to spend their money at large malls in nearby cities.

Rachel searched the small crowd of people standing outside the city building when she approached, hoping to catch a glimpse of Douglas. He was certain to be here. Unsuccessful, she saw Glenn and walked over to greet him.

"There's the lady with the pretty smile," said Glenn, always making her feel special. "So we're going to solve some important problems."

"I'm not really involved in his," she said, her hand nestled momentarily in his large, freckled paw. "I'm just here to observe this time."

"I was really sorry to hear about your husband. How's he doing?"

"Thanks, Glenn, we're handling it." Rachel found the subject still too tender to discuss and quickly switched to the upcoming meeting. "What's expected to happen tonight?"

"Oh, the city's prepared a plan to improve the business community, they say. But I don't have much confidence." Glenn frowned, his eyes sweeping the small clusters of people entering the building. He frequently nodded or smiled to acknowledge a fellow businessman.

"I've been standing here counting the merchants I still know,

136

and who are showing up. That's about forty. I can remember when there were hundreds of them when I was a kid."

Glenn saw Tom Baines, owner of the hardware store, and lifted his hand in a greeting as Baines approached with Gene Evans, family descendant of the 100-year-old Evans Jewelry Store firm. Rachel also greeted both of them.

"Think it's going to amount to anything?" asked Gene, supporting his frail body by holding to a silver-headed cane. Gene's jewelry store was where towns people bought wedding gifts, high school graduation presents and trinkets for long-suffering wives.

"Hell, I don't know, Gene," said Glenn, a third generation businessman addressing a second-generation one.

"Don't know what they can do for us that we merchants haven't already discussed."

"I'm down to a skeleton staff." The older man turned painfully, favoring his left hip, and used the cane to help share the weight. "I almost stayed home. If that tells you anything."

Glenn and Rachel slowly trailed the older men up the steps of the city building, converted from the former high school. Inside the city commission chambers, where the crowd was gathering, Rachel sat down by Glenn and searched the room again.

Douglas was at the far side, bending over and talking to some seated men, including Hooper. It's almost as if the entire Community Committee is here tonight, she thought. She had missed attending the meetings, but was anxious to begin again. Rachel's attendance at the session tonight was her first venturing back into the city's mainstream.

"Why does everything have to change?" said Glenn, capturing her attention away from the clustered group of men across the commission chambers. He began describing how in the "old days" the downtown area was crowded with shoppers and not just on Saturday.

"Women used to come downtown to buy a dress, then a matching hat at a shop across the street, then pick up a pair of shoes at Feldman's next door, " he recalled. "They'd end up at a downtown restaurant for lunch. Everything they needed was right there in a couple of blocks."

It was a good way of life, Glenn reminisced, telling how merchants created life-long friendships, watched each other's children grow up, and said good-bye when old-time friends passed on.

"Too many have gone now, and new ones are not coming in...." Glenn was interrupted by City Manager Bart Hillings and City Planning Director Timothy Brown moving to the front of the room to begin the session.

The city manager quickly turned the microphone over to Brown, who knew how to use it as if he had studied for the radio. Brown realized early in life his voice was a fine instrument and used it now to woo the audience with what the city was going to do about the problem of losing businesses.

A small man with a big voice, and who also appreciated grandiose thoughts, Brown opened his remarks with, "We must gather all our talents and work together to plunge forward into the future. We must be aggressive and challenging."

"Bullshit," croaked Gene Evans' aged voice in a mock whisper.

"I think you are going to be as excited as we are about what we are going to share with you," Brown said, grabbing and adjusting a stand that held flip charts.

During the next twenty minutes, he outlined how the city could obtain federal funds to build a climate-controlled canopy over a four-block area in the downtown area. Some outdated buildings would be demolished and new ones built.

The new "shopping mall" would compete with nearby cities.

Brown waited for the proposal to sink in. "We think it's an exciting concept," he said in the lull.

Then it came, voices raised in angry rejection, expressing fear of allowing the familiar to fade and skepticism of the unknown.

"We have figures to show that the downtown can be revived," Brown added convincingly.

"You don't get something for nothing," said Gene Evans, his old voice breaking with the strain of trying to be heard.

"You are right," Brown agreed. "Government grant funds will pay for closing the streets, building the canopy, adding walkways and lighting. We'll ask merchants to invest in modern store fronts."

Brown studied his audience, his voice soothing. "Some buildings obviously won't survive, but we'll ask those merchants, at low interest rates the banks will set, to build new ones and get in on the growth we're going to experience."

Hooper stood during the public discussion part of the meeting and raised the issue of colored downtown merchants.

"There never have been any. Are they included in the plan?" asked Hooper, capturing attention with his six-foot frame and commanding demeanor. He was impressive to the point people turned to give him their full attention and respect, despite the fact he was one of the coloreds.

"We haven't gotten into that yet, but certainly it's a possibility," Brown reassured. "Garland's coloreds represent about six percent of the population, and that should be reflected in the percentage of businesses."

"We'll see if that happens," Hooper challenged as he took his seat again.

Brown invited the audience at the conclusion of the meeting to come forward and view the architectural drawings on the future concept of the mall.

Glenn McIntire and Rachel were still moving up through the lines of people, taking to other businessmen, when Douglas met them after cutting through the crowd.

"So many of our committee are here, we should consider having a meeting afterwards," he said in greeting them.

"I was thinking the same thing," Rachel said, her eyes searching his face. It had been a long time since she had seen him.

"You need to get back involved," he said to her. "There are some things I'd like to talk to you about. I'll call you about the next meeting. Is everything going all right for you?" he ask, not really referring to the situation with her husband, but she understood.

"Treatment is still continuing, but it hasn't been very effective."

"Hang in there. If there's any help we can give you, let us know."

"You got that right," added Glenn.

"Well, Glenn," began Douglas. "I don't think you're going to like the drawings when you get up front to see them."

"Why not?" asked Glenn, his brow tightening with suspicion.

"They have your building and Gene Evans' marked for demolition and replacement'," Douglas explained. "You'll probably have to do some heavy negotiation if the plan goes."

"The hell you say." Glenn began a hard push to the front of the chambers. "My grandfather started the business, and it's staying right where it is."

"You may have to convince city officials."

"Just watch. I don't have red hair for nothing."

* * *

The annual lawn fete at Sonny's junior high school came on a sunny spring day and Rachel had volunteered to help staff a food booth. She was walking that way now with Sonny and smiled to herself at his obvious anxiety to catch up with some of his friends for the games.

"Do you think Teddy is going to be here with his parents," she asked, suddenly distracted. "Oh, I'm sorry, I didn't hear what you said," Rachel told her son after being slightly startled at seeing Douglas and obviously his family at a distance.

"I said I don't want to hang around with him anymore."

"Who?" Rachel's eyes stole another glance at Douglas's wife and the girls she guessed were his two daughters.

"Teddy. You asked about Teddy."

"You know it's not nice just to ignore him," she answered, giving her son attention again. "He admires you so much, Sonny. We've been close to the family a lot of years now."

"It's all right if my friends aren't around. But they're not gonna be with me if Teddy's around." Sonny stammered in trying to

140

explain to her.

"Just try not to hurt Teddy's feelings," Rachel said. "Uh, tell me. Do those two girls down there, the one in pink and the other there in green, go to your school?" Rachel was ashamed of her question. She thought Douglas's family lived in Columbus, but they could have moved back to Garland. She needed to know, but she was not sure why.

"Don't know'em. But a lot of people come to the fetes that don't go to school here," Sonny answered. "Hey, do you mind if I look around for some of my friends now?"

"Go ahead. Have fun, and I'll see you back home if not before." Rachel stopped on her walk toward the food booth, giving Douglas's family time to move on down between the rows of tents.

She could not help but admire the image of the wife, elegant, even when walking on a gravel path at a lawn fete.

Douglas's family was just about out of sight now and could not detect that she was studying them, even if they looked her way. The tall, slender and blond woman who strolled beside Douglas wore a yellow pants suit of a fabric that just sort of swished against her body. Not a sign of a wrinkle.

Heads turned in admiration, but the woman did not acknowledge it. Probably used to it, Rachel thought.

I'm more than foolish to think about him when he has a wife like that, she thought.

* * *

Because she thought Douglas would want to be with his obviously impressive wife after the lawn fete, Rachel was unprepared when Douglas called her to talk about the Community Committee.

She could not know that Douglas was emotionally drained after a weekend of bombarding arguments with his wife about moving back to Columbus. He suggested to Rachel that they have dinner along with the talk.

Once the words were spoken, there was no doubt it would happen. Douglas chose a quaint, but secluded restaurant about a forty-five minute drive from Garland.

After wine and dinner filled with non-stop conversation on many subjects, they strolled along a path overlooking a moon-reflecting pond beside the restaurant. Both were silent. Then Douglas reached for her hand in the dark. He moved closer, looked down at her.

"I can get a room here, if we want to continue the talk."

That was all he needed to say.

* * *

When the hotel door closed, Rachel put her hand on Douglas' shoulder and instantly his mouth was on hers. Not just a kiss, but a search, a demand for release of the passion they had shared and stored away for so long. His arms tightened around her, blending her to him. She dared not move. Her groin suddenly ached and felt damp, embarrassing.

He had felt her shudder and pull back. "You all right?"

"Yes, it's just, I...." He pulled her back toward him.

Rachel felt awkward, wondering what to do next.

She suggested, surprising herself, "Shall we get out of these clothes?"

There were no questions from him, just quick acceptance. She turned her back, began unbuttoning her blouse, then removing the rest of her clothes, putting them on the back of a chair. Douglas was slower, but did the same.

They both were overwhelmed with emotions, but were moving so slowly, so methodically. Almost impersonal.

His brown hair tumbled over his brow and she saw the dark

hair on his muscular thighs as he leaned forward and stepped out of his shorts.

"I'll be right back," Rachel said, moving naked toward the bathroom, chiding herself to suck in her tummy. Am I shocking him, she wondered.

She studied herself in the bathroom mirror critically. Long legs are good, she thought, and fortunately I'm slim. Feeling calmer now, she re-entered the now dimly lit hotel bedroom, slipped under the sheet and scooted next to Douglas.

When she reached to turn off the one low light, he said, "Let's leave it on."

He raised on an elbow, flipped down her side of the sheet to view her. Then he enfolded her into his arms, kissing her mouth, her shoulders and then her breasts, one at a time, then repeating the kisses.

It was mutual touching, hands exploring, caressing. His warm palms slid over her smooth skin, stopping again to cup and hold her breasts one at a time. Her fingers touched the silky hairs on his arms and chest as his lips covered hers again in kisses that went on for minutes. Do other people kiss like this?, she wondered, the sensation making her dizzy. She thought she would be unable to breathe. Both made short gasps and deep gulps as their lips ground together again and their bodies tightened around each other in a tangle.

Douglas moved one of his legs under her, meshing their stomachs together. The rigidness of his body caressed her. How tenderly he moves, she thought, as his intensity grew.

Words were not needed. Rachel whimpered, sighed, and Douglas moaned as he moved his mouth from her lips and found her nipples again.

She lost track of time as they held each other, caressed bodies, tangled their legs in clinging positions. She thought any second he would thrust into her, but still he delayed.

All Rachel could think was: *This is the way it is supposed to be. This is what passion is. I am so late in learning.*

Although he would have delayed longer, Douglas interpreted the increased tightening of her arms as eagerness for him and slowly began sliding into her, a deep groan coming from his chest. They clung, thrust and merged until they were not separate bodies, but warm clay softening together.

A surprising sound, like a meowing of a kitten, escaped from Rachel's lips, a sound totally foreign to her. He slid in and out of her, increasingly. She sensed he could not delay much longer.

"Go, go ahead," she said breathlessly.

"I'll wait for you" Douglas said, the words from between their mashed lips. "I can go on like this forever."

No, she thought. No you can't. Don't think so much. Just don't think, feel, she told herself, letting her own building sensations increase within her. It was as if a power engulfed them to take them deeper and deeper into each other. A power that only he could control, he had to reach her, rescue her, save her. His final plunge released them both, to shudders and heavy gasps that faded into soft, poorly-controlled sighs.

After he eased down beside her, Rachel rested her head on his arm, running her palm over the dampness of his chest.

"You're wonderful." She was surprised at her trembling voice.

"You're pretty wonderful yourself."

Over the next couple of hours of love making they shared heated, long, and slow kisses, fingers sliding over each other, conversation in low voices on unimportant subjects, drifting from one topic to another with no purpose. They liked the sound of their voices together, merging of the minds still, now that their bodies were satiated.

Contentment. Satisfaction. Completeness.

Rachel felt the hint of a slight release in his body, a relaxing as if he were moving away from her. It was momentary. She didn't move. Then another one, a letting go, a little at a time. He's falling asleep, she thought. But he doesn't let go easily, doesn't lose control easily, a little at a time when he could no longer prevent it. A third slipping, and she knew he was deep asleep now.

She couldn't control her own wakefulness to ease into peaceful sleep beside him. Rachel withdrew as gently as possible from his arms, disturbing him slightly so that his arms tightened. She remained alert, willing herself to lie still, not to disturb him. Finally, she inched out of his arms, slipped out of bed and huddled in a chair by the window.

Rachel shivered, missed the warmth of his body, and wrapped her arms across her naked breasts. She remembered his mouth on them.

It was complete, all I could expect and far more, she thought to herself. He's as good at this as he is everything else, so why am I...so...so restless? She sat a long time, wondering how to interpret her emotions, and recalled her fantasies for years about what real love would be like.

She now knew, she had experienced it, the passion. The hurt, she thought to herself, is that the love is not mine and I can't have it. We're together tonight, but maybe we never will be again. It would be gone, even later tonight, all over.

It has to be a letting go, no need to try to cling, it wouldn't do any good. She shivered again, longing for Douglas's warmth. She moved from the chair, inched silently onto the bed, and slowly slipped down beside his long body. Even in sleep his arms reached out to enfold her to him, his legs shifted tenderly to tangle with hers. She wanted the moment, longed for it, as they held each other closer.

He reacted, his mouth came for hers. His body became hard against her again.

Much later they reluctantly dressed, back to back, dreading the coming moments. They would part now, Rachel thought, perhaps never to be together again.

Douglas, finished dressing first, walked over to her.

"What can I say? I don't want to leave you." He put his arms protectively around her.

* * *

The joy that came into Rachel's life with Douglas's love lingered into the weeks ahead. Their rare meetings, brief and at sites located at a distance from Garland, kept them bonded with a passion that withstood the always lurking threat of discovery and pain to families.

Both Douglas and Rachel recognized the consequences, dreaded them, but at times felt they could not exist apart.

Their separate lives provided opportunities for them in that Douglas lived alone and Rachel had lessening family responsibilities. Sonny was in a development pattern that made little demands on her time. He was active in sports and literary activities at school, but they lived close enough that he could walk to the junior and high school buildings.

His goals were to win college scholarships and pursue his teaching career.

Douglas maintained a weak link with his family, despite efforts for more contact. He visited in Columbus once or twice a month, and welcomed his wife and daughters to Garland when they could make it.

Those visits were becoming more rare. His feelings of rejection and insignificance after each visit, such as after the lawn fete, left him wondering why he bothered.

There were opportunities for Rachel and Douglas to see each other publicly about every other week at meetings of different organizations in which he deliberately involved her.

"Not another committee" became one of her gag comments when he signed her up for yet another organization so they would have more reasons to meet. They kept their distance at these functions and, once committed, Rachel was known as a solid contributor.

The times increased when she was more recognized on her own abilities and was asked to serve on projects without Douglas's influence, such as in various capacities for the new Teen Center, for restoration of a historic water fountain, and on a feasibility study committee for the first apartment complex in the city.

Their special times together came irregularly when they retreated to a secluded hotel or motel in another city.

"I've never known a woman who wants as much love as I want to give," Douglas told her one afternoon as she lay in the tender vice of his arms.

Their muscles then tightened as if on cue, straining toward each other, holding closer, closer until every part of their bodies were touching in what they laughingly learned to call a body kiss.

Rachel and Douglas both knew from the beginning they would not interfere with the other's marriage or family life, never even discuss it seriously.

Although dedicated to their responsibilities, and they told themselves that repeatedly, they weakened when it came to spending a small fraction of their lives together.

They were unable to fight the joy of loving each other, the touching, and merging together in a mind-out-of-body oneness.

Telephone calls were too risky to communicate, so they each signed up for secret post office boxes. Even in those letters they were cautious. They never wrote expressions of love, saving that for private times together, and signed the letters merely, LY, for "Love You" LYMY for "Love You Miss You."

She treasured his letters. They became the incentive to keep her going for days and weeks at a time.

In one letter he wrote, "Certainly my dilemma is one of feeling that I am a problem, rather than a help and a support. Regardless of my circumstances, you have been a great satisfaction to me.

"I now realize that I have turned to you many times for advice and encouragement. You don't need this extra burden even though since I first met you, I have placed more trust and dependence in you than most anyone I can think of. You have been an outlet, a comfort and so many other things....."

This sporadic loving and relief from life's daily afflictions were shattered, when Rachel learned Marty was to be released from the state mental hospital.

* * *

CHAPTER FOURTEEN

March, 1951

Rachel was not mentally prepared for Marty's release from the state institution, even though more than two years had passed.

She had received reports in recent months about how he was overcoming his depression, and that his release was pending.

But the approaching date of the actual day that she would see him again for the first time created a mood of apprehension. She had not visited him for a long time, not since the doctors said he had became too agitated after seeing her and since she had initiated the divorce proceedings.

They were divorcing, but it could not be final until he was released and competent. Physicians said Martin Bradford was ready now to deal with his life. He had accepted the loss of his leg, his family, and was ready to move on with his life.

Attorneys had been their legal contact in the past year, arranging their divorce and property settlement. It meant dividing up the houses, with Marty to dispose of his share of the property. The end of their time together as man and wife was near, not that they had been that for many years.

It would just be official now.

"What do you plan to do? Are you staying in the city?" Those were Rachel's polite questions the first time she saw Marty after his release. He had dropped Sonny off after an afternoon re-acquainting baseball game.

I don't know the man, Rachel thought, it's not Marty.

She watched the man sitting stiffly in the living room of her newest home. She would keep this house that she lived in now with Sonny and another where Alice and Tim lived, while Marty would take possession of the first one they had bought and the home Tina Rose occupied with her family.

Rachel did not regret losing half the real estate she had struggled to accumulate. She owed that to Marty, she felt, and she would work even harder in the future to buy more property.

"I'm not staying here in the city," Marty was explaining in a slow, plodding voice. "I wanta go back home, to Kentucky. I think I can get a better handle on my life there."

Marty sat rigidly on one of the two straight-back chairs in Rachel's living room. She offered him a comfortable, over-stuffed chair, but he decided on the less comfortable one. She chose a similar one beside him.

"You still have family there, so it will be good for you. Do you know what you'll do?"

"Not yet. I'm gonna sell the houses here and use the money for some kind of business. Maybe buy into a grocery. I don't know. That seems like something people keep needing."

Rachel did not want the houses sold. She had saved and pinched to make down payments and personally slaved to renovate them. But it was no longer her decision. This was part of her freedom, and Marty's freedom. The money would help him make a life for himself.

She studied him closely. He was still a good looking man, but not someone who appealed to her. Marty's hair was thinner from the treatments and drugs he had taken. His skin had the yellowish look of someone who had been confined a long time.

He was gaunt. The off-the-rack gray suit hung from his shoulders and the belt puckered the material around his thin waist. But despite Marty's apparent discomfort at being around her, he showed not the least awkwardness or concern about his missing leg.

Occasionally he would lay the palm of his left hand on his knee, and pat or tap his fingers on his leg to emphasize something he was saying. He didn't seem aware that the hand was making its emphasis on the plastic artificial leg. He's tense, she recognized. The tapping didn't make any noise, and he didn't seem aware that he was doing it.

When Marty stood to leave, there was no awkwardness in getting his balance. But she noticed his first stiff-legged step as he moved to the foot of the stairs, the faint squeak of leather, plastic and metal abrasions, and his glance up the stairs to where Sonny had disappeared only moments ago.

"I'll call him down to say goodbye," Rachel said, as the young replica of his father stuck his head over the banister. She had not been unaware of their similarities - their coloring and stiff, black-hair cowlicks until she saw the two faces at the same time. Their son's hair was more manageable.

Sonny thumped down the stairs two steps at a time with all the energy of youth. Nearly as tall as his father now, Sonny hugged his dad, wadding the suit jacket that hung loose around the emaciated body.

"I had a good time at the game, thanks," Sonny said.

"Yeah, me too. You gotta come to Kentucky and visit me now. I'll take you on some coon hunts down there. You won't believe how quiet it is when you're out in the woods all night like that."

"Let me know when."

"I will. You take care now." Marty turned to Rachel.

Overwhelmed with compassion in watching the exchange between her son and his father, Rachel raised her arms to wrap them around Marty's shoulders. She tightened her arms and kissed his rough cheek.

His body tensed against her. "You'll get yours, bitch," he whispered in a raspy voice in her ear.

Stunned, Rachel drew back.

The look Marty returned was one she would never forget.

It left her with a dread that flavored her nightmares for years to come. The cunning, narrowed eyes emphasized the cruel grin that twisted the face she once thought she loved.

Marty turned then, gesturing for Sonny to accompany him out to his car. At the front door, Marty twisted back once to look at her. He winked, and it was not friendly, then he softly closed the door behind them.

Stopping on the sidewalk, Marty opened the door of the car

he had borrowed. He slid into the seat, and threw one hand into the air in farewell to Sonny. He did not look back at Rachel.

She watched as the car blurred in tears and disappeared down the street.

* * *

<u>October, 1954</u>

"I don't think investing in the hat shop would be a good idea at this time," Douglas told Rachel one Saturday afternoon. Their feet crunched on red and gold leaves littering a wooded path near a Covington motel.

It was one of their rare weekends together. Douglas, long her sounding board on varied financial ventures, was weighing Rachel's urge to buy a downtown store that faced going out of business because of mall construction.

"The city and merchants are doing a lot to hold onto business traffic during construction, but it won't get better for awhile, if ever." Douglas responded with gentle nudges of his swinging hand against her hand as they strolled.

They always were reluctant to hold hands in public, even though isolated, but just the touching was part of the closeness they needed. As their hands brushed together, one of her fingers sometimes would stretch out and curl momentarily around one of his. It was not a gesture someone at a distance would detect.

"I'd be afraid of investing just now," he said.

"But Glenn's building his new stag bar. He's excited about it now, even through he said he was ready to kill when the city condemned his building."

"Glenn probably will do all right. He has a long-time business with regular customers," Douglas explained.

151

"I guess hats really are becoming a thing of the past," she reluctantly conceded. "I just hate to see them go."

"You'll be better off in real estate. You've done all right so far."

That prompted Rachel to confide uneasily that she was considering another property investment, one of the stately houses on Chestnut Street. She would live in it one day after Sonny left for college in another year.

"Am I being foolish?" The rents from her four other properties, one a duplex, were paying off the buildings and giving her the incentive to buy a special home for herself and Sonny when he returned home. Rachel had been giving real estate so much of her time, she no longer worked at the paper bag company.

"Not if you looked at all the financial aspects we've discussed. It'll probably be a good investment." His hand clutched at her hand in a passing swing, squeezed it, and released it reluctantly.

They had grown closer in recent years, including overcoming any awkwardness in talking about their families. He knew the agony she felt with Marty's accident, his attack and their divorce. They talked of their children, shared concerns.

Douglas long ago had confided that he had relinquished his role as husband, but not as a father. People thought he and Sandra were a couple, but they only gave the appearance of married life because of her parent-influenced attitude to divorce. She was surviving, existing on country club life and charity work to boost her glamorous young matron image.

Douglas made Rachel aware that she was the cushion he needed to survive the existence he had chosen. They both knew the other was the major force in their lives, and that their love was special.

"Before you, I had never experienced waking up in anyone's arms. I guess I couldn't lie still long enough," she had stated early in their relationship. "How did so many years go by without knowing one of life's greatest pleasures?"

"We're making up for it now."

Despite their delight in being together, loneliness fell heavily on Rachel in living alone. Some single female friends, experiencing

152

the same lifestyle, suggested she find someone to "date". She never considered the possibility, realizing no one could begin to compare to Douglas. Besides, he also lived much of his life alone.

It was better for her, Rachel realized, to have a small amount of time with him than a lot of time with a lesser person.

* * *

April, 1966

"You're going to be busy now, Girl!"

"Why do you say that?" Rachel answered in response to Hooper's remark after a meeting of the Community Committee had ended.

"Well as a candidate for Garland City Commission, I'm going to need all the help you can give me in campaigning."

"You a candidate?" Rachel asked in amazement.

"He certainly is." Douglas turned from talking to other committee members when he heard their conversation. "The steel company's going to endorse his financial support as the first colored candidate for the city commission."

"I'm not an eager candidate, but I've been asked, so I'm considering it," Hooper said modestly.

"You're not considering, you're it," admonished Douglas. Turning to Rachel, he said, "We'll need you to help head up some of the coffees and citizens' campaign meetings".

"Define coffees," Rachel responded, a smile spreading on her face at this exciting venture opening for all of them.

"We'll all work together," Douglas began. "As company public relations man I'll handle publicity, but we'll ask you to contact women in different neighborhoods throughout the city to hold morning coffees and invite eight or ten friends to come and meet Hooper. You know a lot of people in the city you can get involved, and many of them already know Hooper, so it should not be tough."

Hooper was scared and apprehensive in his reactions to becoming the first black city commissioner, but he was the likely candidate. The term nationally now in the 1960s was "Black" instead of "colored", and more emphasis was given to Civil Rights. Garland was long overdue for a Black city official.

"I just hope there won't be any violence as they've had in other cities..," Hooper began. But he stopped. "Why anticipate trouble?"

* * *

Alice was the only discordant note in Rachel's life that spring and Sonny the bright spot, as she volunteered on Hooper's campaign. It involved much more of her time than just coffees, as she learned.

"You're the only family I have here, and you need to spend more time with me to help me through this," Alice whined in what was becoming a weekly, sometimes daily litany.

Alice's increasing arthritis and stomach problems drained her energy. She also had to care for severely-overweight and nearly immobile Tim in the two-story home they rented from Rachel.

"We can't afford to have anybody come in and help," Alice's weak, pathetic voice droned.

"How about your daughters? Couldn't they help run some errands for you, bring in some groceries?" Rachel asked after spending another Saturday morning "helping out", as Alice put it. She glanced at her sister, still with the stretched-tight hair that threaten to pop her eyes out.

"Them, heck," Alice said of the daughters who had married and moved away several years earlier. "They don't have time for nothing except theirselves. You got a college- graduate son to help take care of you. My girls are not gonna bother drivin' down here thirty or forty miles to do somethin' for us. They kissed us off. Just now, I'm so worried, I think I better take another nerve pill."

"Too many of those are not good for you."

"So what is good for me right now? Nothing!"

Rachel felt Alice was taking advantage of her, especially since her sister seemed to move easily and without pain when she thought no one was looking. How much of her illnesses are real, and how much to control me, Rachel wondered.

"I'll help where I can and we'll see if we can find someone to help care for Tim," Rachel said. She secretly decided to wait and see how well Alice managed when she was not putting on an act, as Rachel suspected.

"I guess it's just meant to be," Alice said, "for some people to have more in life than others."

* * *

Housing and decorating were issues in which Rachel became involved with Sonny when he prepared to move into one of their apartments.

He had returned to Garland after his years at college and teaching a few years in another city. Now he wanted to continue his independence by not living at home.

"I'm going to like the high school," said her tall young son in telling her of his new contract to teach at the same school he had attended.

His resemblance to Marty had increased with maturity, but his personality was more enthusiastic and more optimistic in beginning a new experience. Rachel saw herself in him, too, especially in the blue eyes.

"It's going to be strange. They've added a new media center

and enlarged the cafeteria." Sonny's words ran together in his excitement. "But I'm hearing from other teachers that discipline's more of a problem with this civil rights movement."

"You'll settle in and do well," she encouraged, stretching up on her toes to put her arms around his neck.

"I can't take much credit for how you turned out. I was gone a lot working, but you grew up just as I hoped you would."

He squeezed her around the waist, lifted her off the floor momentarily. "You've always been there for me, Mom."

"I'm so proud of you," she whispered.

* * *

Although Rachel attended meetings with Douglas in Hooper's campaign and had secret time with him about once a month, Douglas began traveling more for MVS. He was pushing himself too much, she warned, sometimes cradling him in her arms as he dozed momentarily when they shared a bed.

"You rejuvenate me," he said once after a long embrace.

He had a worn look, was thin, and sometimes lapsed into staring into space. There never seemed enough hours for him to do everything he felt he should do, Douglas explained.

He never complained to her about the company, or talked personalities, but one rainy evening as they walked to their cars after a speech by Hooper at a meeting of the American Association of University Women, Douglas could not resist spilling out what was bothering him. He never kept anything from her, but some subjects verged on the confidential.

"Two things are hurting the company," he blurted, "cost of environmental regulations and imports from abroad. We're diversifying, but I don't know if that's the answer."

Douglas touched her elbow to guide her around a puddle in the parking lot. "Hell, we specialize in making steel. What do we

156

know about managing oil rigs, insurance companies, and any other kind of company they have bought?"

"Have they really gone into all that?"

"All that, and more, and the company attitude is changing, I can see it," Douglas said, the weariness coming through in his voice. "The company's loosing it's small town flavor, and it'll be worse if they bring in an outside chairman of the board as they are considering."

"Hooper mentioned in his speech tonight about how top officials attend school lawn fetes and walk around calling mill workers by name," Rachel reminded.

"It's been like that," Douglas said. "But we're getting too big. That personal contact won't last. I guess that's why it will be good to have someone like Hooper as a commissioner. He's seen a lot, and won't let go of the past too easily."

Rachel suddenly remembered the disruption in the meeting that night. "Can you believe the reaction Hooper got when he said there are drugs in the schools? Is that true?"

"Hooper would know, and I've heard him mention it."

When Hooper raised the subject of drugs in his speech, a loud roar of denial rose from members of the audience. Their looks would have set him ablaze if they could. They didn't want Garland's School District compared to inner city schools with major drug traffic.

"Hooper didn't back off, though, so I have no doubt that he's right," Douglas said. "He doesn't fight the system openly, but he's his own man to the point he says what he thinks."

He had stood up to the jeering audience, feet planted behind the lectern and his tall figure prepared for the onslaught his race had experienced for generations.

"I liked it when he told parents they would only be convinced when their own children were affected," Rachel said, "and that it could be sooner than they think with drugs passing up and down the north and south highways."

"I cautioned him after the meeting not to dwell on drugs too much during the campaign," Douglas said. "People aren't believing him, and he'll lose credibility."

"What are his chances for election?"

"Oh, he'll make it, and he'll be effective," Douglas explained as he and Rachel exchanged glances, approaching their separate cars. Another parting.

"The city can't afford to pass him over just now, with this growing civil rights attitude. Believe me, Hooper's going to be needed."

* * *

Hooper did become a motivating force in dealing with the dissension that struck the city on black and white issues over the next year.

But just having a black commissioner in office was not enough concession for some black residents, who still were not served in some restaurants, could not enter some theaters, and faced job discrimination.

"We had no right to think we could escape it," Hooper said openly of protests and demonstrations that followed. "We have as much injustice here as anywhere else."

Although Hooper gave the image of calm acceptance in his drive for equality, he over reacted when discrimination touched his own daughter. She came home in tears one evening after she and some friends were denied a table at a restaurant.

Hooper, trained to be controlled and soft spoken in negotiations over the years, was ready to grab and shake somebody.

"Damn it, we're going into the seventies, and it's time to stop."

Jaws clamped in determination, Hooper drove to the police department that same evening to file a complaint. He was secretly pleased at the way he was acting officially and setting an example, but he was apprehensive at the common knowledge that Police Chief Pendleton was known for having a racist attitude over the years.

Hooper did not know what position he was putting himself in, because he was aware the police chief was employed by the city commission and he was a city commissioner. He was determined to be heard, however. His daughter had the right to eat in any public restaurant.

"She'll testify against them in court," Hooper said of his daughter to the young officer who had started writing down his complaint at the night desk.

"Sir, you may not have a complaint in this case."

"What do you mean I may not have a complaint? Look, I'm a....I'm a resident in this city and I can file a Civil Right complaint as well as anyone."

"But, sir...."

"Don't but me."

The young officer stopped, then looked up into Hooper's strongly-controlled expression. They both felt the tension.

"I was only going to say the restaurant is not in the city, Sir."

"What did you say?"

"The restaurant's outside the city limits. We have no jurisdiction."

"The hell you say." A smile widened Hooper's face when he realized he had made a fool of himself by acting so spontaneously. "I guess I really never knew that, or never thought about it. It would be county sheriff's deputies then that have jurisdiction, not city police?"

Hooper stuck out his hand to the officer, attempting to make amends. He felt foolish, wanted to end the incident on a positive note, and was able to relate the story later in a humorous vein.

But civil rights incidents mounted in Garland, which lagged behind other parts of the country by several years.

The increasingly active local protest group was comprised of a small band of blacks, five or six adults and about a dozen youngsters, who showed up for protests.

Although convinced changes were needed, Hooper and other blacks who held jobs with the mill over the years and wanted equal opportunities to occur peacefully, preferred to distance themselves from the alleged trouble makers.

Dissenters followed patterns of the Rev. Martin Luther King and NAACP leaders by boycotting stores and restaurants that did not serve or hire blacks, but they were unorganized and ineffective. The group issued printed statements at boycotted businesses and called reporters to cover their protests.

But group members gave the general impression in newspaper photos of being no more than misdirected high school drop-outs.

Douglas, active behind the scenes as much as possible when not traveling for MVS, continued to consult with Hooper, city officials and other black community leaders.

"Changes have to come locally and willingly, we have to work toward that," Douglas encouraged. "We don't want enforcers from large cities coming here and organizing our people. Let's move with the times peacefully."

The attitude didn't guarantee a peaceful transition, however, as restaurants, rest rooms, theaters and public facilities were desegregated. Protests continued.

Hooper, who never favored demonstrations, sounded off. "I support Reverend King and his goals, but I believe more can be accomplished by sitting down at the bargaining table to resolve differences," he said.

Stores did not just suddenly create more jobs for blacks. Scuffles and rock throwing occurred sometimes outside bowling alleys and in parking lots of the increasing number of fast-food restaurants. Tension increased.

* * *

"If we don't reach some kind of accord in the community," Sonny complained one Sunday evening to his mother, "it's questionable the school levy will pass in the spring."

Citizens had never turned down a school levy in Garland, but the community had never been in such a turmoil. Floods and strikes in the past had united residents in a common crisis. Now, they were suspicious and apprehensive, along with city and school officials.

"It's not fair that schools take the brunt of this," Sonny told Rachel angrily. "People don't understand that schools are where integration is most prevalent."

Sonny admitted that in the past the elementary students had attended separate schools, and still did to a great extent, but junior high and high school students had shared classrooms for years in Garland. Not just classrooms, but showers, gym lockers and cafeterias.

Sonny saw the restlessness growing. Black students now were magnifying inequities in life styles and opportunities that they had only mourned in the past. They became more aggressive, taking a little more space in the halls, occasionally bumping white students and mumbling remarks under their breath that they were not yet ready to shout.

"Sure it's got to change," Sonny agreed. "But it should never have reached this point for students. It's taking so much of our time to keep the peace, we don't have time to educate them."

* * *

CHAPTER FIFTEEN

October, 1969

A slender black youth rapped with his pencil on the table, calling to order a meeting of the Black High School Student Union to discuss problems with the 1969 Homecoming game.

"Let's stop talking among yourselves," he said, rapping a little louder with his pencil to get the attention of the thirty or so black students gathered in the basement of the Garland South Side Community Center. He wanted to get the meeting over and get out of the basement's stifling October heat.

"We got all the interested parties here, and we're going to let them tell it like it happened. Leona, tell 'em."

An attractive, tight-skirted black girl with a modified Afro hairstyle stood, turned to whisper to her girlfriend sitting beside her in a studied gesture of awareness that everyone was watching. She straightened, her narrow hips swaying slowly as she moved away from her friend toward the front of the room.

"Well, I think a lot of you already know, but I got a telephone call saying I really hadn't been elected a homecoming queen candidate. But the guy who was to be my escort, Gerald Pierson, there's Jerry.....,"she gestured toward a male student, "really *was* elected part of the homecoming court."

No great shock wave swept the room. As Leona suspected, most of the students knew the story. They listened again to the account, but their purpose there was to discuss what they were going to do.

"How did you say you found out about it?" a female voice

asked.

"I got a telephone call," Leona repeated. "She didn't give her name, but I'm sure it was a white woman. She said, 'Please don't tell anyone about this call.' She was whispering. She said, 'There is still a lot of injustice. I thought you should know about this'." Leona waited for the words to take effect.

"This happened every year in the past. Students voted for the queen candidates and escorts, but there were never enough black votes to get black candidates on the list," Leona explained. "Teachers on the committee crossed off the names of the two white candidates with the lowest number of votes, and added the names of two black candidates with the highest votes."

Leona stood a little taller as she announced she was going to turn down the honor of being in the queen's court. "I want no part of their tokenism," she blurted. "But I think Gerald should stay on the list. He was elected fairly."

Afro-styled heads turned to Gerald, who had a modest haircut. He nodded, indicating he was willing to continue.

A female hand raised and fluttered in the back of the room, which was getting steamy with the warm bodies of the youngsters. They shuffled in their seats, causing a perpetual clatter of metal, folding chairs.

"Rustine, we'll hear from you," the leader said.

Standing, the girl with the fluttering hand said, "I don't think the few of us have any strength in talkin' school people into doing anything. I think we ought to get some adults to meet with us and advise us what we should do."

The leader nodded his agreement as she sat down, but added, "We've already been talking to parents and leaders in our black community. They're standing with us, but they want this to be a student action. Any other suggestions?"

A male student stood without waiting to be called on. "We need to do somethin' to keep people away from the homecoming game. If we ain't part of it, nobody should be."

"That'll hurt us, me and the other guys on the team," said Jerry. "If there's no gate receipts, no sports."

The session ended with students compiling a list of eight

possible actions at the homecoming game, including staging a boycott, organizing an informational picket line at the stadium gates, and refusing to buy items at the refreshment stand.

Students left the meeting elated with their decisions.

They vowed never again to accept "tokenism" in school activities.

* * *

Black ministers stood united in their pulpits the following Sunday to denounce the school's homecoming policy but, at the same time, to call for calm in the community. Safety at the upcoming homecoming football game and future games became the community's obsession.

The attitude was tense - fueled by reports of violence in other parts of the country - when black students, parents, Sonny and other teachers attended a standing-room-only Garland School Board meeting. Again, Leona dramatically rejected being in the homecoming queen's court as a "token" black.

Board members, already alerted to the situation through newspaper articles, listen in frozen positions as Leona and other students ranted about being manipulated as puppets by the school system.

"We're not just things here, we're human beings," Leona said, swiveling at her slender waist to face the supporting crowd of predominantly blacks behind her. Hoots and cheers rolled to a high pitch, accompanied by the thunder of foot stomping.

"Let's have a little control now," the school board's president began, his voice at first not heard. As the room quieted, he continued, "After looking into the situation, I can't say we deny the practice that's been used for the homecoming court. But we didn't know about it."

The nervousness of board members, their fingering of papers in front of them and downcast eyes were not obvious signs to convince any crowd of truthfulness, especially not a hostile one.

"So what's going to be done about it," a deep masculine voice rumbled from the rear.

"The procedure already has been changed," the president said, clearing his voice repeatedly. "Why it was done, we understand, was so black students would be included in the court."

He explained that blacks comprise only six percent of the student body and their votes traditionally were not enough to elect their candidates to the top ten court positions. Gerald, as a popular athlete, did capture enough votes.

During the nearly two hours of comments that followed by mostly black students and adults, they denounced the shallowness of the situation and ended by shouting angrily of retaliation.

When the issue seemed exhausted, other allegations were raised, ranging from the need for more black assemblies to more blacks on the teaching staff. Finally, the last speaker took his seat. The board president waited, and there were no others.

"We'll look into all this," he said, clearing his throat more forcefully. "We regret this has happened and.... feel the school system should move ahead now with the business of education."

Sonny was unaware he was slowly shaking his head. He and other teachers were not surprised when students grumbled their displeasure at the lack of any real action.

"We're going to boycott the homecoming game and dance," Leona defiantly stood and announced. Cheers bellowed from her supporters. "And black students are going to hold their own homecoming dance."

* * *

Hooper did not relish the role he was assigned to play in the growing debate over homecoming. He had been asked by black community leaders to meet with the racist chief of police on increased police protection at the game.

Part of the problem was the location of the stadium on practically the dividing line between the white and predominantly black communities. Incidents had occurred in the past.

Years before when the stadium was built away from the high school in an open field, it was nearly a mile north of the row houses built by the steel company for families of black workers. But the black community had spread north, and the white community south, until the stadium now was surrounded by residences of both races.

If there were any major racial problems, school officials knew the white population would avoid that part of the town for fear of possible conflicts. That could mean loss of revenue, and the end of award-winning sports in the district.

Hooper weighed the problem as he parked in the city building driveway and headed for the double doors of the police department. At the entrance, he saw a familiar emblem that he felt said a lot about the chief.

It was an iron cut-out of a fat, smiling pig, about ten inches long and six inches high, resting on top of a swivel pole a couple of feet high. The pole was stuck in a patch of ivy. The pig spun around in a heavy wind.

Hooper and other residents knew the police chief capitalized on the way criminals called cops ``Pigs'', by picking up on it first. Pendleton had cartoons about pigs put on the bulletin board and had small pig pins made for officers to wear. He took the sting out of the slur, until the men, too, joked about being pigs.

Standing now in the open doorway of the police chief's office, where the secretary had abandoned him, Hooper eyed Pendleton at his desk. He knew he was being kept waiting, as Pendleton continued to concentrate on papers in front of him.

Hooper had butted heads with Pendleton before, and was not optimistic a "talk", as Douglas had suggested, would convince the chief to be generous with more officers' time.

He considered Pendleton a typical dumb, uneducated cop who put on a uniform and took command, although Hooper never would put that assessment into words. Nor would he publicly describe Pendleton as he saw him - a paunchy, balding, hick, gorilla. But he was prepared to reason with the chief, if possible.

Hooper walked on into the chief's office uninvited and sat down.

"I guess we know what we're gonna talk about," the chief said, raising his head and finally looking at Hooper. A former Army man who learned early that an officer's uniform commands respect, Pendleton had pegged Hooper during his campaigning as a show-off Nigger with a taste for power.

He wouldn't even begrudgingly give Hooper credit for his volunteer work in counseling black parents whose kids were in jail for intoxication or fighting. The chief preferred that Hooper stick to the mill union or city businesses and allow him to run the police department.

"We need to provide more police protection at Friday night football games. Parents are upset." Hooper was matter of fact.

"Let me tell you how it is," said Pendleton. He leaned back in his swivel chair, put his hands behind his head, and allowed his full stomach to protrude and spill over the belt that tugged at his waist.

"My men don't want to go down there in Buck town and guard people who want to watch a football game. There's a lot of real crime going on that's more important.

"You know how much they get paid for sticking their necks out and maybe getting stomped in the stadium? Four dollars. A lousy four fuckin' dollars an hour in off-duty pay. That's after they finish their regular work day."

Speaking faster and emphasizing words in a staccato-speech pattern, Pendleton went on to explain how off-duty officers could make more money just guarding parking lots and drive-through restaurants.

As he talked, his hands rubbed down the hair on the back of his head. He didn't touch it in front, where it was combed toward his eyebrows to hide his disappearing hair line.

A cop who had come up through the ranks, Pendleton was either fiercely liked or hated by officers under him. He had respect of mill officials because of knowledge of his job and his toughness, or he never would have lasted until near retirement. Secure in his position, Pendleton did not have to play a role now with Hooper.

"Don't police have responsibility to provide safety for city residents, and out-of-town visitors like football players?" Hooper asked.

"Not on school property," Pendleton fired back. "That's the school district's problem. We provide safety on the streets and public property, on private property only if there is a crime."

Damn, he's got quick answers, Hooper thought. Determined not to be intimidated, he called on some of his negotiating experience in sitting very still, casually slumped, holding his hands rock steady, and staring at his adversary as if indifferent to the outcome. This time it was a struggle. He knew how important it was to succeed.

"You've already made up your mind, the officers are not going to work the football games," Hooper said in a slow, deliberate voice.

"The men made up their minds, God damn it." Pendleton slammed straight up in his chair, hands ruffling through papers on his desk. He searched for something, seemed displeased it was not readily on top of the stacks of paper spread across the desk.

"These officers will do just about anything for me," the chief blasted in a voice that was growing louder. "They know I've laid my ass on the line for them before and I'd do it again. They also know if they shit on me, I'll jerk the uniforms off their backs, wipe their butts with it and rub it in their faces. That's for starters. It's either that or up their hairy ass with a lawn mower." The pudgy hands searched the papers angrily.

"Don't bother me with how you run your office. I'm just asking for the sake of these kids for you to be a little concerned about them," Hooper said in a controlled voice several octaves below Pendleton's.

"Your solution," Pendleton said emphatically, "is to change to *Saturday afternoon football games*. Friday night games are getting too dangerous from all this shit."

"No way! We won't go to afternoon games."

"Then I'm saying you won't have any protection for your players or spectators, and the state athletic association will end your games."

Pendleton eyed Hooper hypnotically.

"Where will you be then? It's not just the hoods here stirring things up." The chief glanced back at his desk where his hands were rooting in the paper stacks. "We're between two metropolitan cities on the interstate. Creeps who can't stand the city heat come here for a few break-ins, sell a few hits in the south end, and hop back home. Now with Buck town here stirred up, we're going to see more junkies heading our way.....ah, here it is..."

Pendleton held up a sheet of paper in one hand, and snapped a finger against it with his other hand. "Let me read this to you, it's from the local Fraternal Order of Police."

Pendleton smiled, relishing the verbal weapon in his hand.

"It reads, `As you will recall from last year, it was at night football games and basketball games where most troubles occurred. These incidences resulted in call-out of the entire department on two weekends in a row. In as much as the schedule of extra work is performed by the Fraternal Order of Police members in their off duty hours, it places a responsibility on us to do what we believe is the best for the citizens as well as for ourselves. The FOP prefers *Saturday afternoon football games to eliminate any problems'*. It's signed by the FOP president, and dated three days ago. I'll get you a copy if you want."

The police chief had saved his final jab. "College and professional football teams hold Saturday games. Why can't high schools?" he asked.

Hooper did not need time to react. He was angry. "We have tradition here. A tradition we are going to keep," he said, standing. "It's obvious you've made up your mind, and your officers."

Pendleton mouth jerked open to speak, but Hooper didn't stop. "I don't know how we will continue the season just yet, but we will."

"Do what you have to do, but don't count on the police," Pendleton said.

"Believe me, we're not counting on you," Hooper said in a

deadly calm voice and casually strolled out of the office. As soon as he was out of sight of the chief, with the door closed behind him, Hooper felt his temper letting go.

He held off until he was outside the building, then he made a guttural moan, clinched his right hand into a fist and slammed it into his left palm.

He again saw the swivel pig sign in the ivy.

Glancing around, seeing no one, he stepped one foot into the ivy, and with the other gave the pig sign a direct kick, sending it spinning on its metal standard. Hooper felt better.

* * *

"You have to come give us a hand," Hooper said in a low, husky voice to Rachel on the telephone. "We need all the people we can get as volunteers, and you know everybody."

"Hardly," Rachel responded, but she was eager to help after hearing an account of the school board meeting from Sonny.

Douglas and Hooper, with school and city officials, came up with a plan they felt could work. Citizens would be asked to take the responsibility of patrolling night football games as volunteers. A lot of responsibility fell on Douglas, as unofficial coordinator of the various groups to be involved.

He also was the voice of the big-daddy steel company that was watching the increasing unrest in the city.

Ministers, black and white, asked from their pulpits for citizens to sign up in this community crisis. The newspaper published similar appeals. Names started to appear on lists.

School Superintendent Howard Briley, a feather-bed personality new to the city and pliable as the baggy suits he wore, fired the emotional pot unintentionally. He announced that members of the local American Legion Post had agreed to help patrol the Friday game.

Irate Legionnaires protested the next day, forcing Briley to correct his statement by saying it actually it was the black American Legion Post in Garland that had volunteered.

Members of the Radio Emergency Response (RER) group, a long-time organization that directed traffic at games, took unprecedented action in declining support this year. Douglas could see the police chief's influence.

"Without adequate police protection. We can not insure the safety and well being of spectators or their property," the organization's official statement read.

Spirits were low the Monday before the Friday homecoming game. Rachel and a small band of other women and some retired men manned telephones in a school auditorium. Their request calls generated little interest. The bank of phones failed to jingle with a deluge of citizens calling desperately to save the Friday-night game tradition.

Superintendent Briley said in a Monday radio comment he was "optimistic" and would check Tuesday afternoon to see if he had a "paper commitment or a body commitment" for the Friday game.

"I feel confident we can find enough men and women to police the stadium and meet state requirements," Briley told the community. "But, we don't have them yet. If we fall short, we will cancel the game," he said, his voice going out over the airway with a bit of theatrics.

It was students, black and white, that changed the community's attitude. They paraded downtown, walked through stores talking to people, waited at service stations.

"You had your games and homecoming in high school, don't deprive us of ours," they asked. The plea captured attention.

Discouraging radio and newspaper accounts began to turn the next couple of days, just as the weather dropped from October heat to the first hint of autumn.

"We're getting calls," Rachel told Briley excitedly.

Not only were individuals signing up, but churches and civic groups were volunteering five or more members each.

"Just give me one hundred volunteers," the school

superintendent, coached by Douglas, said in yet another radio broadcast and newspaper article. "Give me one hundred dedicated people out of this community of nearly twenty-five thousand, and we'll say we have a football game Friday night."

While names were growing on the list, Rachel, Sonny and other volunteers began making yellow-ribbon, crossing-guard-like harnesses to be worn by volunteers at the game.

Rachel tried to involve Alice, but she whined off, saying she no longer had children in the schools.

Glenn McIntire did come forward to help, joking that he would get his own volunteer to stand behind the bar for him.

The number of volunteers never reached one hundred. It stopped at ninety three. However, Briley told the news media on Thursday, "We have our one hundred. We play ball Friday night."

Townspeople, whether they volunteered or not, felt pride in the fact the community had seen a "body rising" and a "spiritual uprising", as Briley said in words Douglas wrote for him.

Preparing to leave for an unavoidable day-long company trip the morning of the first game, Douglas told Briley, "It's the things we don't expect that could go wrong. I plan to be back by game time, but if I'm delayed, tell the volunteers to act natural, but that anything could be a trigger, so be alert."

* * *

The stadium on Homecoming night began to stir with early volunteers at 7:30 p.m., about an hour before the game. Briley, hovered, flitted through the gathering group.

Rachel and Sonny were among those who had assembled in an unheated stadium hallway and were beginning to don the crossed yellow-ribbon harnesses over their heavy jackets.

It was cold. Frost was predicted.

Why isn't Douglas back, Rachel wondered, uneasily. He had

172

been the power behind this effort. She missed the confidence of his presence. Always, always she longed for the comfort of knowing Douglas was nearby. He had been so faithful through the years. Now when tension was so great, his absence magnified the mood of threats.

"I guess we're ready for anything, weather and all," Sonny said, pulling his mouth into an almost invisible line as he struggled to fasten the yellow harness over his frame that was made larger by his heavy jacket.

Rachel straightened the ribbon across his back, leaving a little more slack for him.

"Remember, be casual, but alert," Briley cautioned as the citizens' patrol group left the hallway to take their posts throughout the stadium.

Rachel and Sonny were among those assigned to "be visible" to the football crowd. They were to walk back and forth on the ground between the front row stadium seats and the playing field. Rachel was posted on the home-team side, while Sonny was across the field on the visitors' side.

Other volunteers walked the top of the stadium, while some were stationed inside the building or along the sidelines.

After the kickoff, the slow-paced patrolling began. The crowd was muted, waiting. Anticipation of what could happen off the field seemed to hold more interest for the spectators than the huddles, passes and runs on the brightly lit, grassy area.

Rachel curled her toes inside her boots, hoping to ease the cold gripping her feet as she strolled back and forth. The tense faces along the rows of seats gave off little puffs of blurring, white mist as their warm breath met the frigid night air.

There's too much tension, Rachel thought, forcing herself to smile at the faces to encourage them to relax. It worked with some people. They returned tentative smiles.

Near the end of one of her passes across the front of the stadium, Rachel met Glenn McIntire, who was patrolling the end of the building.

"Looks like everything's going fine," he said in a heavy whisper, his breath also steaming. "Half time's coming up. They say things should be okay if get we through that."

"We'll count on it," she said, clutching a wool scarf tighter around her throat.

High school band members in their green and white uniforms began assembling at one end of the field. Five flower-decorated convertibles were driven through the double chain-link gate beside the stadium and parked in anticipation of the homecoming court's ride down the field at half time.

Hooper, not wearing one of the yellow identification harnesses, leaned casually against a railing near the center of the stadium's home-team side. He selected his location, where the main corridor under the stadium connects the field on one side and the entrance gate on the other, so he would have a full view of the stands. He wanted to move quickly in any direction, if needed.

* * *

At the far end of a darkened side street outside the stadium, another decorated car waited to make an entrance.

It was a beat-up gray junker car, wrapped in black crepe paper and toilet tissue. It's dark appearance blended with the shadows under the heavy branches of a concealing tree.

An adult, about thirty years old, and five teenagers shivered from both the cold and anticipation as they waited for the sound of the band on the night air to signal their move.

"Remember, we don't want no trouble. Don't give any lip to anybody. We just wanna be seen and let them know how they're treatin' our people," said the adult. "This is more than just football, queen and all that crap."

"We're gonna show them, ain't we," said one of the younger teenagers, tossing a rock the size of a soft ball in his hand.

"What ya got there?" the man snapped. "Git rid of it. And the rest of you with rocks or anything else to throw, do as I told him.

174

We're here peaceful."

School band members lined up. The homecoming's royal court left the only warmed shelter under the stadium and hurried to the convertibles. The girls struggled not to react to the crisp wind that whipped their skirts and ruffled the tops of their white dresses as they boarded the cars.

The band and vehicles moved in slow motion onto the field, into the glare of the tall field lights. All eyes in the stadium were on the convertible with the first-ever black male Homecoming escort.

Without his black female counterpart, Leona, Jerry was left teamed in the court with a while female. It had never happened before, a black male student and white female student paired. They sat side by side on top of the back seat in one of the convertibles. Jerry's female partner waved. He did not. The crowd watched.

* * *

Douglas, who had arrived back in Garland about a half hour earlier, had stopped by his home to change clothes before heading for the stadium.

It was what he could not see of the suspicious black car that caught his attention when he crossed the intersection of the side street. The scene was shadowy, but he detected movement.

He squinted for better visibility, then identified the dark-cloud silhouette as a car slowly leaving the protective covering of the massive tree.

Suddenly Douglas was alert to the threat, realizing that it was a vehicle loaded with people heading for a confrontation somewhere at the stadium. Douglas accelerated his car the final block to the stadium, slammed to a halt, and sprinted to a trio of burly volunteers.

"Get this damn gate shut," he shouted as they watched in stunned silence. They saw no threat, and did not move until one of the men recognized him. They then raced with Douglas to swing the

175

two six-foot-high chain-link gates together and flipped a metal bar to lock them in the middle.

"What's happening?" one of the breathless men asked.

A black volunteer at that moment saw the approaching car with its black occupants. "Oh, shit, we're gonna need some reinforcements". He raced to find Hooper.

Waiting in his position at the center of the stadium, Hooper spotted the volunteer hurrying toward him in the corridor and motioned for him to stop. Hooper went to meet him.

"You want to panic everybody? Act calm. What's going on?" Hooper whispered huskily, glancing around to see if anyone was aware of the man's wild alarm.

"Ya gotta come," the man said in a rush. "We got company that may try to get out here on the field in an old beat up car."

"The hell they are." Hooper moved as rapidly back through the corridor as he could without appearing to rush. He kept the other man by his side at the same pace.

At the gate, Douglas and now five volunteers were lined up as a show of force inside the gate as the slow- moving car came to a stop just inches away.

"We wanna be part of the celebration," said the adult spokesman, unfolding his long legs languidly from the gray junker. The teenagers jumped from the car and surrounded him.

Hooper joined the volunteers and exchanged glances with Douglas. They did not recognize the strangers. Probably out-of-town instigators.

"These young men here," the black adult said, indicating the followers around him, "feel they been cut out of the festivities. They wanna parade, too."

Cheers, shouts and power fists in the air backed him up.

"You're at the wrong place at the wrong time," said Hooper taking a place by Douglas in the center of the volunteer line. "Halloween hasn't arrived yet. Come back then."

"What's the matter with you, brother?" asked the spokesman angrily. "You an Oreo that you suck up to whites like them when your own people are shut out of homecomings?"

"You're not my brother. Everybody had an opportunity to

attend the game tonight , and they got here in time to get seats," Hooper said. "You're not from around here. Why don't you get on down the road."

"We can still come in if we want, you know? This little puny fence wouldn't stop us," the man said, a sneer frozen on his face. "And besides......"

"No besides. This has gone on long enough," said Douglas, interrupting, and stepping forward with an air of authority. "You're on school property. We ask you to leave peacefully, or we'll call the police and have you arrested on warrants of trespassing and disorderly conduct. At a minimum, you'll spend the night in jail."

"You an undercover officer then?" sneered the spokesman. "Course you're not, because there ain't no policemen here. And no policemen are gonna come, not tonight."

"They have to come by law if there is a disturbance and threat to the public." Douglas stood hands on hips and stared at the leader in a time-is-running-out attitude. He showed no fear, no emotion at all, but his demeanor was of a vicious bulldog ready to go for the jugular if a wrong move were made.

The black man hesitated, looked around at his young supporters. "Well, if you ain't gonna let us in, we're just gonna wait here a little bit and enjoy the music. That sounds like a good band."

"No you can't wait here. You are trespassing." Douglas dropped his hands from his hips.

"We're waiting." The voice was emphatic, the sneer gone.

"You wait three minutes longer, and we'll have police on the way. Don't think they're not alerted tonight," Douglas said. "They have patrol cars probably a block away, just waiting. You think they'd want to miss anything tonight? They'll be here in a blink."

The man backed away from the fence, slowly. He motioned for the others in his group to get back in the car. "This is not the end of it," he said. "Change is happening, and this ain't gonna stay no little white paradise. Be warned."

"Ya white mudder-fuckers," one of the black youths shouted as he got in the car. The engine roared. "Nigger", one of the teenagers yelled at Hooper. Others shouted muffled obscenities, made gestures.

As the car turned and paralleled the gate, an arm reached out of the rear window and several rock missiles shot forward. One rock bounced off the fence, another went over to slam against a volunteer's shoulder. One hard-ball size rock made a crackling sound as it struck the top of the metal fence, ricocheted, and scrapped missile-fast across Douglas's forehead.

He staggered from the impact, blood trickling down his face, neck and into his collar. Recovering quickly, Douglas grabbed his handkerchief to apply pressure to the head wound. Volunteers surrounded him and began leading him to the first aid station under the stadium.

"We can't all abandon the gate. I'll be all right." He turned to leave, but Hooper and another volunteer went along, hoping to shield him from any football spectators inside the stadium.

Rachel was at the far end of her patrol route when a female volunteer whispered to her what had happened.

"Take over for me just a minute," Rachel asked. "I need to check on something. Won't be long."

She did not wait for the woman's response, but headed at a regulated pace to the first aid station. She was desperate to know he was all right.

Douglas was seated on a gurney in the small crowded room when she opened the door. A woman, apparently another volunteer, was sponging Douglas's forehead and scalp with a bloodied white wash cloth. Superintendent Briley hovered over the woman's shoulder.

"Are you all right?" Rachel asked, smiling and steeling herself into calm. "Word is getting around upstairs, but not to the crowd." What a dumb sentence, she thought to herself. I'm sounding and acting stupid.

"I'm okay," Douglas answered, his eyes staring at her for seconds only. They both looked away.

"Head wounds bleed a lot, but this one doesn't appear serious." The woman tending him washed out the cloth in the small sink. "You'll need X-rays to see if you have a concussion or anything," the woman said tenderly.

I want to take care of him, Rachel thought, forcing her hands to remain at her side. I have a right. I have a right to him. He's mine, she said to herself, knowing that it was not true.

Awareness of how little he did belong to her swept over Rachel. She did not even have the right to be here just now, in the first aid room. He did not belong to her. Not now, not ever.

Rachel turned away, closed the door. She did not have the opportunity to say even a few words alone to him that night, when she felt such a need to comfort him.

* * *

CHAPTER SIXTEEN

October, 1969

Hooper could not shut his mind off and go to sleep after another uneventful Friday night football game. Volunteers had turned out again, but the threat of violence had subdued with the passing of the homecoming event two weeks before.

It was now 2 a.m. Saturday. Where had the night gone?

Hooper still was churning over the week's activities in his mind. He eased himself getting out of the bed, trying to avoid awakening his wife, holding the mattress down with his hands and allowing it to rise slowly when his body left it, so it wouldn't spring up without his weight and startle her.

In the dark, he felt his way around the bed, past the chair, and felt for the doorway that opened into the hall.

When he reached the dining room at the end of the hall, he appreciated the faint light diffused through the window from a nearly street light. He could find his way easily now to the rear family room.

There, he flipped on a light by his favorite chair and headed for the adjoining kitchen for a glass of pop or juice from the refrigerator. He settled for a glass of ice tea left over from dinner, realizing it could keep him awake. What the heck, he thought, I'm awake anyway.

It was a dark night. Hooper couldn't remember the stage of the moon at the time. It must have been a sliver, or it was a very overcast night to make it so dark.

The morning newspaper was in the magazine rack beside his chair, and although he didn't want to read any more about riots, arrests and threats, he had to divert his mind so he could sleep when he went back to bed.

He deliberately avoided stories about the school problems on desegregation or demands for a Black History Week in the spring.

He vowed to pick up on that tomorrow. There was little diversion in the rest of the paper to calm the pressure inside him.

Is anything good happening, he wondered, dropping the paper on the floor in a heap beside his chair with a rustling sound. He leaned his head back against the chair.

He would force his mind clear with thoughts of his daughter, Aimee, he decided. His beautiful daughter sleeping in the room at the far end of the hall.

Aimee was all he and his wife wanted her to be, a good student who had just graduated with honors from college and was job hunting. A clear-headed girl, pretty girl, she was not vain. She could have turned out that way, Hooper realized, if he and his wife hadn't stressed early on that good looks is something given and what really counts is what is inside.

The face you have at age twenty five is the face God gave you, they had often told her. The face you have at fifty is the one you make yourself.

Hooper wondered how he and his wife could be so lucky in a daughter, when so many kids in the black community were getting into trouble - pregnancies, drugs and auto accidents. He was grateful his daughter had survived all that.

Tension began to ease out of Hooper's body like the ice cubes melting in his glass of ice tea. It disappeared even more as he envisioned his daughter moving on in life, finding a job where she enjoyed going to work every day, marrying and having a family. It would all come.

A smile pulled his closed lips back. He slid deeper into the chair, rubbed his right hand back over his hair, which was slightly graying at the temples, then allowed his hand to hang loosely over the back of the chair. His legs stretched out over the ottoman in front of him. He let go even more, sinking deeper into lethargy.

Hooper watched as he lifted his right hand and dropped it on the chair of the arm. He chuckled, the sound rumbling up from his large chest. Drowsiness was coming down on him. The sand man is coming, he thought, smiling at recalling the phrase taught to him by his parents. The sand man scatters sand to make your eyes heavy until you can not keep them open, he remembered.

And his eyes were heavy. In a few minutes he would be empty enough to go back to bed, and curl up next to his wife, and drift off.

Hooper's chair suddenly jumped underneath him as the blast shook the house. He sat upright, startled by the jarring sensation, the yellow flash of light that reflected through the dining room, and the screams of his wife from the bedroom.

He leaped to his feet, raced toward the front of the house and the glow. He wasn't afraid. He was angry, outraged, because he knew his house was damaged and his family threatened.

Through the living room windows, he could see flames racing up the white columns that supported the porch roof and licking around the front door frame.

"Stay where you are," he yelled to his wife. "Get Aimee and go to the back door. Don't go out yet. I'm calling the fire department, and will be there with you in a minute."

Hooper knew his voice was quivering. He gulped air in an effort to keep calm and stay in control as he reached for the telephone.

"A fire, the front of my house is on fire," he said, identifying himself and giving his address. He realizing he was speaking too loud and too fast. "Hurry please, it's not in the house yet. No one's hurt."

They probably knew he was the city commissioner, Hooper realized. It'll be in the newspaper and on the radio, he knew, but his mind was racing too much to think about that now. His family and home were endangered.

His first thought was to grab some trophies off the dining room shelves. Hooper started toward them, then stopped, picked up instead their wedding picture off the hutch and jerked open the hutch drawer to grab the check book ledger. At least we'll have access to money if the house goes up, he thought.

Joining his wife and daughter at the back door, Hooper said

quickly, "Get a jacket for both of you, it'll be cold out there." He didn't want them to see how scared he was, fearful that whoever did this to their house could be waiting out there for them.

He thought of grabbing a ball bat out of the kitchen closet, then heard a siren in the distance, a fire truck, the high-and-low shrill siren of a massive piece of equipment maneuvering through the narrow, car-lined streets in the black community.

Hooper put his arms around his terrified, weeping women, held them by the kitchen door until he heard the truck arrive and the lesser sirens of police cruisers.

"The front porch is on fire, and a window broke from the heat. But I don't think it'll be too bad," he told them soothingly. "Firemen got here quick. Let's go now."

Hooper led the tearful women around the house, keeping a distance from the building, and walked away from the heavy water lines being stretched along the ground and connected to the fire hydrant on the corner.

They stood at a distance and watched their house anxiously, as fast-moving men in thick, shiny yellow suits and helmets grabbed up the connected hoses and directed the sprays of water on the now red then yellow licking flames.

"Think we got it in time, Commissioner," said the deputy fire chief who Hooper recognized. "Doesn't appear it got under the eaves and into the roof. We'll have it under control in no time."

Holding his wife until her sobbing lessened, Hooper told her he wanted to talk to the Deputy Chief a few minutes. He stepped slightly away from his wife and daughter, who quickly were surrounded with gentle, concerned neighbors.

"Are any of ya hurt, dear?" Hooper heard an elderly neighbor ask as she tried to share the faded blanket around her shoulders with his wife and Aimee . He turned away as the woman tried to soothe them.

"It was a firebomb, I think," Hooper said in a soft voice to the deputy chief. "I heard what I think was a bang and an explosion at the same time. It really shook me up."

"Undoubtedly that's what it was, and it's the third tonight."

"What?"

"Yeah, that's why we got here so quick. We were just arriving back at the station. The school administration building was hit with a Molotov cocktail - wick in a bottle - about 45 minutes ago, and general offices of the mill had one thrown through a window. Looks like we're building up to some real trouble."

The glow from Hooper's house disappeared as water smothered the flames and poured off the darkened porch. Spotlights from the trucks and headlights from police vehicles kept the area well lit, while more neighbors stood on porches or crowded onto the sidewalks to see what was going on.

"We've been firebombed," Hooper thought. "And it was our own people." He knew blacks had done this to get back at him, although he had no evidence.

His wife, back by his side, cuddled herself against him, tightening her arms around him to hold him close. She sobbed hysterically. She realized it wasn't just a fire. Someone tried to hurt them.

"We have to move. We have to get out of here," she gasped between sobs. "They'll kill us next time. We have to move."

"Is that true, Daddy?" asked Aimee, moving in close until they were a trio holding each other tightly.

"I don't think it's that bad," he said, not quite convinced himself. They could have been killed tonight, if the fire had caught quicker, if they had not heard the bomb and smoke penetrated the house while they slept, if....... Hooper pulled his family even tighter to him.

We've been firebombed by our own people, some God-damn Niggers, Hooper swore to himself.

* * *

CHAPTER SEVENTEEN

October, 1969

Hooper would have stayed in their home that night, but his wife and daughter panicked. He could not convince them it was safe. There was no inside fire damage, but the smoke smell hung heavily in the front part of the house.

The flames had tried to lick through the crack between the front door and the frame, leaving darkened spots that could wash off with a good scrubbing. The front porch was scorched, and paint blistered on the front wall of the house, but only a few boards would have to be replaced.

The incident could be forgotten almost as quickly as coats of paint could hid the scars. But Hooper doubted it, knowing the terrifying memory would cling to him and his family.

Later the night of the fire, as Hooper and his wife lay in bed holding each other at her mother's house a few blocks away, he weighed what steps to take. There were no vacancies or houses for rent in the black community that he would consider.

He could not afford to invest in buying another house just now, and did not want to sell his original one. Perhaps his best bet, he thought as he held his now sleeping wife, would be to move into an apartment in another part of town and rent their own home until these incidents settle down. Incidents, ha!

They burned my house!

Hooper investigated apartments the next day, deciding on one in a predominately white community near the interstate.

The feeling of security in going to bed safely at night

returned, but he missed his old neighborhood, where there were no comparable apartments. Reports got back to him that people were holding the move against him.

"Oreo", his former neighbors were calling him - black on the outside, white on the inside. Blame came for not only moving out of the black community, but for his increasing contacts and socializing with "Whities".

I guess I can stand the criticism if my family can, Hooper thought. We'll see how it goes. If it gets too much for them, if it affects Aimee too much, I'll step down as a city commissioner. But, damn, I don't want to. I want to be part of making things better. He visited his old neighborhood as much as he could, grasping at bonds and talking to people.

I'm going to be back here some day, Hooper swore to himself. *I promise that.*

* * *

February, 1971

"They say the kids are tearing up the high school," Alice said in a high shrill voice when she telephoned Rachel from her job in the elementary school cafeteria. "I thought you'd want to know, because of Sonny teaching there, an all."

It was Black History Week.

Rachel hung up, turned on the radio, and listened to a live broadcast by a reporter talking to the police chief.

"Everything's under control," Pendleton said. "We have some slight damage in one hallway, but that's all. No one is hurt."

The superintendent had met with some students in the main lobby and everything had settled down, the chief explained. The riot began with name calling and evolved into a gang of students

186

shoving, scuffles and sharing a few blows, he said.

"We blame Black History Week, but we know how to handle these things," Pendleton said, concluding his portion of the broadcast.

Hooper also was alerted by a telephone call, from a black teacher at the school. There was no problem in leaving his office at the steel company, he had long been given permission to go wherever in the city he was needed. He saw this as a must-go situation.

Driving quickly from the office to the mill, Hooper parked his car along the street. He saw three police cruisers parked in a jumble near the school entrance, indicating officers had arrived and left their car engines running where they stopped.

Off to Hooper's left, on a hillside overlooking the school, he saw several black youths talking together. As he approached them, all but one fled.

"What's been going on?" Hooper asked the youth, moving in a non-threateningly manner to indicate he was on the boy's side. Hooper held his hands in an open palm position to show he wasn't about to do anything, just ask questions.

"They said police came in there and started shoving them around," the boy answered. "A couple kids got into it, I guess, but from what I heard it was started by just two white kids and two black kids. Then everybody was at everybody else."

"You all right?"

"Yeah. I really wasn't part of it. I got outa there fast."

They didn't notice that an officer was walking up the hill toward them. When Hooper spotted him, he asked the officer, "Is anybody hurt down there?"

"You gotta come back inside with us, Kid," the patrolmen said. "Anybody not in their classroom gets taken in."

"He's all right. He's just standing here talking to me," said Hooper, suspecting the patrolman knew who he was and unwilling to mention he was a commissioner.

"I said he has to come with me."

"He wasn't doing anything," Hooper said emphatically. "I can vouch for him."

"Come along," said the officer, grabbing the boy by his arm and pulling him.

"Let him go," snapped Hooper, getting angry, and grabbing the boy by the other arm. "You have no reason to do this."

"Mind your own business," said the officer, getting angry himself.

"I'm not going to let you."

"That's it, Mister," cracked the officer's voice. "You're charged with interfering with a police officer. You're under arrest."

* * *

Hooper admitted later it was a mistake that he went to the school. "I should have known better," he told friends and fellow commissioners.

"When it came out in the paper that I hit the police officer, that was wrong. It was just bad publicity. Nothing came of it. But I admit I shouldn't have been on the scene since I'm a city commissioner." Hooper was silent a moment, pondering. "But I'd do it again."

Rachel waited by the telephone in her office most of the day, hoping to hear from Sonny. She knew he would stop by to see her at home after the school day, to tell her what happened, but it was agonizing to put in the hours until she saw him.

When he pulled up in his car in front of her house, she could see his pale, drawn face. At least he doesn't look hurt, she thought. She grabbed him as he came in the door.

"Mom, what am I doing as a teacher? It's not school any more, it's a war zone."

She took his hand, led him to the couch. "This is the first time something like this has happened. You can't call it a war."

"It's not just today. The kids are constantly at each other."
Sonny slumped back against the couch, dejected. He described what

188

he knew of the day's incident, which rapidly was becoming known in the city as the student riot.

"I have seen the anger growing," Sonny said. "Some black students bring those big Afro combs to school. Combs, huh. They're weapons. I don't know what the white kids have, but I'm sure some of them are armed, too. It' going to get worse."

"Are you afraid, is that what it is? That's not like you."

"Afraid for the kids. You're not hearing me," he said, running his hand angrily back over his short dark hair, which at times show the uncontrolled cowlicks of his father's hair. "Sure there are a lot of good kids. You don't hear much about them. We're so busy dealing with the unruly ones, we don't have time to really encourage the good students."

"You're always going to do that, Sonny, no matter what?"

"Ah, Mom, do you have to be so positive all the time. You and your platitudes, that everything's going to be all right."

"Maybe so," she said, wounded by his criticism, "but we have to be optimistic and expect the best. I firmly believe that."

"Why, when it doesn't work out that way? I'm not hearing teachers talk much about how to help kids. They're talking in union meetings about reduced class loads, more time to prepare lessons and especially more money," Sonny said, his voice growing more agitated. "It's Me, Me, Me, not the students."

"I didn't know you were so unhappy teaching."

"I guess I am. It's come down to that. But, bear with me. It hasn't been a good day."

He smiled at her, until she suddenly could see the boy Sonny, who had always been such a comfort to her. Now, she wondered how to comfort him. "If all the good teachers walked away because it got too complicated, who would be left for the kids? You have so much to give, and I've always felt giving to students is part of your happiness."

"I don't know if it is any longer. I haven't made any decisions. Maybe it'll be better tomorrow."

"There, optimism. That's what we need."

* * *

What people later remembered of that February riot was that there were no major injuries. Two white students were expelled for disorderly conduct, and numerous students spent hours in detention.

It was a stigma in the community, however, just as other civil rights incidents were across the country. The positive side was that there was a leveling off of racial equity in curriculum and staff. Changes occurred in text book selections and activities advantageous to black students.

A black counselor was hired, diversity assemblies were held and the community began catching up with what had been happening in the rest of the country since the 1960s.

It was too late, however, to convince Sonny that his future was in teaching. Rachel felt it was a loss to the education profession.

"You have too much to offer", she kept repeating to him.

For Sonny, the disturbance in the school, although he realized changes were warranted, was a turning point in his career. He had seen too many students passed from grade to grade who could not read adequately and lacked comprehension of math. It made him ache.

He made overtures for changes, but felt his lone crusade was inadequate.

The ache had dulled by the time he finally decided not to renew his teaching contract for the 1972-1973 school year. Maybe the steel mill would have a job for him, he speculated, perhaps sales would be a career for him at Miami Valley Steel.

* * *

"Okay, a quick walk to the top of the hill," said Douglas, grabbing Rachel's hand and setting the pace. They were on the walkway along a lake in southeast Indiana. The cool spring air pulled them out of their motel room and into the park atmosphere.

Both believed in regular exercise, Douglas having set up a

bedroom exercise plan for Rachel when she complained about her expanding waistline and that she often felt tired.

Their walk carried them around the crest of the hill until they could view the man-made lake below them, reflecting the Robin's-egg blue color of the cloudless sky.

But they were both breathless at their fast pace when they reached the hilltop, partly because they always talked constantly when they were together.

Conversation included the latest state and world news, and what was happening at the local level. Douglas was the leader because he read three newspapers each morning.

Rachel particularly loved the changes of personality she saw in Douglas, from the gentleness of the caring and attentive lover to the forcefulness of his character when dealing with life's daily issues.

She saw that change during their walk when later she brought up the subject of Sonny's interest in a job with the steel company.

"Tell him it wouldn't be good," counseled Douglas.

"You don't think the company would want him?"

"Not that." Douglas was silent. He was searching thoughts. "You can't repeat this," he said , knowing she never did. "If he were my son, I would tell him it's no place to start a career. It's on shaky grounds."

"The steel company?"

"All that running around some other people and I did a few years ago on behalf of subsidiaries was a mistake, company officials are realizing now." Douglas's attitude deepened to a depth of agitation and concern that she rarely had seen before.

"We should have stuck to what we knew - making steel," he said, grabbing her hand as they picked up their walking pace. He kneaded her fingers between his. "Instead," he said, "our insurance companies have floundered, oil rigs have cost us a fortune in federal fines for spills, and we've lost bundles of money trying to run other companies we knew nothing about. It's catching up with us. You want your son to work for a company like that?"

"I haven't heard anything about it in the community," Rachel said.

"You've heard talk about more overtime in the future?"

"Yes, but that means more pay."

"It means fewer jobs and workers having to put in more time to make up for it," Douglas predicted, unaware he had picked up their walking speed slightly. "The company's trying to work it out, but hard times are here and probably will get worse."

"What do you see happening?"

"Lot of layoffs, and not just factory workers. It'll hit almost all white-collar departments. My public relations staff may even disappear. The company will sell off some assets and try to revive."

"What does all that mean for the town? The steel mill has always *been* this town."

"No one knows. The company's wanting someone to represent them more at the state level, with taxes, environmental and safety issues. Who knows if it'll happen."

Douglas suddenly slowed their pace. "We got off the subject didn't we?" he asked, realizing the question had been a job for Sonny. "Don't tell your son any of this, but encourage him to look for a career in a company somewhere else, with a less uncertain future."

* * *

Just as the school system began changing through civil rights, so did Garland 's business climate evolve as a result of the backwash of the feminist movement throughout the country.

A handful of professional women began pushing for the McIntire Stag Bar to conform and be integrated.

The attitude didn't bother Glenn McIntire at the time, he was caught up in hosting the grand opening of his newly relocated and reconstructed McIntire Stag Bar and Restaurant in the mall. It was modernized with massive oak tables and masculine leather chairs, but still featured the ceiling-high cabinet and brass-railed bar of the former bar business.

The massive wood-burning stove that had served flood victims was enshrined in a rear party room.

"You ladies take a good look now, because it'll probably be the last time you see the inside," Glenn said excitedly to the female contingency of the hundreds of guests flowing in through the new stained-glass front door.

The opening of the first re-located business in the mall generated interest both locally and nationally. The mall was touted as the first of its kind to use federal development funds for a climate-controlled canopy to enclose existing buildings and streets.

Admittedly, some of the nationwide media attention was generated by Douglas in his role of promoting MV steel and the community.

But he was not thinking about that now as he waited near the rear of the restaurant for Rachel's arrival. They had shared messages that they both planned to attend the opening.

When she came through the door, Douglas was not aware that he took a deep breath and relaxed his shoulders. The wait was over, she was here. He only knew he was always relieved to see her, to watch as she greeted friends and to delight in studying her well-known features. Soon, he knew, they would stand facing each other, and he would look down at this feminine creature that dominated so much of his thoughts.

She saw him also. Always, when she arrived expecting to see him, she waited near the side of the crowd, as she did now, until she located him. Their eyes met. They went back to talking to acquaintances around them, then after about ten minutes made their way to each other.

Reaching to shake her hand, and glancing around the room as if commenting on the new restaurant, Douglas whispered to her, "You're looking lovely tonight." He loosened his grip, releasing her hand with a final squeeze.

"You always look great to me," she said softly, also looking around the room as if responding to his comment.

"Glenn really did do himself proud with his new place," Douglas said. "And looks like the whole town turned out."

"Lucky for you guys," she teased. "It's stag, and you'll be

back often."

"And back, and back and back," he countered. "There's a great party or conference room in the back you have to see. The stove's there. Remember the stove and the flood?"

They talked business a few minutes, Douglas taking time to ask about a new program she was working on to provide home care for terminally ill patients.

"We're trying to locate families who can use the service," she explained. "We're finding there's a real need out there."

"Let me know when you're ready to go, and we'll work up a news release together," said Douglas, who was interrupted by a shout from Glenn.

He had spotted them among the invited guests, and called them over to join him as he held court in the ant-hill-like crowd behind the historic carved-wood and mirrored bar.

Glenn's father had joined him, sharing family pride, although the senior McIntire had declined to advance any finance money for the relocated business.

"Looks like we're a team again, Son, if only for one night," Douglas and Rachel heard the older man say as they approached.

The McIntire men threw their arms around each other. The father, no longer physically interested in the business, proved by his attitude that he was present only because of the party. He had already had several drinks, which added ruby color to broken blood vessels in his cheeks and nose. They attested to his lifetime of bar tending and enjoying the atmosphere.

Glenn at this high point had forgotten the gall he tasted when forced by the city to relocate from the historic bar's site into a new structure. Also suppressed just now was the searing disappointment of his father's refusal to put up any financing for the new restaurant. The older man had scooted off to Florida with a large portion of company funds and plunked them into real estate investments.

Although Glenn felt the money should have been banked until the re-located tavern business was established, he was not worried about keeping old patrons. Most of them were here tonight as freeloaders, plus a lot of the town elite. He was counting on all of them coming back as paying customers.

"Have another drink," Glenn bellowed expansively to guests lined up two and three deep at the bar. When Glenn saw Rachel, he came around the bar and kissed her on the cheek with an alcohol breath. He pumped Douglas's hand.

"How about this? Did you think it would happen after all the agonizing I did?" Glenn asked, throwing his arms into the air as if embracing the room full of people.

"Of course," Rachel answered. "We're proud of you, Glenn. It can only get better now, with your construction finished."

"I hope. But other merchants here tonight are pissed , sorry, excuse the expression, that mall construction will go on for another Christmas season. I can't believe it's taken all these years. It's gonna hurt them. Fortunately I just sell eats and drinks. I don't have to worry about a big inventory of dry goods or toys."

"Looks like you're a role model, Glenn, giving people a reason to stay close to home and not run off to malls along the interstate," Douglas said. "But we know it's not easy."

"Is that me? A role model?" asked Glenn, foolishly. The corners of his lips turned up like a teasing leprechaun. His freckles and once-red hair, faded now to a rust brown and white, added to the illusion.

Douglas grinned back. "Others here tonight wish they were as far along as you are."

"But not as deep in debt," said Glenn, a seriousness threatening to take over.

"You better cut everybody off in the next hour or so, or it'll take you weeks to finance all this partying," kidded Douglas.

"Hey, invitations said seven to nine," Glenn said, beginning to move back to his duties at the bar, "and if everyone isn't cleared out by then, unless they're lying on the floor, I got me a neat little Saturday Night Special stashed under the counter that I'll fire off a couple of times to let'em know it's over." Glenn chuckled, shaking his middle-age belly that was beginning to hang over his belt as he visualized himself running the mob out with a gun.

"Whoopee, what a night," Glenn shouted above the many conversations in the room. He did a little dance step as he returned to stand traditionally behind the bar alongside his father and serve up drinks.

Glenn grabbed his father by the arm and they both did a little Irish jig behind the bar to the clapping of spectators.

Near the front of the shiny new saloon, a cluster of professional women stood in one corner, holding drinks and balancing paper plates of hors d'oeuvres. They had no interest in clapping.

"Haven't they learned that stag anything isn't allowed any more?" asked one of the women, picking a black olive off her plate with red fingernails.

"He should wake up and get with the real world," said another woman.

* * *

"It makes me feel like I can't even care for my own husband, to have someone carrying in food," grumbled Alice to both Tim and Rachel on a snowy evening in January. "An besides, we can't afford any luxury like that."

They were in the living room of Rachel's home that Alice and Tim had rented for a number of years now. Rachel was trying to convince her sister to sign up for a noon-meals delivery program.

"The meals are not expensive, only four dollars and fifty cents a week, and it's hot food that Tim isn't getting now while you're at work. You're a good cook, I know, Alice, but it'll be nice for Tim to have a different, hot selection of food for lunch every day."

Rachel glanced over at the large blob of a man melting down into the worn, brown-vinyl recliner.

"I imagine it gets a little lonely during the day when Alice is working at the cafeteria, doesn't it Tim?"

"It'd be all right to have food brought in," he said hesitantly, glancing cautiously at his wife.

"Well, I'm not in favor," said Alice, standing and walking over to stare down at him. He seemed to sink lower into the chair. "I cook good meals and always have left overs waiting for you each noon. If you can't just stick'em in the oven, you can eat'em cold."

She stalked back over and flopped into her own recliner. Her hands immediately went to massaging her legs, as if the arthritis was too much pain to bear.

"We could use that money for something better, like doing something for ourselves once in a while. We could do that now, if the rent wasn't so high."

"Oh, Alice, you know I let you pay half of what I would charge anyone else, including Tina Rose," scolded Rachel.

"I know what you're trying to do. You're just using us," accused Alice venomously. "You keep coming up with all these services in the city, for the kids and for homeless people, and now lunches. But you need people to sign up to make 'em work and make YOU look good. Huh? Well not us."

* * *

An embarrassed Glenn, with a frozen smile on his face, tried to talk to the protesting women the first day they paraded in front of his stag bar during their lunch hour.

"Why you doing this?" he pleaded. "My family has had a stag bar since before I was born. It's not as if you don't have nice restaurants you can go into up and down the street."

"You don't get the point, Mister. It doesn't matter whether we want to come in or not," said one plump young woman, barely able to keep from grinning. She kept glancing over her shoulder, anticipating the reporters that were on their way. "You just can't keep us out anymore."

Glenn held out as long as he could. After a week of the women marching, protesting, carrying signs and shouting comments to passers-by, Glenn relented and open the bar to women.

That did not mean he turned the entire bar over to them. He kept a private back room for long-time cronies who demanded their privacy. It was a special "party room".

Never again was it the McIntire Stag Bar and Tavern. That was reason enough, in addition to concerns about financing the new business, for Glenn to feel an increasing need to have a quick sip of gin behind the bar when he thought no one was looking.

* * *

Tina Rose heard a thumping on the front door, and wondered what Teddy might be doing there. She rinsed her hands in the kitchen sink, dried them on her apron and headed for the front door of the brightly-painted, two-bedroom cottage she and Josh now rented from Rachel. They had moved from the first one when Rachel's former husband had sold it.

She glanced out the window at the side yard, surprised to see Teddy there. He wasn't making the noise on the front door. Her son was squatted on his knees entertaining himself with his prize marbles - apparently enjoying the "Cat Eyes" he had practically demanded she buy the weekend before at the drug store. Just a kid, she thought, even though he is in his thirties. But it got him out of the house and didn't hurt anything. So, humm, who was out front?

Swinging open the door, Tina Rose looked up into the frowning face of a young police officer.

Oh, God, don't let anything be wrong, she thought. Help me, be with us, Lord. Teddy hasn't done anything wrong. He never really does anything wrong, but neighbors get afraid of him. But Teddy's been here all the time. Josh! What's happened to Josh?

"Mrs. Barnes?" the young officer asked, still frowning.

He's so young, she thought. A babe come to hand me a broke world. Oh, no, surely not. "Yeah," she answered, trying to stand taller.

"I've come about Joshua Barnes," the boy cop said.

She noticed how his tongue shot out to wet his lips as she held open the door and he walked past her into the living room. "I'm his wife," she said. Her own lips felt dry. She could not resist wetting them, copying his action.

"Why ya want him?"

"There's been an accident."

Tina Rose had known, felt she was prepared. Still the flush of hot emotion washed over her. That didn't stop her feeling angry, too. *How could he let himself get hurt?* Tina Rose started taking her apron off very slowly. "We'll go with ya to the hospital."

"I can take you, Ma'am but...."

"What?"

"It was a fatal accident, Ma'am."

Fatal. That means...."What happened?" she finally asked.

"I think maybe Mr. Barnes had a fall. No, he did have a fall," the young officer said. His throat seemed to be tight and the words were becoming difficult for Tina Rose to understand. She glanced at him, her eyes searching his smooth young face. No stubble of beard for him even this late in the afternoon. Josh would have a dark stubble shading his jaw at this time of day.

They stood. Neither one thought to sit down. "Tell me what happened," Tina Rose said. *Why don't I cry, she wondered. But if I do, that will make it real.*

"He was working painting a two story house. They said he was near a gable, that's what he was going to paint next, and as he stepped from the ladder to the roof, his foot slipped on a weak board. It held, but it was enough to throw him off balance."

"He fell to the ground then?"

"So they told me. I can take you to the hospital now, if you want."

It was only a short drive to the hospital in the east end of the city, with Tina Rose and Teddy sitting in the back seat of the young officer's cruiser. It was an adventure to Teddy , who liked the shiny car, the officer's uniform and even the protective screen that separated the front and back seats.

Although Tina Rose tried to explain the accident, Teddy's

attention was claimed by the cruiser, he couldn't stop smiling, looking around, and running his hands over the fabric of the seat cushions.

At the hospital, they walked several corridors. The officer turned them over to a nurse at one of the desks. She looked sympathetic and talked in a soft voice. She led them down another corridor to a door, then into a room where Tina Rose at first could only see a partially-clad figure lying on a bed.

"Do you need me to stay with you?" the nurse asked. When Tina Rose shook her head, the woman said, "Press the buzzer on the bed there if you need me."

Tina Rose walked on stilt-like legs to the figure. The sheet didn't cover the face.

"Josh, Josh...." The tears came, along with the release of convulsive sobs. She flung herself on his chest, her arms gathering him up to her. Only momentarily did she react to the coldness of his body, then pulled him closer into her as if to warm him.

Teddy stood motionless at the end of the bed. He laid one hand on the sheet that covered his father's legs. He rested it there. "Daddy?" Teddy questioned.

Tina Rose lost time. It could have been seconds that she laid across Josh, or minutes, an hour. Eyes still blurred with tears, but with the sobs weakening, she raised her head to look at her husband's face. She ached for him to open his eyes and look at her. Never again.

"Tell me ya can hear me," she whispered, thinking maybe the sound of her voice could open those eyes. There was no deep throbbing in his chest, no small pulse in his temple to indicate he really was in there and would come back any second now. There was nothing.

Josh had been washed of blood, although she saw a thin, red crust around one nostril and a small dried patch in a crease of his left ear. He had struck his head. Hemorrhages had allowed blood to seep down and discolor his eye socket and cheek on that side of his face. She moistened her finger with her tongue, and wiped faint patches of dried blood away from the edge of his ear and nostril.

"You are so good at what you do, you couldn't just fall," Tina

Rose whispered. "I've watched you, and I know you're careful." She picked up Josh's right hand. Gray-green paint edged his fingernails. She kissed each one of them. They tasted a little of paint remover. She stood, suddenly realizing Teddy still waited at the foot of the bed, his hand resting on his father's leg.

"Tell your Pa good-bye", she said tenderly.

Teddy took a stumbling step along the bed, put his hand flat on his father's chest, his fingers splayed, pressing and moving in a circle. When Teddy didn't stop rubbing his hand in the circular motion, Tina Rose stopped his hand with both of hers.

"Kiss him good-bye," she said.

Teddy shook his head. "I don't want to, he's cold. Somethin's not right." He backed away, pulling his hand out of hers.

Tina Rose turned, leaned over Josh's once again, gently put her lips against his. Rising, she glanced down at him, memorizing one last time the full lips, long-straight nose, dark brows that nearly bridged the area across his nose.

Reaching again for Teddy's hand, she led him from the room. "Don't ever bring me to a place like this, Teddy. Promise me. They can't do nothing for you here. Don't ever bring me."

At the visitation service two days later, Rachel stayed close beside Tina Rose. There were so few people.

"I'll be here for you, for whatever you need," Rachel offered. Her suggestion of financial help was refused. She pulled the tiny Tina Rose to her, squeezed, and pressed her cheek against the fading blond hair.

Only a few neighbors attended the visitation at a local funeral home. Glenn came. Always an outgoing, caring, talkative man, he was even more so now out of concern for the family and perhaps because of having a couple of drinks earlier at his bar.

"I had to come and tell you how sorry I am," the red- headed teddy bear of a man said in cuddling Tina Rose against him.

"You always was a good person," Tina Rose answered, reminding him again of when she and her family stayed with other homeless people on the second floor of his tavern during the flood. They had a closeness then - Glenn, Tina Rose and Rachel - that remained over the years.

Tina Rose still resembled the slender, soft little blond woman he first met. Only now she seemed slightly faded, distant, barely aware he and other people were there to comfort her.

"We'll be all right," she reassured the few people around her in a monotone voice. "Ya have to be prepared to handle the bad times in life."

Both Rachel and Glenn stayed until visitations were over at 9 p.m. They didn't plan to, but neither could leave the frightened little woman whose eyes were drawn during almost every sentence to the face in the open casket.

"What do you think she'll do?" Glenn asked as he and Rachel sat on chairs along one wall in the nearly empty room. Teddy sat nearby, lost in himself. They watched Tina Rose talking to one of Josh's painting coworkers beside the casket.

"I don't know, and she doesn't either. She hasn't really held a job since the tobacco plant closed, but she's cared for sick people."

Rachel hurt for her friend and for all people with sadness. Why is it so much a part of our lives, she wondered.

"I'll help her all I can with the rent, until she finds a job somewhere," Rachel said. "She's a hard worker, she'll find something. But it won't be easy, with Teddy."

"You think she'll consider putting him somewhere?"

"Never. He's her family now."

* * *

CHAPTER EIGHTEEN

"Glenn's saying he's bankrupt and it's the city's fault for forcing the mall construction on merchants." Rachel glanced from Douglas to Hooper as she shared the information. "He's not remembering that a lot of other people made the decision to go along with the mall."

The trio, the last to leave after a meeting of the Community Committee, was filling a free half hour until Douglas and Hooper were to attend a special meeting with MVS officials at the steel company headquarters.

"I wish we'd never started the damn mall," said Hooper, disgusted with the city's inability to solve the financial woes of the development. "It's only caused problems, and hasn't improved downtown business traffic."

"The city should have realized it needed anchor stores to move in before the mall was built. But that's hindsight," Douglas said. "The only answer now may be to fill the empty store fronts with professional or government offices."

"Do you really see that happening?" Hooper asked.

"Partially." Douglas studied a second or two, a characteristic so familiar to Rachel. "The city has to explore other avenues. Commitments have been made on the mall and there's no going back now. Too many federal funds involved," he said.

"What Glenn and others are losing sight of is what the downtown would have been like without the mall, a dying area of empty stores," Douglas explained.

"But that doesn't help Glenn when he's losing his business," Rachel added. "It may be an attractive business development, but he won't own any part of it."

Douglas glanced at her, appreciating her quickness in sizing up situations. He credited it to her exposure over the years to government and human nature. She can absorb what is going on, and identify intentional or unintentional injustices, he thought. That's why she is so good at her job.

While taking pride in whatever role he played in Rachel's growth, his response to her about Glenn's situation was, "I wish I knew an answer for him."

"Come on, Douglas," Hooper chided. "We consider you an expert on everything. Just lay out what's to be done."

"Ha," responded Douglas, both surprised and depressed by Hooper's assessment, because he had no ready recommendations. "All the city can do is have merchants advertise sales to get shoppers downtown, and seek out lawyers, doctors, beauticians or whatever to fill the empty space. I hope it's not too late for Glenn, but it may be."

After Rachel parted from the two men, they headed for the MVS offices and the meeting on an undisclosed subject.

* * *

Although the meeting with steel officials was brief, it left Douglas shaken and with an overwhelming need to talk with Rachel before he made a decision that could change their lives forever. Our existence can take a different direction in a matter of minutes and our future depends on the decisions we make at the time, Douglas realized in the uncertainty of how Rachel would react.

Douglas called her later at home, asking in a tight voice for her to meet him at one of their secluded restaurants about 20 miles away. She quickly agreed, only too aware of his rare urgent call. He would not have asked if he had another recourse, she knew. Has someone found out about us? Someone at the steel company?

He stood up in a back booth so she could see him as she

entered the roadside restaurant. The booth was by a window, and he apparently had watched for the headlights of her car.

"I don't know that I want to know what this is all about," Rachel said as she sat down, loosened her coat and let it fall off her shoulders.

"I just felt the need to talk to you." Douglas, appearing pale, dropped back into the seat on his side of the bench. His eyebrows were drawn together in a frown and his shoulders hunched over the table. His hands curled around a cup of coffee in front of him. That was an additional clue to alert Rachel because he seldom drank coffee late in the evening.

"You want to tell me?" No amenities. They both knew it was too serious for that. Rachel needed to know.

Douglas dropped his voice, speaking so only she could hear his words. "It's hard to believe, really incomprehensible, but, some MVS officials today asked me, well, practically told me...that I should run for the Ohio House of Representatives......."

Rachel sat stunned. Silent. It was not difficult to see Douglas in the role of a state legislator. She knew he had the talents, capability to do whatever he decided to do. The impact she felt was how it would affect them. Could they spend any time together in the future? Would he want to?

"I had the same reaction," he said when she didn't give a response. "How could anyone consider me a state legislator?"

"Oh, no, that's wasn't what I was thinking. You would be a wonderful one, you know what's going on and how to work with people. I was having very personal thoughts."

"So was I," he said, moving his foot under the table to touch hers. She responded quickly, rubbing her foot against his, feeling his touch an indication that it was not yet over between them.

"My first thought was how it would affect us," Douglas said, still speaking in the controlled voice, "and it hasn't been out of my mind since."

"Any decisions?"

"Not really. I needed to see you. Let me just talk, and get your reaction." Douglas glanced up as a waitress approached. "What would you like?" he asked Rachel, then passed her order along to the waitress, "Coffee, no cream." He paused when they were alone, as if deciding where to begin.

"This is something I would like to tackle, being a state representative, and it could really be a reality with the steel company and union backing me. That's what I've been told, and I agree. The position's opening up because Representative Powers is retiring. That'll make it easier, not challenging an incumbent. But, if I go for this, my whole life would change...."

He waited for her reaction. There was none yet. She wanted to know about the changes he expected.

"Even though we haven't been able to be together all the time, we've been free to see each other frequently and keep in touch almost constantly," Douglas said. He waited again as the waitress approached with the coffee and set it in front of Rachel. He put his hand over his own cup to indicate he wanted no more.

"We couldn't have that much freedom in the future," he said when they again were alone.

That already was obvious to Rachel. "It might be best if you didn't have to deal with the problem of...us," she said softly.

"Not at all, that's not my point. The thing is...well, right now I can think of no other word to describe my reaction except greedy. I think I want the challenge of being a Representative, but I know I want you in my life."

Rachel felt she could breathe again now, not realizing she practically had been holding her breath. Maybe things could work out, maybe a solution so she wouldn't lose him.

"The main thing I don't want to do is stand in your way, or be a handicap of any kind," Rachel said, finding words were coming in a rush now. The real tension was gone. At least he was saying he didn't want to let her go.

"You'd never be..."

"Let me say it," she interrupted. "I've always known you were meant for something like this, something bigger than working for the newspaper or steel mill office. You certainly can handle this. So I support whatever decision you make, and I think you should do it. But....I am interested in what you see for us."

"Rachel, I can't honestly tell you right now. I only know you are important to me and important in my life." He smiled at her, the first time since she arrived. "You just don't know, Lady, what an influence you've been on me. I can't imagine these years without you, or the ones to come."

"Will we see each other after you're elected?"

"If I'm elected, and absolutely. I can't say how or where just now, but I know that for a fact. And if it means giving up the job or you, I'll step down, I pledge you that."

"I would never accept that, so don't even say it."

Douglas' long silence alerted Rachel that he was weighing exactly how to phrase something he wanted to say. His thoughts were always well organized before he voiced them, and there was never any doubts about his meaning. She waited.

"If I'm elected, would you give some thought to moving to Columbus and working in my office headquarters there? It would be a way for us to see each other regularly, without anyone knowing."

She hesitated to answer, although yearning to scream "yes" at him. She was realistic. "Do you really think we could be close together like that in an office and not give ourselves away?"

"Probably not." He grinned at her, and at the answer he had expected. "Somehow or other, though, we will have time together, and I'll work it out so we can communicate by mail the same as we do now."

He was silent again, glancing away from her. "There is something else you should know...."

Here it comes, Rachel knew, the catch that always comes in a relationship like this, because love or not, it was only a relationship. So this really is the end, she thought, resigned. No, don't be so resigned. Fight for him. I can 't. I can't. He has to do this.

"Tell me."

"Politicians need a certain image, so MVS tells me."

"Yes?"

"My image would need my wife and daughters on the sidelines in the campaign. Posing for pictures, helping me cut ribbons, whatever. I don't know if my wife would agree. You know there's been nothing between us for years, but the company doesn't know that. I don't relish telling them."

207

"You could pick up your married life again, since you'll be living in Columbus where she is."

"How long have you known me, Rachel? How well do you know me?" Douglas asked, irritation at the possibility of a resumed marriage revealed in his voice. "If you've heard anything I've said over these years about my personal life, it's that you came and brought me the only happiness I've known. If you didn't listen before, I hope you do now." He downed the last of his coffee, studied her.

"You don't want to be a handicap, and you could never be that." Douglas' eyes held hers. "But if I really wanted this, you are the only thing that could stop me , if you pull away."

You say so now, Rachel thought, aching to believe his eyes. But she sensed the pressures that would be on him to create the image of a family man. She also knew the time Douglas and his wife would spend together could lead to affection between them in the future, shutting her out.

She could not change any of that - either by withdrawing from him now to ease her future hurt or, as her spirit cried out to do, clinging to him for the little time they had left.

She asked simply, "Can I be of help in your campaign?"

"Rachel, you can't imagine how much that says to me." Douglas reached across the table and grazed his hand across hers. "What do I want you to do?" He smiled. "First of all, what do you know about holding coffees for campaign candidates?" His grip tightened on her hand as his lips spread into a wider smile.

* * *

Campaigning began almost immediately in preparation for the election the next fall. That meant a heavy schedule for everyone, with Douglas still handling his steel company job while traveling throughout the seven county area he would represent if elected.

208

Hooper attended a lot of breakfasts and fish fries with him in communities where he could help carry the black vote.

Rachel was the backbone for the campaign, although a steel company official was named the figurehead. While continuing her community services roles for the city, she circulated news releases Douglas wrote, organized women committees to staff the campaign office, had buttons and brochures prepared, and set up a schedule for media interviews.

"Douglas Hodge will get the job done!" was the campaign theme. A vivid shade of blue was selected for the signs as the color best known to attract voters. Green and yellow were turn-off colors, according to Douglas's research, and red came on too strong. Blue was the "sincere" color. Poll studies were made to determine where solid pockets of voters were located, and in-depth studies were made of state issues.

Two other contenders announced they intended to enter the race, but they were not major opponents. The pressure of the Hodge campaign never lessened, despite the lack of strong competition.

Rachel never asked details of the meeting between Douglas and his wife, and didn't want to know them. Choosing to know only that the wife was cooperating, Rachel made certain behind the scenes that she was never around or involved when the wife accompanied him on any public appearances.

Douglas did try to describe the meeting to Rachel, but she quickly ended the conversation. He did not press, actually feeling it perhaps was best for her that she did not know too many details. But the arrangement developed as he had presented it to her. There was an agreement with his wife to participate in his campaign, and portray her role as a supportive spouse. It was only that, but he had been surprised at Sandra's eagerness.

"A State Representative! Why my dear, I think it's marvelous. Daddy will be very excited, too." Sandra's smile added sparkle to her tanned face that she explained was the result of a month of golf at a Naples, Florida, resort.

Preferring not to meet Sandra at her parents' house in Columbus, Douglas had asked her to meet him at a downtown restaurant for lunch. Heads had turned when she entered to meet him. She had aged, too, but oh so gently. Her smooth blond hair, delicate facial features and the vivid royal blue suit she wore captured attention. She knew it. Sandra had a talent for appearing to be indifferent while gazing straight ahead, but she knew exactly who in the room had their eyes on her.

During their first few minutes together over glasses of wine, Douglas quickly outlined his intention to seek election and the role she could play, if interested.

"I want you to know it doesn't mean any more than being seen together, and that may or may not be to your liking," he explained.

"You don't have to say that to me, Douglas. I have a very satisfying life here, but this could add some excitement." Sandra flicked on another smile for him. "The girls are on their own now, and Mommy and Daddy are in fairly good health, so I'm free to help out."

"This shouldn't take much time, just showing up at different functions and looking your usual beautiful self."

"Now that's public relations, my dear. And I know you're good at it." Her eyes swept the room quickly, no longer appearing indifferent, but eager to size up the occupants when she was in an unobserved position. "I can understand how such an arrangement would benefit you, but I'm a little fuzzy on what it would do for me."

"Not much, I'm afraid," Douglas said honestly. "I'm asking this of you as a favor. I can't say I'm proud to do so, but my steel company advisors asked me to give it a shot. If you're not interested, I certainly understand, and I'll handle it alone. I just ask that you not talk to any reporters about our personal situation."

Sandra scoffed at the suggestion. "Can you even imagine I would want to do that? How could you. It's my reputation here, too, you know. And I think it might be good, for a while at least, to be known as a Representative's wife."

"Sandra..."

"Don't worry, my dear. We can carry it off."

* * *

Garland City Commissioners, including Hooper, were tired of Glenn McIntire's ranting about the downtown mall. Their heads turned away from him even now, ears not really listening, as he once again attended a public meeting, weaving unsteadily while berating them.

"You're ruining us. Nobody wants to come downtown any more," Glenn accused during a late January commission meeting. "They don't want to battle the mud and parking problems to get down here and find there are even fewer stores than they had before. What are you going to do about it?"

"We've been wrestling with the problem, Glenn, you know that, you've met with us," Hooper tried to soothe. "There are no easy answers."

"They were easy in the beginning," snapped Glenn, his face appearing almost as red as the remnants of what remained of his once red hair. "I fought the mall hard, at first." Everyone became prepared for what they would hear next. They had listened to Glenn's story numerous times, but no one wanted to challenge the ravaged bar owner in his apparent volatile state.

"I wrote letters to the editor against the mall. Then I decided to go along with it. Your city planner, that Tim Brown, kept talking about the plastic dome city and how great it would be." Glenn glared around the room, failing to find the hated face of Brown, the planner who had deceived him the most.

"Well, your planner talked me into buying two redevelopment lots at $17,000. He even went to the bank with me for the loan. I walked out of the bank with a quarter million dollar check in my pocket. I felt rich." Glenn stopped, hung his head, then gained momentum again.

"The city had sketches of what the new anchor stores would look like. But you know what, they didn't have anybody signed up. They didn't have any anchors. All the city people were talking who didn't know what they were doing. They had nobody signed. We all lost."

Hooper again tried calming words, other commissioners mouthed phrases, but admittedly there were no solutions to the mall's financial situation.

Words came out of city officials mouths about a new plan to hire yet another marketing specialist to bring in new stores. It had been a failed enterprise in the past that would fail in the future, Glenn and other non-vocal merchants in the commission chamber suspected.

"You're just going to let us go down?" Glenn challenged.

"What do you want us to do?" Hooper asked, exasperated.

"How do I know. You're the people in charge and I hold you all personally responsible," Glenn shouted, losing even more control. He felt they did not care. Some of the city officials had not grown up in the city. They had not watched the steel mill import workers as his grandparents had. They did not watch as the mill made the town something special that thrived when other Midwest communities collapsed under the depression.

"You just don't care," Glenn shouted at commissioners. "But I tell you some of us do, and we're going to fight for this town. We're not going to let you destroy it."

* * *

Other mall merchants were just as unhappy that January, following the dismal Christmas season, but they were not in the bar business and were not drinking their supplies to seek oblivion. It was the time of year when they traditionally made the most profits, but not this joyless year.

The ladies' hat shop had closed, a shoe store and a man's clothing store were soon going the same way. Second generation merchants just closed up shop and stood back to watch their long-time friends and competitors struggle against the odds of making the mall work.

They blamed, yet sympathized with shoppers who braved muddy boardwalks instead of sidewalks to reach their destined stores. Shoppers and store owners alike struggled with massive

212

sheets of clear plastic stretched over wooden frameworks to provide temporary doorways in under-construction buildings. The plastic sometimes ripped loose in strong winds, whipping and creating a greater chill.

Not only had stores been under-stocked and overpriced in apprehension of the slow Christmas season, shoppers often had found their cars dusted with debris or sloshed by mud when they returned to them. Why fight it, became their attitude.

Glenn did not let up with his haranguing, including any time or place.

"They're going to destroy us. They're doing it deliberately, and the leader is that God damned Brown. That big-headed toad," Glenn swore in a loud voice to Gene Evans as he and the old jeweler had a sandwich in a corner drug store one day. "He just wants to get his name in some of those national publications with this project, while I'm going bankrupt."

Glenn's trade had almost disappeared. Most of the noon-time restaurant patrons had moved over to the hotel and other outlying food stops to avoid the hassle of wading through the last dregs of mall construction. The night-time trade of cronies dwindled because there was no longer any parking available in the lot at the rear of his saloon. The city had taken the land.

Next had come dreaded notices to merchants and property owners of pending assessments as their share of costs to operate the mall. Payments would be due as soon as square footage was determined, the notices stated.

"I just won't pay them. I just God damn won't," Glenn told Evans. "Just let them try to get another dime out of me."

Assessments, based on square footage of buildings connected to the mall were to pay for heating, cooling, maintenance and security. City officials had talked assessments a couple of years before when the mall was first proposed, but the added costs were always something out in the future when revenues were flowing from the climate- controlled, sparking new downtown shopping area.

Now, one thousand dollars more a year each in property owner assessments would cause even more stores to go belly up and die. Unfortunately, the business community knew assessments would be a lot more than that, they could increase perhaps to three thousand or four thousand dollars a year.

What the average citizen failed to comprehend was that since a large portion of the mall was unoccupied, taxpayer money had to be used to pay the city's share of assessments on the empty space. That cost also escalated as more stores closed and the number of vacancies expanded.

"We're just some God damned guinea pig," Glenn swore. "Brown, don't you hate that guy? Anyway he said it's the first covered mall in the country to include existing streets and buildings. Shit, what's that to us?"

"You don't have to shout at me,'" Evans came back gently. "I'm in the same boat. I've got all my family working in the store. I can't afford outside employees anymore. We probably won't be here next Christmas."

"Let's make them put it back the way it was," Glenn said hopelessly.

* * *

There were only about six patrons in McIntosh's bar on a rainy autumn night. It was the rainfall that would be the death knell for all the vividly-colored trees that draped the Miami Valley.

Leaves heavy with raindrops would be forced overnight to relinquish their weakening hold to mother trees and would be swept to the ground on wet gushes of wind to become only brown debris in the morning gutters.

The same depression saturated the atmosphere inside the darkened, shadowy bar. The few steady patrons were here at their "bitching" hour. The long-time sots, grizzled with life and booze, only showed up at this early hour for gripes and companionship when the reality of a new day was approaching.

A couple of these wasted souls of the night had known Glenn since his boyhood. They watched him grow into a slim, red-headed youth, then into a family man who took over management of the business. Now they saw before them, in their own blurry world, a nearly 60-year old man with a ballooning belly, thinning gray hair, and a thickening nose with broken blood vessels. That was the same way the other "dregs" in the room had seen him. They had drifted into town after having failed somewhere else.

This night was particularly bad for Glenn. He blamed it on the weather. That was easy to do, because he used up every other excuse - ranging from the shit the city put him through to the far lesser reason of his wife not sticking beside him. They were barely staying together now, the main link being their financial indebtedness.

"This weather's enough to rot your bones," Glenn, slurring his words, said to one of the rummies at the end of the bar when he put another shot and a glass of water in front of him. "I can feel it in me, like mold."

"Ya got a long way to go, Kiddo." The man who answered, known as "Howie", had difficulty getting the words over his own thick tongue. "Wait'll ya get to one hundred and ten like me."

"Hell, I'm not even gonna reach seventy," said Glenn. "The city's taken it all outa me. You heard what the city did to me, didn't ya."

"Yeah, yeah," said the men around the bar in chorus.

"How many times you gonna tell that story?" asked one of the men, wearing three layers of jackets he apparently felt were needed against the chill of the night and forgot to take off when inside. He was one of the new faces in recent years, not new really, the face was worn, unshaven, framed with hair that hadn't seen a comb or shampoo in remembered time. "Christ sakes, when you gonna let it die."

"That's not what's gonna die," said Glenn angrily. "It's me, and I can't expect any of you to care. Christ, what am I doing talking to you bums anyway? None of you ever had anything, so what do you know about losing anything?"

"You sure know how to hurt a guy," said Buckie, essentially a "rag man" who lived out of a push cart he shoved around the city to collect rags and bottles out of trash cans. Buckie spread his mouth in a fake laugh to show darkened, misshapen teeth and dark spaces where others had been.

Glenn didn't care if they were watching. He poured himself another shot of scotch and downed it. He did not care if he mixed drinks. "All of you, drink up," he said. "I'm gonna close early."

"Ya can't, it's still going on two o'clock," said one of the men. "What time is it anyway?"

"We ain't leaving till the proper time," said Buckie, wrapping his hands tighter around his glass. No one bothered to look at a clock, it didn't matter. They knew he wouldn't close until the proper time. It was just conversation. They knew that from the way Glenn went to the deserted far end of the bar away from the saloon entrance, and just stood there, staring.

"Christ, he's really out of it. Did you ever think you'd see Glenn like this?" mumbled one of the men to another. He tried to talk in a whisper but his rasping, whiskey voice carried to the end of the bar.

Glenn stood holding to the edge of the wooden counter to steady himself. He had to get out of here, away from these men. They were losers like he was going to be when the bank foreclosed on his loan - any day now. He would have to find some haunt late at night like this, just to have someone to talk to. But the bums wouldn't leave now. They said they wouldn't. He had to get them out. He would get them out.

The gun. He never had to use it before. But it was always there, on the shelf under the bar up front. About knee high it was. All he would have to do would be to reach down and pick it up out of the cigar box he hid it in. It would scare the hell out of 'em. They were pretty good guys, just losers, but they didn't believe him when he said he wanted them out.

Glenn started a slow, unsteady walk behind the bar toward the other end, holding at each step to the solid wood of the historic bar. Step after step, until he was in front of the secret hiding place. He reached. It fit nicely in his hand. The gun felt cool and hard. He was going to show them now.

"I want all of you to just get up and get out of here," he said, turning unsteadily and pointing the gun at the floor. Glenn barely knew in his shaky state not to point the gun at anyone. Accidents happen he thought, finding it difficult to hold the weapon steady and seem in control.

"Hells bells, what ya doing?" asked Buckie, standing from his stool and knocking his glass over. It rolled on the counter and clinked against another glass. All else was quiet. The sight of Glenn swaying in front of them holding a gun began to sink in.

"I said chug-a-lug and get out," Glenn said, gesturing with the gun. No, point it low, he said to himself.

The men stood, a couple downed their drinks, others already had finished. "You better get in control, Kiddo," said Buckie. "You gonna mess up your life if you don't."

"Mess up, ha! As if it isn't." Glenn tightened his grip on the bar. He studied the gun in his hand a moment. "I donno if this is loaded or not," he said, a foolish smile spreading his face. "But you listened, didn't you?"

"We're not going to take a chance," said three- jackets.

"But you listened anyway," Glenn said. Looking up at them, he asked, "Do you think Tim Brown would listen if I went to his house and told him he was a prick and I want the city to put the mall and our bar back the way it was?"

"Come on, Kiddo. It's time to close up and go home," said Buckie.

"Who says? The night's young, and I got me a gun." Glenn shook his head to steady himself. He felt he was moving in slow motion. "I know where Brown lives. He'll listen to me now, just like you guys are."

Glenn backed a few steps, kept the gun in his right hand pointed low, and flicked a switch with his left that shut off lights above the bar. Other dim wall lights were on the other side of the room. Glenn ignored the men and headed unsteadily for the back door. "He'll listen to me now," he mumbled to himself.

Three-jackets stepped into his path and faced Glenn. "You don't want to do this."

"Like hell," Glenn shoved with his left arm. "I'm gonna kill me a city planner. A big toad who took away everything we had. I'm goin' toad hunting." He staggered on toward the back door. As he passed the man in jackets he was grabbed from behind, his right wrist squeezed in a vice and wrenched, causing him to drop the gun to the floor. He turned and struggled weakly to free himself.

"You got no right.....", screamed Glenn, tears suddenly streaming down his flushed cheeks, twisting, jerking, soberness growing with the realization he had failed again. No power, strength, nothing left. Glenn fell in a slump against the jacketed-chest. Strong arms wrapped around him and held him momentarily.

Glenn looked up into strong, steady eyes in the liquor blotched face.

"Why'd you stop me?" he asked. Glenn saw intelligence in the eyes that were so dark blue they looked black. A leader, he probably was a leader at one time, Glenn thought, as he was held tightly against the cushion of jackets.

The arms released him.

"It's easy to be a loser. You don't belong there," said the man, swooping down to pick up the gun. He flipped open the chamber. It was loaded.

* * *

CHAPTER NINETEEN

<u>October, 1975</u>

"This has been my life. I planned to retire from the company," MVS staff photographer Dick Warren complained to Douglas the day he got his layoff notice from the steel company.

"God, Douglas, I'm forty two. How am I going to find a job out there in today's market?" Dick kept his eyes down as he loaded some of his personal equipment into supermarket egg cartons. The photo lab already was looking empty.

"You're a qualified, experienced photographer. There will be work for you out there," said Douglas, who in his role as State Representative was visiting the steel company headquarters to help boost the morale of some of his fellow workers. He was there both out of personal interest, and at the company's request. "You may have to face relocating to another area, though."

"Sure, and do you know how my wife is going to feel about that, leaving her job at the insurance company and pulling the kids out of school?"

It was not that Representative Hodge, only a year into the state post, could do anything. They both knew that. But the photographer had to share with someone who he felt cared.

Although Douglas was no longer with the company, he knew its history and was familiar with the staff. Mill hands were accustomed to the annual winter lay-offs and summer hirings to fill in for vacation seasons. There were no surprises, because it was routine postings of what jobs were on or off.

But white-collar workers had been insulated over the years

and felt victims now of the blood-letting. Rarely had workers lost jobs in the past. Staffers felt secure in taking on long-term home mortgages, planning for their children's education, and buying motorboats to go with their cottages along southwestern Ohio lakes.

Now they were caught in the company's "Down sizing", laying off workers to economize and conditioning remaining workers to do two jobs at existing or reduced salaries. Nearly one third of the six thousand MVS mill workers already were off the job. And shocking for the industry, two hundred eighteen white- collar employees were being dismissed or encouraged to retire over the next eighteen months.

"What does the company expect us to do?" asked Dick, who had been with the company fourteen years. "God, the pay and benefits have been great. Where else are we going to find them?"

"It's happening all over the country," Douglas said, hurting for the uncertainty his friend and other staffers were feeling. "The company is going to help with relocation, and my office will give you all the help we can."

Douglas realized it would not change anything, but he reminded Dick that steel companies particularly were having a hard time because of foreign imports and environmental mandates. And it did not make it easier to realize the company had turned out some pretty poor products in the past that turned off customers.

"We can't change any of that and it's really not important to me now." Dick dropped some outdated appointment books into the box with a thud. "I have to think about feeding my family."

"I realize that," Douglas quickly agreed, "but sometimes knowing why something is happening to us helps us understand better and accept."

Douglas had just about exhausted supportive phrases in talks with other employees in recent weeks. Words were such a small tool, he realized. Douglas had been called on by the company to give emotional support to "displaced employees" and, as he recognized, to take some of the heat off MVS officials. He took it on as a personal obligation to help where he could.

Many of the mill workers being laid off permanently had similar stories. They had followed their fathers into jobs and expected their children to follow them. They admittedly took for granted the eight weeks of vacation each year, and the salary that paid for their pick-up trucks and bass fishing boats. But they still owed mortgages on their homes and were putting children through school, on a lower scale pattern of the white-collar workers. Were they going to have to move to find another job, would they lose everything?

Douglas had no real answers. He was struggling behind the scenes at the state level to increase the length of time for unemployment benefits, but few people knew this. He did not mention this to workers he counseled. He did not want to raise their expectations, not hold it in front of them as an enticing carrot of hope, in case it never happened.

The constant flow of displaced workers passing through his State Representative's office in Garland, such as Dick, was leaving Douglas emotionally burdened with the sharing of their apprehensions and feelings of abandonment. It was not as if he could do any good or change anything, but he worked at an exhaustive pace to let them know someone cared about what happened to them.

Douglas was well aware he was being used by the company, placed out front as a spokesman to provide credibility to promises that employees would receive severance pay based on length of employment, that employees forced into early retirement would receive health benefits, and efforts would be made to find them other jobs. He did not mind. These were his friends and fellow workers, and he had an overwhelming desire to ease their agony.

Also he felt an obligation to the company for helping him get elected as a State Representative. Although he mentioned it to no one other than Rachel, his new role spared him the experience he would be having now of being fired. He barely missed being one of them. He felt guilt for getting out in time. There was no effort he would not make for them now to compensate.

"The company could pull out of this and expand in the future. It could mean a call back." Douglas really wanted to believe that.

"That's the worst crap I've heard yet," Dick said, his mouth spreading into a grin as he turned to Douglas.

"I just thought I'd try that one on you. Hey, the Ark floated, even with elephants on board."

"Must have included a bull, too, huh?"

"You guessed it. And now that's we're on a light note, we mustn't leave MVS without carrying with us the memory of the *BFR*".

"God, I haven't thought about that for awhile. I still have pictures here somewhere." Dick, his mind suddenly diverted, walked to a file cabinet in the corner of the lab and searched through a drawer. "I was the one sent there to take the first picture."

Douglas had not yet joined the public relations staff, but he was familiar with the story of the memo from the head office telling about a massive stone found at the site where the company was digging a pond at it's MVS Employees Association Park west of the city.

"Let's find some use for this", was the directive at the end of the memo.

Weeks passed and the rock remained on the pond bank.

Another memo came down from the head office, passing along word from the park association to the effect that "the big rock has to be moved because docks are scheduled to be built in the next couple of weeks. Find some place for the rock and get a crane to move it."

More time passed, to the frustration of the park association management. The delay prompted another message, "Get the big fucking rock out of here."

"Here it is," said Dick, handing over a photo of a crane lifting a rock the size of a small car onto a flat-bed truck. "I followed it into town, and took pictures of them unloading it in front of the building."

When Dick got his assignment, it was to go to the Association Park and take pictures of the *BFR (Big Fucking Rock)* being loaded onto the truck. From then on, it was always known as the BFR. "Plans are being made for a plaque for the BFR", "a dedication ceremony is scheduled for the BFR", "invitations have been mailed for the BFR event".

"I met you shortly before then and I covered it for the

newspaper," Douglas reminded.

"I know", Dick said, searching, until finally he said, "Here it is." He handed Douglas a picture of smiling people gathered around the massive stone in front of the steel company's headquarters. It was set in a small garden area, with benches and flower gardens.

"And what was so funny," Dick said, "was that not one word was said about the `BFR', yet everybody knew about it."

"My favorite part was the plaque," reminded Douglas, "stating the rock was dedicated to `BFR - Beauty, Friendship and Rest'."

The two men exchanged glances over the photo. "I'm going to take a copy of this picture with me. I guess it's one of the funny things we'll remember," Dick said.

Douglas walked to his friend, put his hand on his shoulder. "You'll be all right."

"Thanks, Douglas."

A handshake. A parting. That last look of friendship with the knowledge perhaps of never seeing each other again. It was a pattern developing in the city.

* * *

Except for not living in his own South End community, Hooper began to feel life was good for him and his family. He was not caught in the company lay-offs, he was grateful for that. Except for the agonizing employment shakeup at the mill and city loss of income tax revenues, other aspects of government had improved. He enjoyed his city commissioner duties and had been re-elected to a new four-year term.

The inflammatory Civil Rights movement had lessened in the city in the mid 1970s, although tugs of war occasionally erupted over perceived hurts and slights continued. More black employees were hired by the city. Restaurants, buses and swimming pools were integrated, and the amusement park six miles away had finally conceded to opening its doors.

What made Hooper's life particularly rich at this time was the pending marriage of his daughter Aimee. He felt Jerry Carson, her fiancée, was a good Garland kid.

Although somewhat of a hellion in high school, Jerry never got in any major problems like other kids in the black neighborhood. He had not owned a car, so he never wrecked one, nor did he ever put a scratch on his parent's car.

Jerry had changed when he came back for his first Thanksgiving break in college, Hooper recognized. His clothes were more casual, he laughed longer and talked louder, and he seemed to turn any chair he sat in into a bed. His legs would flop over an arm of a chair, his body slink down on the cushion, and his head would rest back on the chair as if he would nod off to sleep any moment.

Hooper and others did not find this change totally offensive, since his Aimee also came home from her first year of college in baggier clothes and attitude. It puzzled the adults, however, and made them question how much they were investing in schooling and if they could see the results in their children.

The day of Aimee's wedding, Hooper felt a tightness like a vice was around his chest as he blinked his eyes to keep dampness under control. He had told himself he would not do this. Aimee was not going away. She would be living nearby, in their old house that had been rented since the fire, but nothing would be the same again. She had a job now, in a lawyer's office, and Jerry had landed a marketing job at an auto factory in a nearby town.

"I'm proud of you, Hon," Hooper told his daughter as they stood at the rear of the church before he led her down the aisle. "Your mother and I will always be grateful you are our daughter."

* * *

Glenn was alone when he locked the doors for the last time on the McIntire Stag Bar, although it no longer would have that name. He was leaving its fate up to the bank that held the mortgage.

His parents, in Florida enjoying their retirement funds, ignored his repeated requests to help save the business. Fortunately his long-gone grandparents did not know what had happened to the dream they worked to make possible.

He went home to get ready for his new job that night. His goal had been to find some kind of work, and stay out of sight. Work at the mill was a joke. He did not want that anyway. He loathed the idea, and always had, of walking into the fiery pits every day, and leaving coated with grime and depression. He had seen too much of that in the men seated in his bar night after night. Well, it used to be his bar, he reminded himself.

The only job alternative he considered was what he knew, tending bar. He had found an opening in a road house near Dayton. It was good enough. The work took him out of Garland, away from faces he knew, and the drive back and forth was not bad. He had to drink less, though, he knew or else he could not get out on the highway. The bar duties let his body move mechanically through chores he had handled since a boy. He did not have to think.

* * *

Rachel stared into the darkness outside the window of a Pittsburgh motel, waiting for a glimpse of car lights that would signal Douglas had arrived.

No longer could they meet at restaurants or motels in outlying Garland. Only very rarely now could they meet at all because of his role in Columbus. Even that was in more jeopardy as each month passed. She had seen newspaper articles and Sunday magazine layouts about the Hodge family, pictures of him with his delicately beautiful wife. In some of the photos, he was shown at social or sports events with his daughters.

Although Rachel did not ask, Douglas had assured her he

enjoyed having the opportunity to get to know his daughters better, and that the relationship with his wife was for public show only.

Rachel, staring now through a two-inch opening of the drapes in the motel room awaiting Douglas, had been giving the impression of accepting his lifestyle and knowing all along she was being gullible.

She only wished she had someone to talk to, a close friend who could give her some feedback. But she had severed any close friendships, preferring to be free to talk to Douglas or be with him when possible. Certainly Alice could not be a confidant. Rachel tensed at the thought of her sister knowing about Douglas in her life.

Rachel's parents were gone now, too. Her father had died first of a stroke several years ago, and her mother followed a short time later of a ruptured appendix. She could not even imagine trying to talk or share with either one of them.

And Sonny, dear Sonny, she could never tell him. He was settled in a new life now in Indianapolis in a management position with a drug manufacturing firm.

"To call it a position is an exaggerated word at this point," Sonny had said, laughing, when he first told his mother of his job. "And it'll mean some traveling across the country, but I think it can grow into something." He spoke rapidly and excitedly. "I'll be based generally in Indianapolis, but that's no more than about two hours away," he said to relieve her concern about his pending move from Garland.

She regretted seeing him give up the dream of teaching, but she recognized that he had found a good job he apparently appreciated when so many other qualified people in the city were floundering. She now wanted more than anything for her son to find someone to love, have children and be settled in life.

"I guess we have to keep striving for something," she thought to herself, realizing she had always done that in adding to her real estate holdings. She supposed she could be considered by some to be a wealthy woman now, based on her properties, but she did not consider herself that. She was frugal in her lifestyle and limited travels, preferring to concentrate her time in the civic roles she played. Housing, food, child care and health benefits for the needy were her dedications.

Her only personal comforts were the time with Douglas, his messages and telephone calls. But they were more and more bringing a gnawing awareness that she could be destined to spend the rest of her life alone.

Her thoughts were interrupted as the flash of car lights struck the window and glared into the room through the small opening in the drapes. She closes the drapes tightly, rushed to the bathroom mirror for a glimpse at herself, smiling, knowing the lipstick or makeup would not last long,   then returned to wait by the door.

At the knock, she opened the door and stood back, not to be seen from outside. Always cautious. Douglas entered. Glancing at her warmly, he turned, bolted the door, then reached out an arm that circled her waist and pulled her to him.

As their lips met and their bodies tightened together in a deepening kiss, she felt his tall muscular body molding into hers. They did not know how long the kiss lasted, did not care, as it was followed by another and another.

Finally they pulled apart and studied each other. He looked gaunt, tired, his face with a sucked-in-cheek look. She brushed her hand across his brow, as if to erase some of the strain she felt within him.

Douglas sensed similar tension in Rachel, confirming an attitude he had developed through their telephone talks and messages. He kissed the fine lines around her eyes and on her brow, feeling an overpowering urgency to lose himself in the mind and body of this woman who been so much a part of him over the years.

From that embrace, they began undressing each other and then were holding each other for hours to come. She marveled at the intensity in him, the desperation of his body pressed against her. It was almost as if he wanted to lose his own identify completely by being absorbed by her.

Spent, their damp, perspiring bodies slick against each other, they lay in a tight embrace, fearful if they let go of each other, the emotions they felt would pass also.

Choked with emotion, Douglas later murmured against her shoulder, "I've realized that's what life is about, loving someone."

Rachel found it difficult to control her own feelings. They knew they loved each other, but they seldom talked about it. Talking about it led to wanting solutions, and they had long ago given up seeking that. They clung together.

For the rest of the night neither slept, but dosed fitfully between love making and tender stroking of each other. They became aware of the dawn. More loving, petting and caressing into the morning hours. They showered together, then dressed slowly, and later carried their overnight bags to their cars. As they ate breakfast, their feet touched under the table.

"I have to tell you," he said when they were on their second cup of coffee. "I maybe needed you too much when we first got together yesterday. Everything just went out of my mind."

"I think it was mutual. It's been a long time."

Rachel wanted to shout, *So what are we going to do about it?* But she said nothing. She had held it all in over the many years they had been together. She would not lose control now. But she wanted so much to be with him, more and more as she grew older, more vulnerable.

"It gets more difficult all the time, having to part from you," Douglas said. "It doesn't mean I can do anything about it, about us, I mean," he said. "That's what makes it ....so damn hard to handle."

It was what she had heard before, always expected to hear. I'm tired of being strong, she thought. I want to lash out and tell him he has to be with me. I'm weak in not doing so, because if I do, he will leave and all this will go out of my life.

As close as they were, and as much as they shared, she could not demand that he be with her. She hurt, but it was not in her character to order him to do something for her own good, or that would hurt him and possibly his family.

These were not new thoughts to her. They were old ones, packed away to be brought out regularly and weighed like the Lady Justice holding decisions in her hands. In this case, there was no decision to make.

Depressing thoughts always passed swiftly. There was too much to share when they were together to settle on gloom, their conversations were so fast in contrast to their periodic sad thoughts, they barely escaped interrupting each other.

Douglas was excited about legislation he was helping introduce in the House, he described new environmental laws pending that could help MVS steel, and also took time to describe his daughters' activities.

Also sharing, Rachel told of Glenn's new job at the roadside tavern, how her sister Alice was growing more cantankerous with age, described Tim's failing health, and that she had lost track of Tina Rose since she moved away after Josh's death.

"I didn't want her to move, but she said she could no longer pay the rent," Rachel said. "I told her it was all right, but she just moved out with Teddy and went who knows where."

It hurt Rachel to share that information, but she had happier news about Sonny. "He's enjoying his job and the travel. He was in San Diego two weeks ago," she said.

"I'm just glad it worked out so well for him," Douglas responded, then glanced at his watch. "I can't believe how fast the time has gone. I never can."

Leaving the restaurant and deciding they had enough time for a short walk in a nearby park, they shared glances at each other and reach for each other's hand when they felt they were concealed in a wooded area.

The sharp October wind prompted him to shove his hand holding hers into the deep pocket of his jacket.

"It always amazes me how much we have to share, and how much I enjoy whatever we do. Even a simple thing like this walk," Douglas said.

"It's not a simple thing. We're together," Rachel said softly, her blue eyes glancing up at him under thick lashes that appeared slightly damp.

"When we get behind that big tree over there off the path," Douglas said, "I'm going to hug you enough to last until the next time we're together."

* * *

229

Teddy sat slumped in the hollow he had created in the worn brown couch. He strained his eyes against the late fall sun flooding through a window opposite him as he watched a wrestling match on the black-and white television screen.

Smoke from his cigarette made a whirling, golden cloud around his face. It didn't occur to him to pull the shade. He usually sat in the same position every evening as the sun sank below the paint-faded residences across the street and spilled sunbeams through the window.

He glanced over at his mother, Tina Rose, resting on the daybed under the window. One of her hands fluttered over the tattered quilt, which had been her treasure since her mother passed it down to her years before.

Ma always bragged on the quilt pattern, Flower Basket, Teddy remembered. The bright print patterns had dimmed over the years. Ma didn't like it being used every day.

She hadn't said anything about it for a long time, though. Teddy, grinding out his cigarette in a brim-full ashtray on the floor, pushed up from the couch, heaving out of the hollow, and walked toward his mother.

"Ya okay?" he asked, leaning over her.

The sun's brightness made Teddy drop his shoulders lower to shield his eyes, as he rested his hands on the bed, so he could see her face. He detected a groan.

"Time for more medicine?" he asked. When there was no response, he shoved himself upright, causing Tina Rose's hand to flutter again as the day bed shook.

He stood and turned toward the kitchen. The wooden breakfast table, with three chairs that didn't match, was still cluttered from remains of lunch and other meals. Grease had congealed in the left-over canned beef soup. A parade of ants was attacking crumbs from a cracker.

Ignoring the table, Teddy headed toward the crude wooden shelves over the stained sink where he kept the bottle of peroxide. Only a little liquid sloshed in the bottle as he shook it listlessly.

Teddy grabbed up a cloth lying on the edge of the sink. It

was dry, stiff, from the last time he doused Tina Rose's sores.

"I'm gonna pour some more on ya, Ma," Teddy said as he stood over her again. His hand reached for the edge of the quilt.

"Don't look at me," Tina Rose whispered in a quivering, weak voice. Teddy remembered how Ma's strong voice had carried nearly a block when she called him as a kid. Now it seemed she was talking through a tiny little box.

"I won't look," Teddy said. It was the same every time. He knew Ma didn't want him to see her in only the soiled, cotton gown that kept slipping around to expose her. Even though she wanted him to take care of her, instead of a doctor, she wanted to be kept covered.

That made his job hard, Teddy realized. He could only guess where her sores were, and try to pour the peroxide there. Ma had put her hands on the quilt, identifying underneath where the hurts were. Sometimes they changed, but he guessed he was pouring on most of them. He knew by now where the worst ones were.

Turning his head, Teddy lifted the quilt, dribbled a little of the liquid on a spot where her bony hip formed a sharp mound in the quilt.

"Ohoooo, ohoooo," Tina Rose moaned when the impact of the medicine soaked her wound, and spilled onto the mattress that was still damp from the previous treatment.

"It won't hurt long," Teddy soothed. "Only last couple minutes." Still with his head turned and holding the quilt up several inches, he aimed for the spot on her left ankle. She had allowed him to see that before.

He could have looked now at the leg, but he didn't want to. It hurt him to see the open sores, black around the edges, red and milky stuff.

For the next several minutes, Teddy splashed, sprinkled and soothed as Tina Rose moaned and gripped the edge of the quilt. It was as if she gained comfort and strength from the material, the loose wrinkles over her knuckles tightened in her grip. The last of the medicine was sprinkled.

"That's all I can do right now, Ma. I'll have to git some more when I go cash your benefit check tomorrow. I doctored you pretty good now. Want me to put a dry towel under ya?"

"After while. Sleep now," she said softly in that weakened voice.

"How about somethin' to eat? There's soup left and an apple." No answer. "You do wanna sleep, don't ya? Well, I'll be right here, when ya decide ya want somethin'."

Teddy put Tina Rose's hand gently back under the quilt, then pulled it closer to her chin. He walked back across the room, lowered himself into his hollow in the couch. He sat the empty peroxide bottle on the floor at his feet, and turned to watch the television screen, squinting against the sun.

He wished Ma would hurry and get better. Things were not very good right now. They had not been good since they lived in the house by the river with Ma and Daddy. For a time they even slept in a car. It got wet at times. Then Welfare got them this apartment. It was not a good place. He did not like the people in this part of town. He wanted to be back near Sonny.

Teddy wondered a few minutes where Sonny might be, but then he went back to watching the small television screen.

* * *

Ma hadn't eaten much in several days. That worried Teddy. He prepared soup for her, and held the spoon close to her dried and shriveled lips. He couldn't remember them being blue before. She slept most of the day. Teddy shook her, and called her name regularly. At first he didn't worry much. Often she took spells of sleeping a lot.

But that evening, when the street lights came on and gloomy shadows settling in the room to soften the harshness of peeling paint, Teddy felt the need to waken his mother and talk to her. He was lonely.

He shook her shoulder gently as she lay curled up on her

232

side. He shook her a little harder, realizing the movement would make her moan. It didn't.

"Ma, ya all right, ain't ya?"

He turned her slightly so he could look at her face. No movement. He leaned closer to hear her breath, or feel it on his lips. She was breathing, he realized, as the rancid odor from her mouth swept upwards into his nostrils. "Come on, Ma. Ya gotta wake up now. It's gettin' dark, and ya won't sleep tonight, if ya don't."

Teddy slumped to sit on the edge of the bed. She'd never done this before. He was doing the best he could. Was she just mad and punishing him? Was she mad that he ran out of medicine? Well, he'll go get some more. She wouldn't be angry then. He shuffled to the hall, grabbed open the door.

Magazines and papers stored on the top shelf avalanched on his head and shoulders. He kicked them back as far as he could, jamming them into the piles of boxes and accumulated debris. Grabbing down a jacket from a hook, and stretching his arms into the sleeves, Teddy glanced back at his mother.

She had not moved. He walked back over to her, his knees pressed against the day bed, as if touching would make him closer to her. "I can't go out and leave ya like this," he said. "Somethin's not right. It's real wrong."

Teddy began walking back and forth by her bed. He glanced at her again, as if seeking directions. *Why was she sleeping like this? She'd know what to do, if she would only wake up.*

"We gotta have help, Ma," he said, falling to his knees beside her. "I can't do it alone no more. I'm going to the house across the street an ask 'em to call a doctor. You said no doctors, but I can't do it alone no more."

* * *

Teddy stood in the lobby of the hospital emergency room.

Ma was really going to be mad. She always said no hospitals. But the men who came in the ambulance just took her.

Nurses had wheeled Tina Rose through double doors that swung open and then closed to block his view of his mother.

He stood staring at the doors where he had last seen her, knowing she would be mad at him when she woke up. She never spanked him when he was growing up, but he always felt bad when he thought she didn't love him.

He didn't want to face her now . He slapped the chest pocket of his shirt, where he kept his cigarettes. It was flat. Had he left them home, or was he out? Well, he was out now. Where to find cigarettes in a hospital? He headed down a hall, hoping someone could tell him where to find cigarettes.

* * *

Kathie Landley's soft blond hair was falling in her eyes again as she hurried to finish one patient in the short- staffed emergency room, and get to a new one paramedics said needed immediate attention. It was an older woman, they said, a patient Kathie immediately identified in her mind as a "Crinkly".

"Crinkly" was the humorous term she privately used for old people because of their wrinkled skin. Sure, it was callous, no, maybe more of a protective attitude. You give them swift, tender and sympathetic care, but you don't get attached because they may not last long.

Kathie had a lot of experience caring for older people, and knew what to expect. They were terrified of what was happening to them and what will be done about it. Men and women alike were either abrupt and belligerent because they were depending on someone else, or they were overly affable because they want to be liked and get good care. She didn't blame them. Many already had been through life's shredder. She had sympathy, which she was prepared to give now.

The child-size woman lying on her side on the gurney appeared skeleton thin as Kathie approached. "What's our problem here?" she asked, pulling back a top sheet and hesitating with reluctance to touch the underneath layer of a tattered and stained quilt that was covering the woman. With a quick gesture, to make as little contact as possible, she flung back the quilt.

"My God. Oh, my God." A bitter gall flushed up into her throat. She would not be sick. She would not, Kathie ordered herself. She grabbed back the gold plastic curtain shielding the bed from other emergency room patients and stumbled toward the main desk. "Get Dr. Blare to Unit Three immediately, and get a social worker here."

The round eyes of the reception clerk at the desk widened in surprise. Voices raised in alarm were frowned on, under hospital procedures. "I mean now," Kathie's voice thundered.

She whirled and raced back to the woman, not wanting to go, but compelled to care for the body that was in the most devastated condition she had seen in her seven years of emergency room service.

Kathie didn't start cleaning the body - that's the only way she could think of the woman - a body. She waited for Dr. Blare so he could have the full impact of what they were up against. Instead, she began speaking to the body in a calm, low voice, trying to bring the woman to consciousness.

I wouldn't want to wake up either, if I were you, she thought to herself. Tears flushed her eyes, and trickled down her cheeks. A couple dropped on the thin, gray strands of the tangled mass of what may have once been blond hair like Kathie's

The metal rings holding the dividing curtain clinked as Blare shoved it aside and entered the unit.

"What do you have?" he asked, his eyes switching to the silent patient. "Good Lord. What the hell happened to her?"

Blare pulled away the last of the quilt, held tightly in the woman's bony fingers, and dropped it to the floor. His attention focused on the woman's hip, where bone protruded about three inches. The swollen, raw wound was both red and black, with maggots squirming over each other as they gnawed at the putrid flesh.

Three broken ribs jutted from the woman's shrunken chest, where the breasts were only sagging flat sacks of flesh. Bed sores on her back and legs were infected. Her feet were black with gangrene, crawling with maggots. The doctor listened to the woman's heart, lifted her eyelids to peer into her eyes, and checked reflexes in her hands and legs.

"Start an IV. Get someone in here to help you clean her up, including shaving her head and pelvic area. She's infested. And get her weighed. We need that for the record," Blare said. "Can you believe this?"

"Have you seen any worse?" Kathie asked.

"Not human."

* * *

Teddy reached for his second cigarette as he ambled back down the hall toward the emergency room. He inhaled the first cigarette in practically one breath after finding the machine in a snack area.

He saw the policeman as he put the cigarette in his mouth. This policeman looked big, but they all did. Teddy admired all the things they wore, that made them look bigger, like the gun belt, and holster, flashlight and that club thing hanging down the back, and the handcuffs. He would like to be a policeman.

He remembered the policeman who took them to the hospital the day Daddy was sick. And Ma told him never to take her to a hospital. He had done wrong. Ma would be mad.

Plopping into one of the chairs in the emergency waiting room, in the smoking area, Teddy glanced up at the television set that was playing, without seeing what was playing. Ma is going to be mad.

The policeman stared at him. Teddy glanced at the officer,

too, the big man in the blue uniform. He was not so tall, he just appeared big, Teddy thought as the officer walked toward him.

The shirt under Teddy's arms felt wet. He liked policemen, but he did not like them so near.

"Did you just bring in an older woman who has a lot of sores?" the officer asked, looming over him.

"She's my mother."

"Christ, your mother!"

"She's gonna be all right?"

"Did you get a look at her?" the officer asked.

"I been taking care of her."

"I'm gonna have to talk to you about that. We're going down to the police department."

"But I can't leave my Ma here. No, I can't leave her. She did not want to come here," Teddy said, struggling when the officer touched his arm.

* * *

Tina Rose died at the hospital three days later without regaining consciousness. Nurses testified at Teddy's hearing in municipal court that the numerous bed sores on her body were so severe the ulcers exposed bone. A wound-skin specialist said the sores were months old.

Rachel learned about Tina Rose's death by reading the newspaper two days later. By that time, Teddy's hearing was over. He was charged with neglect and non-support of a dependent. Whether Tina Rose Barnes was the victim of financial or medical neglect was the issue of the hearing.

"She weighed eighty-two pounds when she was admitted to the hospital, "testified Kathie, who along with Dr. Blare, described Tina Rose's open wounds, exposed bone and maggots.

Rachel shuddered when she read the newspaper report.

Other testimony indicated Teddy had cared for his mother for an undetermined number of years, living off her monthly Social Security checks of $275. Reports stated that at one time they lived for weeks in an abandoned car. A spokeswoman for the Department of Human Services testified they lost contact with Mrs. Barnes until she was hospitalized.

* * *

Rachel was in the courtroom the afternoon the judge returned a verdict. She previously had tried unsuccessfully to reach Sonny when Teddy was being evaluated in a county clinic.

Teddy, handcuffed, dressed in jail clothes, shaven and his hair trimmed short, was ordered bound over to the grand jury on a charge of involuntary manslaughter.

As he was led from the courtroom, Rachel called his name. Teddy turned his head. Rachel doubted that he recognized her. She wished she could touch him. He seemed puzzled about where he was and why he was there.

His confusion was the same when Rachel visited him several times in the detention center. He recognized her, but seemed lost, kept asking about his mother.

Teddy did not go to jail. The grand jury ignored the charge of involuntary manslaughter. He later was found guilty of a charge of neglect, and was placed on probation. Tina Rose's cause of death was listed as malnutrition, multiple bed soars and overwhelming infection. She was buried in the city-funded cemetery near the grave of her husband, Josh.

Rachel and Sonny attended the simple ceremony, their flowers the only ones to soften the harshness of the somber gathering. Teddy was not there. He already was lost somewhere in the state mental health system, with welfare officials declining to reveal information about a recipient to anyone other than a relative.

July, 1977

Rachel lost track of time. It was about two years later when she read about Teddy in a brief police department article in the newspaper.

A patrolman had found Theodore Barnes dead of "natural causes" in a rented room a couple of blocks from where he had lived with his mother. There were no known relatives. He was buried near his parents in the city cemetery.

Rachel remembered a small smiling woman in a pink-flowered feed-sack dress, blond curls, and the smell of tobacco.

* * *

CHAPTER TWENTY

April, 1984

Rachel sat at the mahogany desk in the sunny, ground-floor office of her home holding the letter she had received from Douglas two days before.

She had taken it out of a wooden box in a locked drawer of the desk and already had read it several times since it arrived.

It was not different from his usual pattern, there was nothing that referred to any future meeting so she could add it to her calendar.

But the letter was another treasure that brought her as close to Douglas as she could get when he was not in her presence -just words, carefully written in his large and slightly slanting style, words which she had often relished in the past and now even more so when she was unusually lonely and discouraged.

"How I miss you.....,"she read the first sentence again, the same words they had spoken to each other so many times over the years repetitiously like a child exhausting its first phrases.

"But yet how you brighten the dark spots. When things are not so good, I think of you and they get better. When things are great, I think of you and they get better. What an inspiration you are?

"Do I miss you and love you? That's obvious! It bothers me to leave you. It's over too soon. It's comforting to know I'm going to see you when we have something definite scheduled.

"But what a void when I see nothing ahead..."

Nothing ahead! That's how Rachel felt now. Other

independent women live solitary lives, she reflected. I've done it for a long time, so why does it seem like it's all falling apart now?

It's the long separations. It would be better if we could only spend more time together, but more and more the time demands on him were separating them.

This latest crisis with the steel mill!!! Why did the mill always have so much impact on the community and their lives?

The battle cry of some Garland World War II veterans at reports that a Japanese firm was buying forty- nine percent of the steel mill had become, "The Japs are going to win the war after all". Controversy was dividing the city.

When Douglas spent time in his regional office in Garland, such as he would today, she felt that mill officials and union representatives jerked him back and forth in a tug to make him stand on their side. We let the mill dominate us, Rachel thought. It broke Marty's spirit and if Douglas is not careful it will destroy him - and us.

Rachel gently tucked the pages of the letter back into the envelope with the Columbus post office stamp, and her slow-moving fingers folded the flap back into place. The gesture caused her to glance at her hands momentarily. They are beginning to look like my mother's hands, she thought, with prominent blue veins crisscrossing the backs like a road map. She laid the letter down on her desk, and raised her hands slightly above her head, until the veins lessened. They looked normal now, giving more of an impression of youth.

We know that youth is gone, she thought and nothing has come to take it's place - at least not daily companionship and feeling of being cared for. There I go again, Rachel thought. Why am I whining? I've raised a son who has done well and is enjoying the travels with his job. Would he ever marry and have a family, though? I've gotten what I've worked for, the houses and apartments and this home, Rachel thought, reflecting on her four-bedroom, three- fireplace residence. But youth, it goes too quickly.

She pulled open the desk drawer and lifted the lid of the wooden box that stored other letters from Douglas. She placed the latest one in front of the packets and closed the lid. Locking the drawer again and placing the key in a partly concealed inkwell in the desk, Rachel took the precaution realizing that if something happened to her in the future the letters would be found anyway, along with the stored messages in the attic.

I will take control of my life and provide my own interest as I always have, Rachel told herself as she determined to improve her mood. It's my responsibility.

As she stood and prepared to begin her work day, she smoothed the skirt of her beige suit over her slim hips and then touched the front of her hair to make certain no strands were beginning to slide out of place.

Her hair was a dark chestnut now, not the natural near black color before she began tinting it. And she liked the way she was wearing it in a smooth page-boy style with a lion-mane sweep back from her forehead.

She hoped Douglas would like it when he arrived at his downtown Garland office.

* * *

Glenn McIntire apparently was just leaving a meeting with Douglas when Rachel opened the door of the Representative's office and entered.

"Am I late?" she questioned, although aware that her volunteer receptionist duties were not scheduled to begin for fifteen minutes yet.

Douglas' secretary, seated at the front-office desk, rose to leave for her own office and allow Rachel to take over manning the telephone.

"He arrived early today," the secretary said, nodding her head in Douglas' direction.

"My favorite lady," Glenn said, turning from Douglas and reaching for Rachel's hand. Although seemingly uncomfortable and in a hurry, Glenn never failed to make her feel special.

"Sorry I haven't been seeing you at the Community

Committee meetings," Glenn said, "But it's been a pretty busy schedule." They talked only moments, then, giving her a quick kiss on the cheek, Glenn left, saying, "Take care, now."

"He wants a job", Douglas said when the door had closed. Then, "Good morning", to her. He smiled, the attempt at cheerfulness failing to disguise the tiredness his total body exuded. As Douglas dropped into a chair in front of the desk, Rachel wanted to lay her hands gently across his eyes and make the dark areas around them disappear. She wanted to comfort him, lay her hands along his graying temples.

"What time did you arrive?" She watched the open door to the secretary's office as she stashing her handbag into the bottom drawer of the reception desk.

"I left Columbus about 6 o'clock. Have a lot of meetings scheduled this morning, and I want to get out into the district this afternoon. Feel like I've been ignoring them out there." His words were slow, his chin drooping. "And I didn't expect Glenn."

"He's asking you for a job?"

"One with the state. Said he's willing to cut grass along the highway, anything. I told him I thought we could do better than that. Maybe road construction inspection. and do you know what he said, 'For the rest of my life I will owe you'."

"That sounds like Glenn," Rachel answered. "It must have been torture for him to ask for help."

Rachel felt sorry for their friend, but she was just spouting words. Mainly she was studying Douglas. His appearance worried her.

"You going to be able to spend time in the office today?"

He glanced up at the question, recognizing that it meant if he were in the office they would be together, although apart. They could talk face to face and perhaps have lunch together, even if they did always include the secretary.

"Not much today," he answered, his eyes holding hers. "I'm to be out at the mill by ten o'clock with the union. We're going on a tour to talk to some workers. They're hot, but it's not going to be easy to control."

She read the look he gave her in recognition that she longed for them to be together.

Their feelings for each other were rich between them when his secretary abruptly re-entered the room. They always maintained a professional attitude, but Douglas was falsely energized by Rachel's presence and his demeanor became that of a man that was younger by a decade. The smile and quick motion belied the increased drain on his energy reserves.

"You're to call the union office before you leave here," his secretary said, handing him a piece of paper. "And I was to remind you that the banquet in Preble County begins at seven o'clock tonight."

Douglas headed with quick steps to follow the secretary back to their offices. As he left the room, he said over his shoulder to Rachel, "I'll get that information sometime today, and telephone it to you this evening, probably early."

That meant they would talk that evening, before he headed for the Preble County event so that he could leave for Columbus from there. Since she could not see him the rest of the day, just talking on the telephone later would help. Realizing his condition, it would be enough - for right now, she thought.

* * *

Rachel had finished a light supper and was reading a book near the telephone next to her living room couch when she was interrupted by a jarring knock on the front door.

Although not wanting to be away from the telephone very long, she hurried to the door where the heavy knocking continued. Seeing Alice waiting outside, she reluctantly opened it.

"Why don't you use the door bell?" Rachel asked, impatient to make her sister's visit short.

"I don't think you always hear the doorbell in this big house, so I just knock away," Alice said, walking heavily and with obvious

244

pain as she enviously admired the wood-paneled entrance hall of Rachel's brick, Tudor-style home. "Why do you need such a big place for just one person?"

"It's an investment, and it suits me," Rachel responded, pacing her words in an effort to be patient. She also was a little suspicious of her sister's exaggerated limp. "I'm in a bit of a hurry, Alice, and I can't visit much just now."

"I didn't come to visit. I just brought the rent," Alice snapped, huffing a little as she padded to the living room entrance and saw the open book on the couch.

"What you busy doing?"

Rachel thought fast. "Finishing up some paper work for Representative Hodge. You know I volunteer there regularly. He's trying to obtain some state park funds to help build the overlook along the river next year."

"That river bank thing won't amount to anything. You might as well forget that," Alice predicted. "You're wasting your time spending all those hours in Hodge's office. You just must like being around him. I have to admit he's still pretty good looking."

"It's another community service job, like some of the others I perform in the city."

Don't let her trap you, Rachel thought.

"Not as I see it. You spend more time with him."

"Is Tim doing all right? You still should let me sign him up for the noon lunches."

"He's doing okay. Here's the rent," Alice said, shoving a bundle of crumpled bills into Rachel's hand as she passed her on the way back to the front door.

"When you get a little free time for your family, remind me to tell you how our apartment, which we are paying that much for, has a laundry tub is the basement that's dripping and the back screen door has a rip in it again. Of course, you're pretty busy taking care of everybody else."

* * *

July, 1984

The phone call in the middle of the night on a weekend awakened Hooper and his wife in their Garland apartment. Terror flooded his mind.

Why do tragedies always prey on people in the middle of the night, he thought, fearing the worst as he reached for the telephone beside the bed. The glowing face of the clock on the night stand showed 3:20 a.m. It was a hysterical voice on the phone, Aimee screaming something about her husband, Jerry.

"Hold on, calm down," he said, springing to an upright position on the bed. "I can't understand you."

"Jerry's dead, Daddy," his daughter's voice caught, sobbed again, before struggling with the words, "I found him on the bathroom floor. Oh, Daddy, please come. Hurry, Daddy."

"Are you all right? Anyone with you?"

"I called the police. Hurry, Daddy."

Hooper laid his hand gently on his wife's shoulder, saw that her eyes were open in the gloom and recognized her paralyzing fear. "We have to get dressed and go to Aimee,"he said. "There's a problem." Hooper did not want to tell her yet. Not yet.

"Has there been an accident?" she asked, throwing the sheet slowly away from her and sitting up unsteadily on the side of the bed.

"Yes," he answered.

"Is Aimee hurt?" she asked, twisting to look at him, her nightgown falling off her shoulders.

She's such a lovely and fragile lady, Hooper thought, regarding his wife tenderly. I wish I could spare her this. "It's Jerry. We have to hurry."

Hooper walked around the end of the bed, took her hand to pull her to her feet, and wrapped his arms around her. She held to him tightly a moment before he led her to the closet. "Don't worry about what you wear, dear, just put on something."

She stood dazed momentarily, still struggling to pull out of the cotton-like insulation of sleep.

"Where are we going?" she asked. What will we find, she

246

wondered?

Two empty patrol cars with flashing lights were parked at the curb of their former house when Hooper and his wife arrived. It reminded him of the night they had been firebombed there.

From the glow of their house, probably every light was turned on. The yellowish light reflected on a gathering of neighbors who stood on the front walk and in the yard, wondering what had stricken the family. But tragedies were not uncommon at night in the Black community, particularly on a hot July night.

"Hooper," several low voices called as neighbors recognized him. "What happened?" asked an older woman who had been one of Aimee's baby sitters.

"Don't know yet. Aimee called us. We don't know any details."

"Is she all right? How about Jerry?"

"We think she's all right. Don't know about Jerry."

Hooper propelled his wife through the small gathering. He did not want to stop and talk. He was impatient, wanting to get to Aimee. He did not like the irritation he felt at these friends who would unintentionally delay them.

At the front door, which again was a reminder of the bombing, a patrol officer took quick steps toward them as they started to enter.

"You can't come in here," said the stiff young officer, taking the voice and stance of authority.

"Get out of our way."

"It's all right. Let them in." The voice came from a plain-clothes detective just inside the living room. The young officer dropped back. "Hello, Commissioner," the detective said. "Your daughter's been wanting you."

Hooper and his wife walked the short distance down the hall to Aimee's old room. She sat up on what had been her bed as a teenager. Sobs racked her as she held out her arms and waited for them to cross to her.

"Baby, my baby," her mother said as she dropped on the bed and grabbed Aimee. Hooper wrapped his arms around both of them, leaning down protectively. They let her cry and waited until the body-jerking sobs eased.

"We're here. We're here for you," Hooper said.

"I didn't even know he had any of the stuff," Aimee said, reaching for the pocket of her robe where she had wadded some damp tissues. Her mother grabbed up some fresh ones from a box on the bedside table, and handed them to her.

"He said he was going out to get some cigarettes and he was gone awhile. He was happy when he got back, so I felt good about it. I didn't even think of drugs. Not till he started acting crazy and out of his head. Before that, he was excited about work coming up next week."

"Wasn't he working? Did he lose that last job again?" Hooper asked.

"We didn't want to tell you until he had work," Aimee explained, the repressed sobs threatening to erupt again.

"How about you? You doing drugs?" her mother asked timidly.

"I'm not, Mom. Daddy. Believe me." Aimee's eyes searched their faces, wanting reassurance. "I never got into any of the strong stuff. Just some marijuana, and everybody did that."

"What was Jerry on?" Hooper tried not to sound too severe. He did not want to throw his daughter more off balance emotionally.

"Probably, coke. That's what he was into before. But I told him if he didn't get out of it, I'd leave him," Aimee sobbed again, recalling their violent disagreements.

"But I probably wouldn't have left him." Aimee clutched her parents tightly, needing their strength to get her through the coming days and weeks.

Jerry's death was the fourth drug overdose in the city that year. It was the second overdose that same weekend.

Police speculated a bad batch of cocaine was traded for cash at the Kentucky border, and ended up in their community.

The local newspaper targeted Hooper's family the next day with the headline, **"Drug Overdose Hits City Commissioner's Family."**

No mention was made in the newspaper that a second victim to die that weekend of a drug overdose was a Garland police officer.

Both obituaries appeared in the newspaper the same day. Information on the officer said the cause of death was "still pending".

* * *

September, 1984

Rachel had slipped into a depressed state that left her listless, impatient, and dissatisfied with any activity she sought to fill the void.

She could not tell Douglas about her feelings. She did not complain to him in their letters or telephone conversations, but Rachel knew she was not coping well. That was very unlike her, not like the Rachel who had stood alone and unbending these many years now.

So what am I? Just a wimp, feeling sorry for myself?, she chided herself. Douglas's letters, bundles of them over the years, became even more of a crutch for her.

She should not have allowed herself to become so dependent, she realized, but it was the primary method to stay in contact with him. They were sharing less and less time together. Their moments alone had to compete with his state legislative duties and increasing unrest at the Garland steel mill.

One particularly low day after Rachel left Douglas's regional office - he had not had time to come into the district for the second time - Rachel grabbed up several packets of dated letters, poured herself a glass of white wine, and headed in the late afternoon for a shaded lawn chair in her backyard.

She considered the letters a treasure. Many of them she had not re-read over the years. New ones were always arriving in her post office box. Through the written words, she now began reliving their years together. So many years, so many moments, and yet so little time together.

What memories, Rachel thought, when she unfolded a letter from him in response to one she had written years ago when she was thinking of ending what they had between then. It was when she was traumatized by Marty's mental sickness and her guilt feelings for having him committed to the state hospital. She was overwhelmed by feeling responsible for the tragedy in their marriage.

"Certainly my dilemma is one of feeling that I am a problem, rather than a help and a crutch," Douglas had written. "Regardless of my circumstances, you have been a great satisfaction to me. I now realize that I have turned to you many times for advice and support.

"Right now, you don't need this extra burden even though since I first met you, I have placed more trust and dependence in you than most anyone I can think of. That is what looking yonder and missing yesterday has been all about for me. You have been an outlet, a crutch, a comfort and so many other things....The Almighty did not place us on this earth to punish us. If that were the case, then our entire existence would be a farce."

The closing was always "LYMY" for "Love you miss you." You have been such strength for me, she thought, folding the pages back together. Who else has ever helped me so much, or cared about helping me?

Still another letter. "Was thinking about how apprehensive you are about the future and that 1978 was not a good year. It occurred to me that perhaps this might help. This thought just popped out and several people thought it was pretty good. Will now expose it to my most severe critic. What occurred to me was that no matter how severe or painful the thought of tomorrow's problems might be, they will pass and become part of the past. So, no matter how bad things might be, time solves the problem in one way or the other. So much for today's philosophy."

She savored paragraphs from the past, "Keep well and stay your warm delightful, wonderful self. You will be in my thoughts constantly, and the days will be brighter, except for the ache."

Rachel read page after page. The wine glass was empty. Dusk was approaching. She remained melted into the lawn chair pouring over the words he had written to her. So many letters, so many, dozens, some slipping off her lap and onto the ground.

"Thought you might be back here."

The unexpected high-pitched voice of Alice stunned Rachel, causing her to jump and her hand to grab at her lap to keep the last of the letters from falling to the ground.

With quick, evidently painless steps belying her arthritis, Alice swooped up a handful of the spilled papers, backing away then as her eyes scanned the pages.

"Hand those here, hand them here right now," Rachel commanded and she stood and rushed toward her sister.

"Ha, love letters," Alice chortled, backing away. "I always thought ya had somebody."

"You have no right, Alice. Give those to me. Of course they're not love letters." Rachel scoffed as she grabbed for the sheets. She fortunately could move a little faster than her sister, and jerked hard when her hand grasped them. A couple of sheets tore. Alice twisted away, pulling the document closer to her face.

"LYMY. What does that mean? It's certainly not a name."

Rachel at the same time said, "Look what you've done!" She grabbed again and rescued now what were scraps of paper.

"What ya trying to hide. It's all right for people to have love letters," Alice was taunting now to find out whatever she could. "Of course who ya trying to hide might be the question here."

"I told you they are not what you think." Rachel hurriedly folded the sheets, collecting them into a bundle that required both of her trembling hands to hold it together. "Now I don't know what you want here, but I don't much appreciate you surprising me in my backyard like this."

"I rang the damn door bell, but ya can never hear the thing. What am I supposed to do?" Alice dropped into the lawn chair where Rachel had been sitting. "I just wanted to stop by and tell ya I'm ready to sign Tim up for the noon carry-in meals. And here I find ya mooney eyed reading your old letters. Who is it? Whose the guy?"

"Alice, I'm not going to have this. You just leave now."

"Looks like ya had a little wine too. Or was it a lot of wine."

"Goodbye, Alice, I don't appreciate you coming here and

acting like this. How I live here alone is my business, and if I have letters from someone, that's my business, too."

"Oh, if I think long enough I'll know who it is. Maybe it's that bar guy, that McIntosh. Nah. He's too much of a lush. Unless you go for that kind of thing, with your appreciation of wine and all."

"Did you hear what I said. I want you to leave." Rachel stood as tall as she could, loomed over her sister with her hands full of the letters. She dared not set them down. Alice would grab them up again.

Hawkishly watching Rachel's face, Alice thumped her fingers slowly on the arms of her chair.

"Then I always thought you spent a lot of time with that Hodge guy, working on his committees and campaign, and all."

"You're just fishing to try to come up with something. I've had enough of this."

Rachel turned to walk into her house. She planned to lock her door and just ignore Alice.

"That's who it is then, ain't it, that Hodge representative. You can't fool your sister. I can't wait to get home an tell Tim. He'll love sharing that with his old cronies at the barber shop."

Rachel stopped. She did not turn back. She did not want Alice to see what she surely felt must be her very flushed face. A give away.

"Why are you doing this, Alice. You are deliberately trying to hurt me."

"Hurt ya. Why my dear you don't know what that means. You've always had everything ya wanted. How did that make me feel?"

"What are you talking about. None of that had anything to do with the way you've been acting. I'm going in now. Let's just forget this."

"Forget. No way. This is the juiciest gossip I've had in a long time." said Alice, chuckling.

"An I'm gonna share the wealth. Rachel Bradford and Hodge. Is it Ken? No, Douglas is his first name. People are gonna love it."

Tears were very near for Rachel.

She had to end the mounting terror she felt. So long, so very long Alice had wrestled for control of her in many ways. Now it was like a vise tightening on her.

"Alice, you wouldn't do this?"

"My girl, of course I would."

* * *

CHAPTER TWENTY ONE

The world closed in on Rachel. Fearing to struggle against Alice's grip because of the potential backlash against Douglas, she cloistered her life.

Rachel's immediate reaction after Alice's visit was to collect Douglas' letters from the desk and attic, and store them in a bank safe deposit box. She thought long about where to hide the key, and finally decided on the secret compartment in her mahogany desk.

She was surprised, relieved, yet apprehensive that she did not hear from her sister over the next week. She determined not to be the first to telephone, feeling it would reveal her vulnerability. The unknowing was racking, the uncertainty of how her sister would use knowledge of the letter to hurt them. She could destroy Douglas' career, his family, and her credibility.

Feeling defenseless and at risk of exposing Douglas to scandal, she continued to write him routine letters, but stayed away from his office on various weak excuses.

He telephoned several times, "just checking up on you", he said, but never guessing from the tone of her voice or chatter that anything had changed. It has changed, perhaps forever, she feared.

Unable to concentrate on any one project for very long or find activities to keep her mind and body active, Rachel languished behind the locked doors of her home. Unable to sleep, she bought over-the-counter pills to close out the nights.

Nights were the worst times. That was when Rachel paced through the rooms of her large house, turning on lights, not seeing the furnishings or atmosphere she had created. No joy or pride. The house was only big and hollow sounding to her now. She took even more sleeping pills to help her get through the nights.

Rachel cautioned herself one evening to be very careful when she decided to go out for a late drive. You have to be very alert, pay attention and do not let your mind drift off to anything except your driving. You are vulnerable, she told herself. Be careful.

She just drove. Although knowing she should not, Rachel drove past the house where Douglas had lived years ago with his family. The exterior of the house was familiar, but she had not seen the interior.

She had known very clearly what kind of relationship she had entered into years ago. She never considered it a relationship then, or realized how much he would come to mean in her life. Over the years, she had pushed away thoughts of his wife, believing him when he said it was a sham marriage.

Rachel knew they did not live together in Columbus, but were known as husband and wife and still occasionally attended functions as a couple.

"We've missed so much together," she said aloud to herself. After passing his house, Rachel drove aimlessly through the city. Thoughts came of many people she had known, from Marty to Sonny, Tina Rose and Glenn, and Hooper. She longed for any one of them to say a word of comfort in her agonizing loneliness. But, they did not, and could not, know her need. She returned to the emptiness of her house.

Rachel convinced herself she needed to call Sonny, not to worry him, but to let him know she was all right. Lie. Lie, she told herself. She needed a comforting voice.

Just when she needed him, she could not reach him. Sonny was traveling, on the road a lot, Rachel was told by his secretary. She was assured the message would get to her son, and he would call back. He did telephone, several days later.

"Are you all right? You sound like you have a cold," Sonny asked in the long-distance telephone conversation.

"Just a sinus infection, but it's getting much better. You should have heard me yesterday," Rachel responded by misleading him, increasing the huskiness of her voice. She gave a false chuckle to let him know everything was light and upbeat.

"You sure you're all right?" Sonny repeated, then at her reassurance said, "They're really keeping me busy here, but it's great, Mom. I'm learning all the time. I'm finding the medical profession and drugs a challenge. And you can't believe all the new drugs coming on the market, or how many years it takes to get one through the testing process."

"You're not wearing yourself out traveling, and everything?" she asked.

"Actually, I like it," he said. "I'm getting to see a lot of the country. Right now I'm in Lansing, Michigan, part of my district. But they've sent me as far as Seattle and Houston for conferences. And, Mom, it's a hundred times better than being confined in a classroom."

"As long as you are happy, Son," she said. With her final pronouncement, Rachel mentally ended her obligation as a mother for the time being. It left her free to turn inward to the cocoon of her life, take a sleeping pill, and muffle the world.

* * *

Alice's face stayed blurred for several seconds as Rachel opened her eyes and looked up at her sister. Alice's body appeared to be massive rolls of fat hovering over her and undulated as she shook Rachel's to consciousness on the living room couch.

"Wake up now, wake up," Alice said in a strong voice, commanding attention. "What are you doing sleeping in the middle of the day like this? You look like you been here a week."

Awareness came slowly. Rachel, shaking, weakly resisted Alice's dictate to go upstairs immediately with her and take a shower, change clothes. Alice insisted, showing unusual concern.

She gripped Rachel's arm.

"How'd you get in here?" Rachel asked, uneasy at her sister's friendliness but allowing herself to be led up the massive wooden staircase to her room.

"Those French doors on the patio never were much good. Just one good hip punch and I was in. I could see you through the window, and you didn't answer."

"Guess I fell asleep."

"Fell asleep? How'd you let yourself get like this?" Alice's round face above Rachel was stretched smooth by her tightly bound cap of gray hair. "You've lost so much weight, I wouldn't recognize you. I didn't know you'd been sick or anything."

After a shower, Rachel gratefully took a couple of more pills Alice handed her, then eased her body slowly between the cool, slick sheets. Again, she wanted nothing to eat. But aroma of hot food later stirred Rachel awake as dusk darkened the house.

"Time for you to start eating something now to begin getting your energy back," Alice said, looming large beside Rachel's bed. "I made you some soup and brought some crackers and fruit. They'll get you started."

Rachel perched unsteadily on the edge of the bed. A fuzzy, white robe Alice found in her closet warmed her shoulders. A few sips of soup brought a comforting feeling, but Rachel had nothing to say to her sister. Alice was intruding.

"Now I want you to take another little pill to help you relax."

"Didn't I take something before?"

"It's just one of my own nerve pills. See how little it is, but it'll help you."

"I don't want medicine."

"Just try it. I take them all the time for my nerves, and they can't hurt you."

Rachel took several more spoons full of the soup, then laid back on the bed in a fetal position, pulled the sheet over her again.

"That's right. You get a good night's sleep now, and you'll be all better in the morning," Alice said. "Tim's coming over to spend the night with us, and we'll look after you."

"I don't want you to do that. I don't want you here, not after what you said," Rachel mumbled.

"Why, Hon, do you think I'd do anything about them letters? I was just angry I guess. Don't you fret about that." Alice's voice was fading away. "Here now, take the pill."

Not convinced of Alice's words, but relinquishing any responsibility for her own care, Rachel took the pill and washed it down with sips of water from a glass Alice handed her. Soon she was drifting off again into the oblivion where she was most comfortable.

Rachel's condition was unchanged in the next week, despite Alice and Tim moving into the house and caring for her. Mostly she spent time in her room. When she managed to come down to the living room and sit in front of the television in her fireside chair, she generally held a book, pretended to read.

The pills helped. They were served up by Alice three times a day now, two little white, oblong pills at a time. Her sister was generously sharing her own "nerve-pill" prescription, plus a second one she had gotten for Rachel from her own doctor. Rachel could sit for hours now facing the television, no longer shamming the act of reading, indifferent to what she was seeing or hearing.

Her mind was less frantic. She sometimes thought of Douglas. He became blurred. She did not remember when he had last called. She was not told that Douglas' secretary had come to the house personally to inquire about her, and was told she was fighting a virus.

"What's wrong with me?" Rachel asked her sister in one of her more lucid moments. It was almost time for more pills. She was anxious for them.

"You just wore yourself out, that's all. It'll take a little time to get back to normal."

Rachel watched placidly on the days Alice carried paper bags of groceries into the house. Her sister's quick steps and easy handling of the bags denied the arthritic pain she often claimed.

Maybe the pills are helping her, too, Rachel thought in her listless state. From her chair in the living room, Rachel could see into the kitchen where Tim sat on a high kitchen-counter stool and helped unload the bags. His obese condition would not allow more effort than that, Rachel was aware, but she felt no compulsion to help them.

"You don't mind if our girls come over for dinner tonight? I thought not," Alice asked, coming out of the kitchen to question Rachel in front of the television.

Rachel forgot what she answered. It did not matter.

The daughters, their husbands and children were in and out of the house often after that. Rachel stayed more and more in her room, in a fuzzy fog most of the time. She wondered if her son was all right. He had not called, at least she did not know if he had.

From the window of her room, where she often sat in a chair staring down at the street, Rachel one day saw a woman drive up to the curb, come to the front door and leave moments later.

She puzzled over it briefly, then realized the woman was one of her renters. Come to pay her rent, Rachel guessed. What time of the month was it? Was it the first again, when rents were due? She wondered about the rest of them. I'm not handling things very well. Have to talk to Alice, she thought.

Rachel walked slowly down the stairs, holding to the railing. Be careful, she told herself. You're not yourself. You could fall. Alice was in the kitchen, apparently putting something in her handbag, which she laid back on top of the refrigerator.

"The lady at the door." Rachel could not remember her name. "She came to pay rent?"

"That's right," Alice said, bustling solicitously across the room to steady Rachel as she sat down on a counter stool. "You know you're not well. Have to be careful going up and down stairs alone anymore."

"The lady and the rent?"

"It's okay. Tim and me are taking care of everything for you. We know you been sick, and we're just going to handle things like you was doing it yourself."

"What's the matter with me, Alice?"

"You had a breakdown, the doctor said." Alice rested her heavy buttocks against the counter in front of Rachel, folded her arms under her melon breasts and looked intently down at Rachel as if to say it's time for you to know.

"I don't remember seeing a doctor. What happened?" Rachel asked, trying to sort memories through the medication controlling her mind.

"You must have had some kind of tragedy, or something that set you off. I guess you rejected whatever it was and it made you sick," Alice said in a soothing voice. "Tim and me have been trying to help, but it's been a burden you know, with neither of us feelin' as good as we should."

The urge to resist stirred in Rachel, but it was so easy to coast. There was something she wanted to ask Alice.

She remembered what it was later that evening - the rent money, the woman had brought the money. When Rachel asked Alice about it at bedtime, when her sister brought the pills to her room, Alice was not as sympathetic.

"I told you Tim and me are looking after you. We have to buy groceries, and your medication. How you expect us to live?"

Rachel did not want to drive Alice away, knew she needed someone. She was not her physical or mental self just now, but the whereabouts of her rent money stirred her business instincts.

She puzzled a long time the next day, trying to think who it was that could help her find out what was happening, and realized it was Sonny. It was a long, slow, and dizzy process down the stairs to the kitchen again, but the effort was a failure when she could not find her address book with his telephone number.

"What are you doing up?" Alice asked brusquely when she entered the kitchen to find an unsteady Rachel searching through counter drawers.

"I want to call Sonny, but I can't find my address book."

"What do you want to call him for. We keep him posted about what the doctor's saying. You'll only worry him if you call in the state you're in now. Look at you." Alice's shaggy, gray eyebrows pulled together in a fierce frown.

Rachel did feel weak and confused. "I won't worry him. I just want to talk."

"Well, we'll have none of this. Look how shaky you are. Here set down." Alice grabbed Rachel's arm roughly and forced her down on one of the counter stools. "Looks to me like you need your nerve medicine early." She walk to the sink and jerked open a door above it, took out a bottle of pills.

"I don't need the medicine," Rachel said, her voice trembling.

"Look who says," Alice shot back. "You have to know that you're making it difficult for us to take care of you any longer. Your breakdown's making it difficult on the whole family."

"All I said was I don't want medicine right now."

"You keep this up, Missy, and you'll find yourself over in the Cedar Grove nursing home. Don't think we haven't checked it out."

Rachel was stunned. Devastated. Vulnerable. She fought tears, not wanting Alice to see.

"I don't need a nursing home. I have my own home." Rachel tried unsuccessfully, wanting to show her strength. "You can't force me to go there. I won't go." Then her will collapsed. Vivid images washed over her of the mental institution in Columbus long ago.

"You're punishing me aren't you? Doing to me what I had to do to Marty - locking me up. You're putting me in the institution, aren't you?"

Alice's cunning latched onto this latest weapon of Rachel's fear. "Why, Honey, no. Never that. And I'm not saying that is what we're gonna do. I just said we've had to look into it. Now, come on, take these two little pills to feel more relaxed."

Hesitantly, Rachel reached for the pills. Watching Alice closely, she put them in her mouth, drank the water she was handed.

The little pills came regularly during the next week and despite the lack of mental pressure she felt, Rachel's guilt grew along with her dim realization that she was turning her life over to Alice. There was less communication with the world outside her room now - she no longer was led downstairs to watch television, she had no access to newspapers, and she even lacked the diversion of a radio in her room. Sleep when she could, that was the best.

Thoughts kept nagging her, though, and sometimes she remembered what it was - rent money. Remembering seeing the woman bring the rent money to the house that day, Rachel in lucid moments sat by the window and watched the street beyond the sculptured shrubs and green lawn below.

Sometimes it was pleasant just gazing, even if no one arrived with rent.

Her vapid stare was nudged into awareness when an unfamiliar car pulled up and parked on the street in front of her house. It's not Alice, her car is in the driveway, Rachel thought. She watched with apathy as a man stepped out of the far side of the car. He was not a renter she recognized.

When the man, with a cap partly hiding his face, came around behind the vehicle and stepped onto the curb, Rachel noticed the way he favored his left leg in shifting his weight. Something is wrong with his leg, she realized with indifference. She watched him take a few steps up the walk, caught a glimpse of his profile as he glanced up toward the house and the realization jarred her that it was Marty.

No, not Marty. He had gone back to Kentucky. Leaning closer to the window pane now, hypnotized by the approaching figure, Rachel knew with certainty it was Marty.

* * *

September, 1984

Douglas' slow-moving car edged some of the mass of angry steelworkers off the darkened driveway as he approached the union hall in a search for a place to park.

His anger matched theirs, because he had driven past Rachel's house and had lacked the nerve to go up and knock on her door. Her absence from the office for over a month, and her lack of letters for several weeks, worried him. The soft-glowing lights in her house and the cars in the driveway, gave him some slight reassurance that she was all right. If he did not hear from her when he was in his Garland office the following Thursday, he would storm her house personally with his secretary.

Tonight's mood also was darkened by the fact Douglas knew he faced a hassle. He had willingly agreed to drive down from Columbus at the union president's frantic request to meet with some of the incensed steel workers, but he'd be damned if he would park a half mile from the hall.

Tempers were too explosive for him to be walking about in an angry crowd by himself. There was too much anger and unrest over the pending Japanese partial take-over of the mill - some vandalism, isolated fist fights between pro and con adversaries, and even one stabbing.

Cars were scattered in a jumble as far as Douglas could see, but he was determined to park as close to the union hall door as possible. The space he settled on meant double parking and allowing his car to extend partly into the driveway, but it would have to serve, he decided.

The mob of people milling outside the hall undoubtedly included all the hundreds of MVS laborers who were not working the evening shift. Douglas surveyed the multitude of shadowy faces, rustic steelworkers who looked his way when he stepped from his car.

Hundreds of sour, frowning workers were huddled together in all directions, smoking, talking in low voices berating the company, shuffling, shifting, swearing and spitting.

What could he say to settle down a teeming pack like this, Douglas wondered. He had not reached any conclusions to that question during his drive from Columbus to Garland.

"It's the politician," said one of the workers, recognizing Douglas. "Come down to give us some advice? Bet that's all you'll give us", the man jeered with twisting mouth. "We're sure need something more than that, or else we're gonna have to beat them Japs a second time."

"I don't know what can be done, but I'm here to talk to your officers," Douglas said, moving through the crowd toward the entrance to the union headquarters. Some of the men he recognized, shook hands with them, slapped them on the back. Others he faced with a smile, hoping it evidenced confidence and calmness.

Douglas almost choked from the smoke when he finally squeezed his way through the pack of men jamming the doorway.

There seemed to be no circulation in the room. The blue-gray cloud hung from the ceiling like some frothy school-prom decoration. The rapid puffing of the many smokers in the packed hall continued to escalate the offensive mass. Douglas' eyes stung, but he identify the union president standing a head taller than anyone else in the room and headed in his direction through the solid tide of bodies, thundering voices and odors.

"We've been waiting for you," said the president, "Shorty" Walburn. "Some of the guys said you'd never be here, but we proved 'em wrong, didn't we."

Walburn pulled Douglas by his arm through the crowd and into his office to fill him in on details of the Japanese take over.

"They sold us out," Walburn said of MVS. "They sold off nearly half, but not quite, of the company. But you know what's gonna happen? We're gonna have squint-eyes around here telling us what to do. An, you can bet, these union guys, many of them World War Two veterans, are not gonna take it."

Douglas was well aware how the community had experienced convulsions of the steel mill's down-sizing in recent years, its massive layoffs and staff reductions through attrition. All had major impacts on Garland, but nothing compared to the emotions now aroused over the Japanese firm buying into MVS to keep it solvent. But he realized it was only a small percentage of the workers and townspeople that might be capable of triggering violence.

"Our mill's not unique," Douglas reminded Walburn when they were alone in his cluttered, paper-littered office. "Steel companies throughout the country are barely surviving because of production problems. Many have already gone down."

"This company may, too. An it'll all be because they brought in the Japanese," the union president predicted.

"Is that what some of your members want, for the company to fail, just to get even?" Douglas asked.

"Course not. Hey, we're just taking a stand to let the company know we don't like it. But there's some pretty rough guys out there. You don't know what they'll do. Most of them still have the rifles and shotguns they brought with them out of Kentucky."

Walburn knew that for a fact, because he was one of them. "Man, I never thought it'd be like this, being union president."

"What the men have to realize is the company is just trying to stay in business. It's lost money the last six years."

Douglas wondered if talking to Walburn were useless, if his words were having any impact. "What kept the company going this long was its farsightedness in the past in putting in building, new facilities, investing millions. But some of the equipment is getting obsolete now, and the company can't continue unless it upgrades. You can't do that without making money."

"Well, will you talk to the guys, just say something?"

Douglas was right, Walburn had not followed his reasoning.

The union boss had a slump to his shoulders that now appeared to have shortened his giant frame by several inches. "I think they won't go home tonight unless something changes."

"I don't know what I'll say, but I'll talk to them. Not in that hall, though. Get me something to stand on, a microphone and some lights. We'll move it outside."

The shuffling crowd fell silent as Douglas stepped onto a concrete railing, faced into a parking-lot street light, ready to address the men.

"Do we have to fight the Jap war again, huh, Hodge?" shouted one of the men.

"He's not going to do nothing for us," another thick, male voice said as the crowd silenced to listen. "Get him down."

"Friends and union members," Douglas began when he felt the time was ripe. "I don't have a great sense of pleasure in being here tonight as a great American enterprise becomes internationalized."

A few boos were heard, but the mass again fell silent "We are here because this company has changed ownership so that the United States and Japan are now partners in this venture. For many of us who fought in World War II to maintain freedom in the world, who remember President Roosevelt's word when he stated that the attack on Pearl Harbor was a day that would live in infamy, the economic victories that are being won by our former rival are against those ideals.

"But I must remind all of us that General Douglas MacArthur, who survived Bataan and returned to liberate the

Philippines, who was assigned the responsibility of being the military commander of Japan once peace was declared, saw that his first responsibilities were the maintenance of peace, the restoration of a war torn country, writing a constitution based upon our own standards, and rebuilding the economy of that nation that had been dedicated to war and aggression.

"Resistance to his policies were non-existent in part because the Japanese nation was weary of war, devastated by the dropping of two atom bombs, and most important, by the trial and execution of those who had led the terrible campaigns of aggression and cruelty. The Japanese war criminals were now only sentences in the books of history."

Loud shouts interrupted Douglas's words.

"What are you getting at?" one man shouted. "Get on with it," another said, "you sound like you're on their side."

"Hear me out," Douglas asked, his words over the microphone increasing in volume to reach those at the rear of the restless crowd.

"Many of you know I fought in the war. I'm saying now it's difficult for us today to realize we must look at a new and different Japan. While their standards, culture and outlook may be different than ours, thanks to General MacArthur, Japan is now a democratic nation, stripped of its military. It has entered the new industrial world of today."

Jeers rose from some crowd members, angry shouts of "Not here. We don't want it here", while other workers urged loudly, "Let him talk."

"We have to face the fact," Douglas continued, "that competition is no longer the store next door, the other steel companies, or Ford versus General Motors. What is important is that we hold the export of jobs from the United States to other countries to a minimum. The production of steel here in Garland is far better than a new plant being built in another land using non-United States labor. Our task is to maintain jobs in our land, to raise the quality of our products so that they are the best in the world, and to take pride in the United States setting the standards which the whole world recognizes as tops.

266

"If we do this, then Americans will once more be willing to invest in our future, and take the risks that we have always known would win over any competition anywhere in the world.

"And so, we must look deeper into our souls, do what is best for our nation, and win another war, the one on which the economic survival of our great nation depends."

Douglas paused, looked around at the faces of his now silent audience. They were not all in agreement, but they had listened and were thinking.

"Then one day," he concluded, "we will be able to say that the American spirit, which made us the envy of the world, won this newest conflict with brains, guts, determination and American know how, without a single battlefield casualty."

That was it, that was all the reasoning he could draw upon to convince the workers to accept this newest change invading their lives. They had to accept. The crowd waited.

"I guess the only thing left to say is the future is in our hands," Douglas felt uncertain where to go next. "In every strife this country has faced, it has endured. So in this, as in the past, God bless us."

Douglas handed the microphone to Walburn and stepped down from the concrete railing. Some hands reached to support him. A few stern-faced workers turned away.

It was when Douglas was driving his car away from Garland on the darkened two-land road toward the interstate highway back to Columbus that he noticed the car following him.

Awareness of the vehicle behind him had been slow in coming. His mind had shuttled back and forth between the confusion and inflamed workers to disappointment that he had been unable to contact Rachel during this brief trip. He would the next time, for certain.

Douglas was jarred into suspicion when the car, which had maintained a controlled distance behind him since they left the lights of Garland, accelerated abruptly as if to pass at a high rate of speed.

When the vehicle zoomed past Douglas' car, a bullet struck the front windshield, startling him and causing him to veer to the right side of the road. The wheels caught on the edge of the elevated blacktop and he was unable to swerve back onto the roadway. He lost control.

The wheels skidded in the soft ground along the road, then spun off to the right as Douglas' car went over the embankment and rolled down a steep hillside to land on its top. The windshield shattered and shards of glass spread out over the deep greenery at the foot of the hill. Evidence was destroyed. No one ever knew, ever suspected that a bullet hole had led to the accident.

Hours later, at Garland City Hospital,
Douglas Hodge was pronounced dead
Of multiple injuries from the traffic accident.

Rachel, in her panic and drug-inducted state, was not aware that Douglas died on the same evening Marty had returned as a threat in her life.

She cowered in her room, fearful that Marty had arrived in Garland at Alice's request to help commit her to the state mental hospital.

She sensed Marty would relish the act of revenge. Rachel remembered his whispered words the last time she saw him, "You'll get yours, Bitch."

While Rachel was oblivious to the closing of Douglas' life over the next five days - the praising and honoring eulogies, impressive memorial ceremonies both in Garland and Columbus, and the numerous emotional pictures taken at the public functions of his grieving wife and daughters - Rachel's numbed mind was searching for her own survival.

Marty's back, she realized, shrinking more into herself. His car would be in front of her house one day, and gone the next, but it always returned. He's coming back into my house. Rachel flinched at the thought. Alice is letting him in. But Alice hates steel workers. She always said stay away from steel men. What are they doing together? What are they trying to do? They're going to take me away!

The house remained very quiet. Even when Rachel crept awkwardly to her bedroom door one afternoon and opened it to hear voices, trying to confirm Marty was downstairs, there was only silence. Rachel waited, trying to come up with a plan, but where was the help for her? She could not contact Douglas for fear of involving him.

Alice continued to carry her meals up to her, and deliver the little pills three times a day. The nursing home threat was repeated periodically, "Take your pills now, or you know what...."

"They're not helping me."

"Sure they are, and that way you can stay right here in your own home. Take 'em." Alice shoved the glass at her and waited while she took sips. "Looks like we may have to get some hired help in here. Caring for the house, the lawn and all, is a little much."

When Alice heard Rachel's bedroom floor squeak one day and confirmed her suspicion that her sister was moving around her room more, Alice sneaked up the back stairs and caught Rachel standing in her open bedroom doorway.

"What you doing out of bed?" Alice bellowed, grabbing Rachel by the arm and leading her stumbling back to her rumpled bed. "You're just trying to speed up everything, ain't you. Do you want to go to the hospital tomorrow, how about today?"

"I thought I heard someone," Rachel answered timidly, although she had only listened for voices and had heard no one. "Is someone else in the house?"

"Get under them covers until you get better. Nobody here you don't know about."

"But it's so lonely here by myself, and quiet..." Rachel thought to test her sister, "....except for the strange man's voice I thought I heard."

Alice roughly raised one of Rachel's arms until she could pull the sheet up to her chin with the other hand, and then dropped her arm. All the time Alice was plotting. A radio in the bedroom might give Rachel some diversion and prevent her from hearing any talks with Marty when he came to bring her share of the rent money in the future, she thought.

Alice was aware of Douglas' death and had ruled the letters out as a threat now. If there had been anything between her sister and the politician, Alice realized it had little importance now.

269

Rachel also had less chance now of learning about Douglas, because all the news stories about him had ended days ago. When somebody is dead, they are forgotten, Alice reasoned. Yes, a radio would serve a good purpose.

* * *

The news broadcast that brought Rachel back to near awareness came at 6 p.m. several days later when the commentator spoke about a replacement to fill the vacancy caused by the "recent death of State Representative Douglas Hodge."

Rachel struggled to be alert, to overcome the lessening effects of the noon drugs. She tried to follow the details of "how the late Representative Hodge's political party was considering who should be appointed to the post".

She waited, hardly breathing, to hear more words about "death."

The news segment ended with a brief statement about how Douglas had "died of injuries suffered in a traffic accident after attending an emotionally-explosive meeting at the Miami Valley Steel Mill in Garland".

Rachel remained motionless a long time, mentally tuning out other words and music that followed on the radio. She tuned out her surroundings, going in her mind to her lover's side, feeling the grip of his hand over hers, looking up into his dark eyes and seeing every feature of his dear face that she had held in her thoughts for many, many years.

Long into the night, long after Alice had found her curled numbly on her side and forced the nerve pills on her, Rachel relived their moments together that she had treasured as the riches of her life. She resisted, wanting to stay in the past, but the pills carried her even farther away into silent nothingness.

* * *

CHAPTER TWENTY TWO

Daylight's brightness aroused Rachel from her stupor and to the realization that Douglas was gone. He had left her world without either of them saying a word, without a farewell.

She lay listlessly on the bed, her initial escapism of the night before slowly evolving into an emotional awakening that brought anger and terror at a future ahead without him.

Her body began reacting, rising off the bed, her hands lifting and softly striking the bed on either side of her, the tears releasing as the hits increased into pounding and pounding as she leaned forward over her knees and wept for Douglas. No sounds again in her crying, as she had learned years ago in the farmhouse while watching the agonized twisting of the wind-whipped grape leaves outside her bedroom window. She felt that agony now, that wringing of her thoughts, body and her very soul.

After a lost, indeterminate time, awareness came to Rachel, her mind more clear since most of the nerve drug had worn off during the night, that she was vulnerable if Alice entered with her morning breakfast tray. She must not be found this way, she realized. Slowly, thoughts of her safety forcing her, Rachel crawled to the side of the bed and began inching her way awkwardly toward the bathroom. Put a wet cloth on your eyes, she told herself, do not make Alice aware you have been crying. She may tell Marty. Then what might they do to me?

Still in the bathroom twenty minutes later, Rachel heard her bedroom door open and heavy footfalls as Alice entered the room. She was on schedule with the breakfast tray, Rachel realized, glancing again at her face in the mirror.

"Come on out now. I have your food," Alice said toward the

direction of the closed bathroom door.

"I'll be out in a minute." Rachel patted a little more makeup on the circles under her eyes, which still showed the redness of tears. I'll keep my eyes down and blame it on a bad night, she thought, but, no, it was from tears, tears for Douglas. The fact that he was dead swept over her again.

"What you doing in there? You all right?" Alice asked, suddenly knocking viciously on the door.

Silence, then, "I'm coming." Rachel opened the door and shuffled slowly across the room to her chair by the window. She looked at the floor as she steadied herself by touching the end of the bed, the edge of the bureau and the chair itself as she sat down.

"I think you get slower every day," Alice grumbled. "We may even have to think of getting you a wheel chair to speed you up."

"I don't need that."

"Well you need something." Alice set the tray on the table beside Rachel's chair. "Take a bite of this toast, then I'll give you the pills," she said, indicating the two white objects she had picked up from a napkin on the tray and was holding in the damp-looking palm of her hand.

"Just leave them, I'll take them."

"No such thing. I'll wait until you get a bite of food in you and see that you take them. Can't have you backsliding on us now and getting worse." Alice shoved the piece of cold toast at Rachel, stood impatiently while she took a bite and chewed it, then Alice reached for Rachel's palm.

"See, that wasn't so bad, was it," Alice said after Rachel tentatively picked up the pills from her hand with two fingers, put them in her mouth and took a drink of water. "Eat up now and I'll be back for your tray shortly." Alice padded heavily toward the door and closed it behind her.

Rachel realized she had to eat to get her energy back. She eyed the cereal, toast and fruit in front of her and knew she must force herself to eat all of it. Before she started, however, Rachel reached under her tongue and removed the soft blob of the pills.

* * *

Over the next several days as Rachel remained a recluse in her room, she continued to remove pills from her mouth that Alice gave her, ate all the food brought to her and watched out her window for the car she had seen Marty parking regularly in front of her house.

Strength and a clear mind had returned after several days, her body was rid of the residual of the drugs, but Rachel continued to portray an invalid when her sister was in the room. Alice was the only person she encountered during the days, and it was easy to put on the act when meals were delivered.

The confrontation was coming, and soon Rachel realized, as she continued to build her energy and resolve.

Rachel was ready the morning she saw the car already parked on the street below. She had not seen it arrive, but that mattered little. Marty was downstairs and she had to face him - face them all - alone.

Rachel stood at the top of the stairs. She could not hear voices. Straightening her shoulders, placing one of her hands on the glossy, wooden banister, she began her descent.

Alice, Tim and Marty were seated at the kitchen counter on tall stools when Rachel opened the swinging door slightly and glanced in. They were having coffee.

"We'll have to figure out some plan to have all the money sent or delivered to one place the first of each month," Marty was saying. "There was just too much running around this time."

"Nobody knew things had changed, that different people are in charge," Alice explained as an excuse. "We'll get it organized."

"I don't think so," Rachel said in a strong voice, swinging open the door and entering. She stood away from the door with her hands behind her back, like a teacher ready to pounce on a room full of unruly children.

"What the hell," Marty jumped to his feet, jarring the counter and overturning his cup of coffee. "You said she was crazy and confined to her bed. A vegetable, you said...."

Although mentally quivering, Rachel commanded herself to

273

be strong. *Attach, attack, before they can attack you*, she thought.

"You can see I'm not crazy or confined to bed," Rachel said challengingly, walking forward with a firm, strong tread.

"You're not able to be down here..." Alice stammered, her face flushing red as she scooted her stool backwards in a grating sound on the hardwood floors. "I've been caring for you. I know how weak you are. How did you get down....."

"Obviously you are mistaken" Rachel said sharply. Her hands behind her were trembling, but she willed her fragility toward strength. Her stance forced her chin up and shoulders back, giving her the appearance of determination and control. She felt none of those characteristics. But she was more confident from the fact they had not detected her weaknesses.

Marty shoved his stool away and started toward her, as Tim cowered away.

"We should not have done this," Tim said, his round, pasty face scowling. Alice, ignored his remark, remained frozen with her mouth partly open.

Resisting the urge to step back as Marty approached, testing her, Rachel watched him move closer with his limping-gait, never taking her eyes from his face, expecting him to raise his arm to strike her. She gripped her hands together tightly to disguise their trembling. She was prepared to let him strike her, just to show she was not afraid.

"What are you going to do, Marty, **hurt me?** Are you going to **cut me** again? Do you have your **knives** with you?"

She took him by surprise by going on the attack.

Startled, Marty stopped abruptly, his plastic artificial leg squeaking faintly like automobile brakes grinding to a halt.

The grating sound was a trigger that brought back Rachel's memories of the past life they had shared - Marty's fear of the steel mill, the railroad accident, and her quest for more real estate that had brought them all to this present-day greed.

There also was another powerful memory of a knife as she sensed he was ready to make a motion toward her.

"You realize if you lay one finger on me, you will spend the rest of your life in that institution." Rachel added in a loud, challenging voice. ***"They won't declare you cured again after you are locked up twice!"***

Marty stopped. The impact of her words was reflected in his narrowed eyes and the tightness of his lips.

"All you have to do is lay one hand on me, and they'll lock you up. Is it worth it?" Rachel held Marty's gaze. She gained strength.

"I'm not afraid of you anymore, Marty. I think you know that. And I think you realize there's nothing you can gain here." Rachel had enough confidence now to turn from Marty and glare at Alice. "None of you can gain anything."

"Who said I was going to hurt you?" Marty remained standing threateningly over her.

Rachel swiveled back to look at him, freezing into position, rigid as a granite statue.

Tim's voice whimpered to Alice, "Let's go back home now."

A faint tick tugged at the side of Marty's mouth. Rachel watched it again. A nervous tick signaling the retreat of his threatening, belligerent attitude.

Suddenly Marty wheeled back toward Alice and Tim, saying accusingly, "Alice told me you were sick and not able to take care of the property anymore. She said I owed it to you and Sonny to carry on and look after the apartments and houses. Hell," he looked back at Rachel, revealing something of the old Marty that had slipped away to Kentucky so many years ago, "how was I to know she was lying."

Alice's feet hit the floor with a thud as she sprang from the stool. "It wasn't all lies," Alice's words gushed breathlessly. "She was sick, and she really did have a breakdown and it was all because of that ugly, old affair...."

"Shut up, Alice," Rachel commanded, suddenly feeling she was sounding like her own sister. "You're making excuses. We all know what's been going on here. But it's over."

"I want no part of this, now that I know you're all right," Marty said, glancing first at Rachel then at the couple near the counter. "I'll let myself out the front door," he said, moving away.

"Not alone, you won't," Rachel said sternly. "No one has a

free run of my house anymore." She led him silently to the front door and opened it.

Marty started to leave, then turned back to her. "When you talk to Sonny, tell him...well, just tell him, hell, this was more than I expected to get mixed up in. I didn't plan to take anything from you."

"You mean the rent money?"

"I'll give back..."

"I don't want anything from you, Marty. I just want you out of my life." This time, Rachel did not watch sympathetically as he walked in muted-jerking steps to his car as he had years ago.

Back in the kitchen, Rachel faced her sister and Tim.

"I want you both out of here this morning," she said to the now cowering couple. "You can send one of your daughters back to pick up whatever clothing and other items you have here."

"Aren't you even going to listen to our side?" Alice began.

"Are we talking about sides here, Alice, when you tried to rob me of my health and my property?" Rachel, suddenly aware of the viciousness pouring out of her, turned away.

"It didn't seem fair that you had so much," her sister said, weakening and laying her hand on Tim's shoulder.

"And I'm going to keep it," said Rachel, fiercely voicing her independence, determined to restrain her vindictiveness, yet remembering her vow as a child never to be forced again into anything she did not want to do -such as drowning kittens. "I think you both should leave now."

Like a Terrier reluctant to let go, Alice's mood flicked from submissive to dominant. "That's the thanks we get for trying to take care of my sick sister, for taking her in years ago in the first place," Alice said venomously, reaction from knowledge that the financial security she had surreptitiously arranged for her family was fading.

"You can leave now, Alice."

"It's all going to come down on you, you know, what you been doing all these years." Alice's voice rose to a high-pitched whine. "I tried to protect you, but now it seems I'm going to have to tell Sonny. He'd like to know this juicy sick story, wouldn't he?"

"You've always done what you wanted to do anyway, Alice, but it's not going to affect me any more," Rachel said with strength of character that amazed her.

Alice recognized it too, that finality in her sister's attitude. With no more weapons, Alice yielded. "I'm asking you, though," she asked submissively, "to let Tim and me stay in the house we've been renting from you. I don't think we can make it anywhere else."

"I'll have to think about that," Rachel answered, recognizing that she would relent. "Otherwise, all this is done. We'll never mention it again."

* * *

April, 1985

Rachel was not aware of the misty rain that formed droplets and plopped off the canopy of brilliant-colored umbrellas.

She stood in a chilled, damp crowd of people on the riverbank, momentarily numb to the presence of seniors her age, young couples and children. They attempted cheerfulness, despite growing restless at the delay of the dedication ceremony

April was not the ideal month for an outdoor gathering in this steel-making town cuddled in a bend of the river. Especially not this year. The winter of 1984 proved vengeful, layering the valley in an icing of whiteness that chilled bodies and spirits.

The ground had finally emerged from under the dingy mounds of plowed snow banks, but the reluctant sun hovered in recent weeks behind dense gray clouds.

Undaunted, city officials stuck to their April date for dedication of the Great Miami River overlook where the river curved around Garland.

It was being dedicated in the name of Ohio Representative Douglas Hodge, for his volunteer leadership in the city over the years and his efforts in obtaining federal recreational funds to build the overlook.

Rachel did not feel the same chill as others who were buffeted by the stiff gusts from the river. She was engrossed in memories of the man who had been the most vital person in her life, the man who had shared her existence for so many years.

City officials viewed the overlook project as a milestone in moving beyond the steel mill setbacks and tragedies of the past. A renewed community spirit of optimism was brewing. Survival and progress were new community themes.

"Rachel." The familiar rumbling voice made her turn and watch as Hooper approached on his way to the speaker's platform.

"Glad you could make it, although nobody wants to be out in this weather." Hooper patted her elbow affectionately.

The chairman of Garland City Commission was bundled like other city officials in a raincoat over a business suit, but in contrast to their pallid faces, the richness of his cinnamon-color skin conjured images of a tropical sun. His public appeal, wide smile and genuine community concern over the years had erased all the old conflicts when he was the first black man elected to city commission.

"Did you ever think all this would happen?" Hooper asked.

"Are you talking about the overlook, or all that's happened since we've known each other?" Rachel smiled at Hooper, letting him know she was being whimsical.

"Who wants to get into all that in the past?" he asked. "Right now we're looking at the view over the river, I don't want to remember the flood. Look at all those bricks we sold to build the walkway along the riverbank over there. Now that's quite an accomplishment."

"You're right, Hooper. You should be proud."

"Not me, but we really have something to celebrate today. I'll catch up with you later," he said, moving away toward the flag-decorated platform, where he joined city officials, school board members and some minor politicians.

Douglas would have been up there, Rachel realized, her eyes moistening but not releasing tears.

Hooper, always quick to tackle disorganization, stepped purposefully to the front of the platform. Others around him checked the dampness of the folding chairs and sat down.

"It's a glorious day for the city," Hooper began, his teeth suddenly gleaming white against his brown face that was framed by his close-cropped white hair. "Well, not glorious weather wise, but certainly where progress is concerned."

Never relying on a prepared speech, Hooper plunged into describing how federal funds were used to create the overlook and dig out the new channel in the river for water sports.

Rachel glanced from under her umbrella to the river below. The dark gray sky reflected into the river as it flowed at the foot of the sloping banks.

Who would have thought the river that was such a threat only a few years ago, maybe not so few, would become a place of beauty and recreation, she reflected. Well, it probably would be beautiful if the sun would come out, she decided.

Rachel felt a touch on her shoulder and turning, faced Glenn McIntire. He leaned closer to her ear and asked, "Are we ready for another meeting of the Community Committee?"

"Almost all of us are here, and I imagine all of us are here in spirit," Rachel said not flinching at her sentimental words. Glenn's silence left her sensing her words had been more serious than he expected.

She glanced at his face, which looked fresh and healthy. He no longer had the bloated look of an excessive drinker. His outdoor work as a job superintendent with the state highway department must be good for him, Rachel concluded as they remained silent to listen to Hooper's remarks.

"This is a positive sign," Hooper was saying of the new construction, sharing his enthusiasm with the crowd. He stood tall, ignoring the heavy mist blowing in behind him from the river.

"For a time, it seemed like we only had negative headlines about our city. For years we've been saying Garland was going to turn around and the steel mill would be booming again. We're seeing that happen now because we've all cared. You mill hands out there, you know there was a time when I worked right beside you."

Male whoops and whistles burst from the crowd, enforcing the bond that linked workers who risked their lives in pouring steel as they sweated or froze together in the drafty plant.

Glenn leaned close to Rachel again, linked his arm with hers, and asked with a puckish grin on his face, "What's Hooper doing?

Running for election again?"

"As long as he's been a commissioner, we probably could say he's always running for office. But who could beat him?" She squeezed Glenn's arm against her side. It's good to have friends who knew us when we were young, she thought. It's the only way to keep us young.

Rachel glanced toward the south end of the city, but she could not see the 30-acre steel mill complex. It was too far away.

There was no red smoke hovering over the area. Only gray sky. No red smoke from the coke plant for years now, not since environmentalists began cracking down on polluting industries in the 1970s.

"It's not the same company we knew, but it survived," Hooper continued. "What helped pull this community through was the people. A lot of people."

Hooper look proudly around at the crowd gathered in front of him facing the river. His eyes searched out Rachel and Glenn.

"When I said it took a lot of people to make this city what it is, that wraps up a whole lot of people, including our late friend and leader, Douglas Hodge."

Rachel stiffened next to Glenn. She did not want this hurt of remembering today. She felt the squeeze against her arm that was linked through his.

"Other people deserve recognition, too," Hooper continued. "Some who worked because it was their job, and others who volunteered to make this a better community. Garland is what it is today because of the efforts of so many."

Hooper looked out at the damp, upturned faces in front of him. He had known so many faces over the years. Many of those were gone and the crowd had changed. There were a lot of young people out there now, with children of their own. A whole new generation ready to take over.

"Our city has been here through the years, and it will continue to meet its challenges and conquer. When you think of the word Garland, you may think of a rope of flowers, or something," Hooper explained.

"Well, Garland means that, but the word also stands for

'thing most prized' and 'a royal crown'. It's both of those. That's Garland. That's our city."

Hooper hadn't expected to feel emotional.

He hadn't anticipated damp palms, either. It was supposed to be just a simple little ceremony to dedicate the new river bank construction. But, damn it, so many memories had swept back today.

Hooper stepped aside as other local officials made brief remarks. He then cut the ribbon, officially opening the platform and walkway to the public.

People were moving away now. The crowd was breaking up. Glenn continued to hold Rachel's arm and began leading her toward the walkway.

"There's something I want to show you," he said.

About halfway down the path constructed of ordinary red bricks that were engraved with names of donors, Glenn stopped and pointed for her to look down.

The brick at her feet was inscribed with the name, "Douglas Hodge." Rachel's eyes moistened. Her throat tightened.

"He's with us today," Glenn said, "I wanted to show it to you personally. And look, I'm right here."

Glenn pointed to an adjoining brick. "And Hooper's name is on that brick, and there you are, with all of us in a group."

Rachel looked at the bricks with their engraved names, but they blurred through tears.

"Hey, it's all right to get a little weepy. I did it myself once." Glenn put his arm around her shoulder. "We decided to do this, put us all together in a cluster like this, during the time when we heard you were sick several months ago."

"You don't know what it means....." she whispered, struggling to keep her voice steady.

"Sure I do," he said. "We're not all here today, but I guess what's left are survivors."

"There's something I want to do, Glenn."

"What's that?" he asked.

The silence stretched into several seconds as Rachel struggled with her response.

Her mouth suddenly curved up at the corners and her eyes

held his. "I don't know, but I'll think of it. We all need to have something ahead to accomplish. That's what keeps us going."

ANOTHER BEGINNING

* * *